Firebrand Books
Ithaca, New York

Book and cover design by Nightwood

Printed in Canada

10 9 8 7 6 5 4 3 2 1

Library of Congress Cataloging-in-Publication Data

Clarke, Caro, 1954—
The wolf ticket : a novel / by Caro Clarke.
p. cm.
ISBN 1-56341-099-0 (cloth : alk. paper). —ISBN 1-56341-098-2 (pbk. : alk. paper)
I. World War, 1939–1945—Fiction. I. Title.
PR9199.3.C5263W6 1998
813'.54—dc21 98-14328
CIP

To Fiona

Pascale

I

Pascale looked at the last refugee standing on the platform. The rest of the crowd had been shuffled away by the soldiers. Only this one had somehow remained, wistfully assessing the train as it idled and steamed. Pascale had seen thousands like him, gaunt, hardened, bleak. She glanced at the letter in her lap, a friend from home who had not been able to resist telling her the latest news, then wiped the window to look out again at the lone boy.

He was probably from Poland, judging by his shock of blond hair, his high cheekbones. Typical wreckage of war, stranded now in the closing gap between the Red Army and Allied advances.

A squadron of Dakotas roared overhead toward the American air force base south of town. The refugee looked instinctively for cover as their engines shook the sky. Pascale stared. Something about him reminded her of the faces back home, of her mother's sister, the same look of wariness in a strange land. Pascale was surprised that his desperation could touch her. She had thought her heart numbed by the pain of too many refugees too lost, too needy, too bereft for any help she could give.

The train's whistle blew. The general must be settled in his suite.

Steam billowed across the platform. The refugee leaned forward, fists clenched, and his eyes met hers through the window. Pascale knew, in a heartbeat knew, and was on her feet, out the compartment, wrenching open the carriage door, shouting, "Come!" over the locomotive's grunting chuff. *"Kommen! Przychoć!"*

He looked at her outstretched hand.

Pascale gestured. *"Przychoć!"*

His eyes lit up; he started across the platform. The train began to roll and he quickened. The train was faster. Pascale braced herself on the handrail and leaned out. He ran full tilt for her, greatcoat streaming behind him. Pascale's hand touched his, gripped his sleeve. His fist closed around the handrail and he heaved himself on board, was on the step gasping, pressed against her for a second as he slipped, regained his footing, and now Pascale did know. The train shot free of the platform.

As it gathered speed, the bombed town rushing past them, Pascale found that she was holding onto the refugee's lapel like a police officer onto a ruffian. "Come inside," she told her in Polish.

The refugee stumbled up the steps. Pascale closed the outside door, the woman's breath rasping in the quiet, and took her to the compartment. The woman looked around as if at a palace.

"Sit by the window," Pascale said, careful to keep her word endings masculine until she saw how the woman played her masquerade.

The refugee sat and wrapped her greatcoat around herself, trying to be even smaller and less significant than she was. Pascale settled opposite and, knowing that the others would be returning soon, said urgently, "I don't know how long you'll be able to stay on this train. You'll almost certainly be put off at the next stop. Are you Polish or Russian? Were you a soldier for the Soviets? It's important."

"No," said the refugee. "I am Polish only."

"That's good." Pascale was relieved. "If you were Russian I'd be required to detain you. Are you trying to get back to Poland?"

The young woman gave her a wintry smile. "Poland? Where is that? All that is east is Communist territory."

"Where are you hoping to go?"

"West. Netherlands, France, anywhere that is not here." The woman studied Pascale's uniform. "You are an American soldier?"

"Yes, but I don't fight. I'm a translator in the Women's Army Corps."

"Your Polish is very good."

"Thank you. I also speak German, French, and a little Yiddish." A shadow across the woman's face made Pascale ask, "Are you Jewish?"

"No. That is why I am alive."

They avoided each other's gaze, saying no more as the bleak landscape sped by.

"What is your name?" Pascale asked her at last.

"Witold. Witold Rukowicz."

"Is that your real name?" Pascale asked. It was a man's name and could not be.

"It is what I am called."

That was how she was playing her game. Very well. "This is an American army train, Mr. Rukowicz. I haven't the authority to keep you on board, but I'll get you as far west as I can before they take you off. From there, you should try to find a displaced persons camp."

"Displaced person? That is what I am now?" Witold shook her head. "I will not go to a camp. They will send me back."

"Not everyone is returned."

Witold looked mulish. Pascale knew that look, had seen it through the past months on hundreds of people whose desires were being crushed by the policies of governments. She remembered the Russians who had served as forced labor under the Germans, how they had screamed and begged for death as they were herded into trucks for the Red Army exchange points. Her face must have reflected her thoughts, for Witold said, "I know that you are trying to help me."

"These few minutes might be all I can give. The others, my unit, will probably call my lieutenant and have you dealt with."

"You will intercede with him for me?"

"She. Lieutenant Bergman. We're all women."

"Women." Witold's expression was closed. "Perhaps they will be kind."

"They are kind, but they must obey."

"Everyone obeys something." Witold smiled a small, tight smile and looked out the window.

Pascale studied her. Witold had made herself convincing: cropped hair, waistcoat, faded twill trousers, scarred British army ammunition boots, and, beyond these, a gaze of masculine levelness, a lack of eagerness for approval. But Pascale knew this was a woman. Something she had seen in her, something she could hardly name, perhaps from being half Polish herself and knowing the way her aunt and mother looked, how the people at her aunt's church looked, perhaps being what she was, open to women, and when pressed against Witold for that instant on the step, already knowing what a woman's body felt like beneath heavy clothes.

The thought made Pascale hunt for her letter. Most of what it had to say was elliptical where it was not censored, but Diana's glee filtered through. Pascale had seen too much to care now about Diana or Edie or anyone back home. The woman in front of her was from a different world. The shadowed look in Witold's eyes, the scars around her wrists from the wire Russians used to bind their prisoners' hands together, told of ordeals terrible past Diana's understanding, past Pascale's understanding. She wanted to say to her, *I know, rest, drop your shield,* but what right had she to take away the secret that had kept Witold safe, had kept her alive?

Witold returned Pascale's scrutiny. Coloring slightly, Pascale did not look away.

"What is your name?" Witold asked.

"Pascale Katarzyna Dobriniewski Tailland."

"Pascale Katarzyna Dobriniewski." Witold rolled the words around as if tasting them.

"My father is French Canadian, my mother Polish. I'm first-generation American." Pascale said the last part in Russian, a technique she used in official interviews to catch the unwary.

"I know some Russian words," Witold answered in Polish. "I know what you are speaking and what you are doing. I come from Poland. I am not Russian."

"I had to know," said Pascale. "I mustn't smuggle a Russian national from Soviet territory."

"Contraband?" Witold's half-smile came and went. "Put me in a sack and call me onions."

"I've seen Russian soldiers bayonet sacks," said Pascale.

"As I have. I have also seen sacks bleed."

A chatter of women's voices came down the corridor. Half-rising, Witold said tensely, "Your friends—"

"Are kind," Pascale repeated with as much conviction as she had.

"Professor!" They saw Witold as they opened the door. "What's this?"

"My goodness! Wherever did you find this boy?"

"So that's why you wanted to be by yourself. You're a dark horse, Tailland."

Witold stood and pulled off her cap while Pascale, obscurely proud of Witold's meticulous impersonation, said to the others in English, "I couldn't leave him. Just for once, I couldn't."

"Well, well," said Velma. "We'll have to squeeze together to let this young man sit down. Dot, Marie, park yourselves on that side, you're the smallest. Does he smell? Does he have bugs?"

"I've not noticed," said Pascale.

"Heaven help us if he does. Binty, Jeeter, crowd our little professor and make her pay for being a Good Samaritan."

Dot smiled at Witold and patted the empty seat beside her. "Sit yourself, pal."

Ducking her head, Witold said, "*Dziekuje*," and shrank into the corner.

"When did he get aboard?" asked Binty.

"At Gultenheim."

"Where the general joined?" Dot whistled soundlessly. "How did he sneak his way on?"

"I helped him," said Pascale.

"You?" Marie squeaked. "How could you do such a thing?"

"Let me ask the questions," said Velma. "Pascale, did you really get this boy on board at the same time as the general?"

"Dragged him on, actually," said Pascale. Dot and Jeeter exchanged a look across the compartment that she knew how to interpret. "I couldn't bear to leave him." She did not need to continue. They all had watched the Russians screaming.

"Is he a Soviet?" asked Velma.

"Polish through and through. His name is Witold Rukowicz."

At the words she recognized, Witold lifted her eyes from her boots.

"I'm explaining why you're here," said Pascale.

"Because you knew that I had nowhere else to go."

"Why didn't you point him in the direction of the camp at Gultenheim?" asked Velma. "As a Pole, he'd have been pretty welcome."

"It's common knowledge that the men there are going to be repatriated any day. He hates the Communists. He doesn't want to go back."

"He's not stupid on either count," said Jeeter.

"Now that he's here," Velma asked, "what are you planning to do with him? What do you think the lieutenant's going to say?"

"I've told him he's certain to be put off at the next stop."

"I should think so!" said Marie. "Especially with the general three carriages down."

The women fell silent, contemplating this enormity. Witold glanced around them, then at Pascale.

"It will be all right," Pascale told her hopefully.

"Well, girls," said Velma with a sigh, "we can't throw him out, and it's a long time before we stop. By the look of him, he hasn't eaten for a while. Let's ante up."

They groaned, but searched their pockets, Witold's wary gaze following their hands.

"Chewing gum?" Velma demanded. "Jeeter, what good's that going to do him?"

"Helps me when I'm hungry," said Jeeter. "And it's all I got, Sarge."

Marie had a bar of chocolate, Binty two packets of soda crackers, Dot a handful of dried apple slices wrapped in her handkerchief. The women passed their collection. Witold thanked them, laid Dot's handkerchief across her knees as a tablecloth, and broke the crackers and chocolate into pieces, eating each fragment separately.

Velma asked Pascale, "Does he want to go to the States?"

"Anywhere," said Pascale. "Anywhere safe."

Witold finished her meal, picked up the crumbs with a moistened fingertip, was at a loss over the chewing gum, and returned it and the handkerchief politely.

"We've got to feed him better than that," said Jeeter.

"Maybe Binty could wheedle something from the cooks," Marie suggested slyly.

Binty snorted. "If you think I'm going to get myself in hock with those jerks, you're mistaken."

"You're the only redhead on the train," said Dot.

"Except that captain."

"Got an eye for the captain, do you?" Jeeter leered, and they laughed, the captain being a jug-eared South Dakotan with pale, moist eyes. "Any kid you two had would be born a carrot."

"Please!" said Marie.

Witold was sitting forward, hands on her knees, watching their conversation alertly.

"They're planning to get you more food," said Pascale.

"I would like more." Witold settled back.

"He's not talkative, is he?" asked Dot.

"The only person he can talk with here is the professor, and she's the same," said Binty.

"I'm tired of talking," said Pascale. "All we've done is talk. To Nazis. All that talk of theirs about how innocent they are, how they were just following orders, how we're so alike, how deeply grateful they are that we've come."

The others laughed shortly in agreement.

"Does he have identification papers?" Marie leaned forward to look at Witold's profile. "He could be a German trying to pass as a Pole. We've seen plenty of those."

"His German is too terrible to be false," said Pascale.

Witold was watching a bullet-pocked village approach and recede.

"What are you looking at?" Velma asked her in German.

"I look at the countryside," Witold replied in the same language. "It is like Poland, a little. My German is not good."

"You said it," Velma nodded.

"I am not Soviet," Witold continued. "I am not German. I am Polish."

"How old are you?" asked Dot.

"Not so old," Witold answered guardedly.

"Have you any family?"

"Dead."

"I'm sorry."

"I was, also." Witold turned to Pascale and said in Polish, "It is easier to stop caring."

"What's he saying?" asked Velma.

"That he has nothing to return to."

"Poor mutt," sighed Binty.

"Was he a soldier?" asked Marie. "He looks old enough to have been a soldier. He's wearing a Red Army coat."

"That means nothing," said Pascale. "We've seen Ukrainians in British uniforms and G.I.s with iron crosses around their necks."

"I was only asking," said Marie. "Is he a draft dodger?"

"From the Polish army?" Pascale asked, brows rising. The Polish army was entirely volunteer.

"Don't get on your high horse," said Marie. "I won't say another word against your new pet."

"You're going to have to make sure he wasn't a Red Army or German soldier, not even a conscripted one," said Velma. "You know the rules."

"I'll question him again after he's rested and has had a better meal," said Pascale. She looked reassuringly at Witold, who gave a small smile and returned to her study of the passing villages. Apparently engrossed, she never quite relaxed; Pascale saw her eyelids flicker at each change in the women's conversation. If she felt trapped, Pascale suspected, she would fight like a wild animal.

The others settled into their usual routines. Marie took out a spiral of crocheting, Dot re-read a wartime issue of Fitzgerald, Velma allowed herself a cigarette, Jeeter and Binty compared the G.I.s they fancied to the officers they also fancied.

"Howie's awfully nice," said Binty half-shyly.

"Howie's a small-town boy. If you like them tongue-tied and bashful, you should grab him." Jeeter snapped her gum. "But you'll be heading straight back to the farm."

"Better than that slick Romeo you were dating last Friday," said Binty. "That man just can't control his hands."

"How would you know?"

"One dance too many on New Year's Eve, back in Fontaine. Should have seen my footwork to stop myself being waltzed into an alcove. Basic training finally paid off."

"They say his old man's got bucks."

"Better see the color of it before you let him sweet-talk you into an alcove of your own," said Binty.

Dot, whose fiancé was fighting in northern Italy, said, "What would it take to get you two to talk about the weather?"

"With that brazen attitude," Marie added, "you'll never get married."

"I'm not worried." Jeeter smiled sweetly.

"The way you're going through them—" Marie began.

The door slid open. "What the hell is that?"

"Lieutenant! Francine!" Velma sat up in a hurry. "This is, uh..."

"This is my business," said Pascale sternly, putting her hand on Witold's arm.

"What's a civilian doing here?" Francine stepped in and slid the door closed behind her. "On this train, in this goddamn compartment?"

Witold stood and doffed her cap.

"I can explain," said Pascale.

"She dragged him on board," Marie interjected.

Francine leaned back against the door to get a good look at them all. "Yeah?" She put out a hand to Velma. "Got one, Turner?" Velma handed her a cigarette. Francine lit it, stared at Witold as she sucked a lung of smoke, and said through the exhaled cloud, "Okay, Tailland, give me the *megillah*."

"He was on the platform at Gultenheim. He must have slipped through the MPs' cordon or been hiding there before the general arrived. He looked—I thought—I thought I could carry him out of the war a little, if only to the next stop, to Bremerstadt. He's been nowhere but this compartment. He's not a security risk."

"You hope. What the hell's so special about him that you'd pull a stunt like this?"

"He—" Pascale, unable to think of a reason as convincing as the truth, especially to Francine, said lamely, "He looked alone."

"He wouldn't have been alone in the Gultenheim refugee camp."

"He wants to get as far west as he can."

"I bet he does." Francine surveyed Witold with disfavor.

Witold straightened her tie as if to convince the lieutenant of her respectability. Smiling at this, Pascale said to Francine, "I wanted to get him safe."

"She's smitten," said Marie, sharp-eyed.

"Don't be a dope," snapped Dot.

"What's going on, Tailland?" The lieutenant frowned at her, puzzled.

"I've taken to him," said Pascale slowly, knowing what they would make of her words. "I want to help someone, one person, in this war, and I want it to be him. It has to be him."

Francine smoked. "You can't keep a man here all day," she said finally, slightly emphasizing the word *man* without looking at Pascale, and Pascale knew she was sickened and angry.

"Sure we can, Lieutenant," said Velma. "It'll be fine. We'll eat in relays and bring food back for him. We'll keep the door locked. We won't even let Norma and the others in on it. All you need to do is make sure that none of the officers or G.I.s surprise us."

"That's all, is it?" Francine smiled grimly. "If you want my advice, you'll toss him out at the first slow curve. I'm not covering for you, Tailland, and I'm not going to let these girls take any of the blame. He gets found out, I never saw him and you take your licking. Savvy?"

"Yes, Ma'am," Pascale nodded.

"Right," said Francine as she left the compartment. "Don't tell me another word about him."

At Pascale's gesture, Witold sat down.

"Whew!" Binty pretended to mop her brow. "I didn't think she'd bite."

"The lieutenant has a soft spot for the professor," said Marie lightly.

"Lucky for Mr. Rukowicz." Velma was firm.

"Lucky for everyone that the lieutenant won't be holding us responsible for an army-shy Pole," said Marie.

Witold caught Marie's tone and regarded her mildly. Marie flushed but said, "He might be one of those sly, clever ones."

"Maybe that's why he's still above ground," said Binty.

Pascale, pensively noting the approving way they now glanced from her to Witold, was still touched, saying to them, "Thank you. Thank you for helping."

"Like you said to Francine," Dot sighed, "let's save at least one."

Pascale answered Witold's querying look. "The lieutenant wants you off as soon as possible, but if we keep you a secret she'll look the other way."

"She, too, is kind," said Witold. "You have put yourself into trouble."

"It's worth it," said Pascale.

"Why?"

Pascale was silent, not able to answer.

"Is it because I am Polish, as you partly are?"

"Does it matter why?"

"No," said Witold. "I am happy to be going. I hope you will get me as far as you are able."

"Even if I'm in trouble for it?"

"Of course. I think you will not be shot. Anything less is unimportant."

Pascale laughed. "I won't be shot."

Witold nodded and looked out at the rain falling on the bomb-scarred fields. Eventually she dozed, but when Dot made a move for the door, Pascale saw her sleep turn feigned and her hand slip inside her coat for some weapon as she watched the women's reflections in the window through one slitted eye.

"When are they going to call us?" asked Dot. "I'm famished."

The first sitting for lunch was announced as she spoke.

"I'll stay with him," said Pascale, putting a hand on Witold's knee in a pantomime of waking her. Witold tensed, then faked a yawn.

"We aren't a waitress service," said Marie.

Velma glared. "Shut it, O'Dowd."

The women left. Witold stretched her legs with a sigh.

"Do you have a gun?" Pascale asked.

Witold's eyes flashed in surprised appreciation. "Knife."

A man would have shown it to her. Pascale had no intention of demanding that Witold surrender it, asking rather, "What would you have done if you hadn't got on this train?"

"Found food. A place to sleep. Tried another train tomorrow."

"There was a Red Cross camp in Gultenheim."

"I know this. Camps are for those who have surrendered to fate. I would rather starve by the side of the road than join the defeated."

"How long have you been hiding?"

"Evading." Witold's smile came and went. "Sometimes fighting. Not hiding."

"You were a soldier?" asked Pascale, appalled.

"When the war began I was too young," Witold said easily. "When I was old enough, all the Home Army units had gone underground and made themselves too hard to find. I enlisted when they rose up to join the Soviet advance against the Germans. After we liberated Lublin together, the Communists arrested us and killed our officers. I was a soldier for three months, then I was a prisoner for three months. That was my military career."

"You escaped." Pascale stated the obvious.

"It was a prison farm. I was a field laborer. I worked stupidly hard until they decided I could be ignored, then I went."

"Went," Pascale repeated. "Did you like being a soldier?"

"It was difficult," Witold shrugged. "Do you like being a soldier?"

"Sometimes," said Pascale. It seemed natural to add, "I confirmed my mother's fears."

"Of what?"

"That certain women are attracted to the Women's Army Corps because they hate men, yet want to be like them. That's what she believes, and I was attracted to the service."

"You disagree with your mother?" asked Witold.

"I had skills I thought should be put to use."

"Do you hate men?"

"If I did I wouldn't be here trying to help them, though I prefer them no closer than a handshake."

Witold laughed. "American women! You are so free to say such things."

"It's more than that," said Pascale.

"I must assume. Were it not, you would be married. You have the heart and face of an angel."

Pascale's eyes flew to hers. Witold could not have understood. She wondered how to enlighten her.

"If you debate inside yourself about what to say to me, do not speak," said Witold.

Pascale was taken aback. "You read me very well."

"We come bearing gifts!" Dot opened the door.

Their shoulder bags produced buns filled with butter and cheese. Binty demurely proffered a teacup of diced fruit and, with greater modesty, a spoon.

"Never let it be said that our unit can't forage in hostile territory," said Velma, lifting out a milk jug filled with coffee.

"He'll have to eat his dessert before he drinks anything," said Binty. "We couldn't get another cup."

Pascale shared the food with Witold, giving her the greater part. Witold ate with the same concentration as before.

"How far to Bremerstadt?" Pascale asked, watching her.

"We'll be there about six," said Velma. "I know you want to bring him clear out of Germany, professor, but we can't have him here tonight. He's got to get off at Bremerstadt."

"If he's going to a camp, I want to take him. I could speak to the commandant on his behalf."

"He's a grown boy. He can look after himself," said Marie. "He's done it so far."

"I'd like to take him," Pascale repeated to Velma.

Velma tapped out a cigarette. "Let's cross that bridge later, okay, professor?"

The women settled into naps, reading, or quiet conversation. Witold fell asleep again with the ease of a combat veteran. Pascale studied her, following the angularity of bone from temple to jaw, the fine skein of lines around her eyes, Witold's disguise made more convincing by the hardships that had stripped softness from her face.

Pascale contrasted her with Edie. Edie's tough swaggering, which Pascale perforce indulged, had never quite hidden her lack of grit. Pascale remembered the first letter Edie sent after Pascale had been posted overseas. Its loving phrases could not disguise the fact that Edie was with someone new. Pascale had known before she joined the WAC that Edie would not endure loneliness for long and had made it plain that she would not begrudge Edie any comfort. Pascale did not equate love with physical constancy. She had told her so, saying bluntly that she valued only love. The hurt from Edie's letter came in her lack of faith that Pascale had meant what she said.

In the end, Pascale had written back urging Edie to stay in the apartment until she herself was demobilized. Diana's letter told her that Edie had indeed managed to find a new roommate, that little South Carolinan from the Accounts Department, did Pascale remember her? Pascale did: a woman who would never trouble Edie with peculiar principles.

Witold was looking at her as if she had spoken. "What is making you unhappy?"

Pascale's heart jolted. She forced herself to say, "Nothing worth mentioning. It isn't useful thinking of the past." She added abruptly, "Sergeant Turner intends to send you to the camp at Bremerstadt."

"I need not go. Let me slip free at the station."

"I can't. Sergeant Turner will place you in military custody and you'll be escorted there."

"Then I shall escape."

"It's not a labor camp. The United Nations doesn't have them. You could do worse than UNRRA."

"It is a prison camp. I have spent five years evading camps. Concentration camps. Slave camps. Detention camps. Poland is one big camp and it is full of the dead."

"Your only chance of reaching a free country is through a refugee camp," said Pascale. "Many places accept immigrants."

"America?"

"We have strict rules. Perhaps they'll be relaxed after the war. Do you want to go there?"

"I had not thought of it before I met you."

"You can't evade your way across the ocean. One person can cover only so much distance."

"I could do it," said Witold. "I will."

"Some things can only be done by people in groups. Winning a war, for example. Hospitals. Schools. Taking people across the Atlantic."

"I have seen groups," said Witold. "Villagers chasing an escaped Jew or a lone Russian soldier, kicking them, taking sticks to them, delivering what was left to the Germans for favors. I have seen village elders sell their towns to Soviet captains for their own protection. I learned to avoid groups."

"Yet here you are on this train."

"Because of you alone," said Witold.

"Perhaps you made a mistake." Pascale bit her lip. "It will get you nowhere but the camp in Bremerstadt."

"It was not a mistake."

"You've lost your freedom."

"Temporarily." Witold was untroubled.

"A camp is better than dodging death in the war zone."

Witold looked at her sardonically.

Pascale understood. "Please stay long enough to be fed and rested."

"Then I go."

"What will you do when the war's over?"

"Find work, somewhere to live. Learn the language."

"You'll be a foreigner for the rest of your life."

"I have lost my family, my home, my village. I have been hungry and a prisoner." Witold looked at her without emotion. "What is precious is not a country, it is ten minutes without fear or a corner from the wind."

"Is that all life holds for you?"

"That is all there is. Stripped of trinkets, that is all life is. Eat or die. Stay warm or die. Evade the hunters or die."

"That makes us no better than beasts."

Witold nodded to the ruined landscape outside. "You have been in this war. We are worse."

"This is what I wish I'd never seen." Pascale's voice cracked in spite of herself. "This is what I can't bear."

Velma leaned forward. "What's going on?"

"Witold's telling me how he spent the war."

"Bet that's a barrel of laughs."

"I have distressed you, Pascale Tailland." Witold's mouth tightened.

"The world distresses me," said Pascale. "I used to feel that injustice could be dealt with by honesty, that people would behave better if they could be made to think, but having seen what I've seen, I can't believe I was fighting so insignificant a battle. I've seen tortured people, I've seen mass graves. Humans aren't capable of living any of their beliefs."

"You think these are the first atrocities visited on the earth just because you have witnessed them?" Witold answered with a curl of her lip. "You Americans know nothing of our history. What of the Prussians? The Swedes? And Poland is only one country. The past is everywhere the same. It is cruelty, massacres, and war."

"Do you think there are ultimate truths?" asked Pascale.

Witold shrugged. "One only: life is better than death."

"That doesn't absolve us of morality. Life itself gives meaning."

"How? The only meaning I see is the law of the wolf, kill or be killed."

"We aren't wolves," said Pascale. "We're human. We can't take morality from Nature. It's preposterous; things like altruism have to be made absurdities of self-interest." She paused at Witold's puzzled scowl. "What I mean is that basing our morality on Nature makes our actions toward others conditional on our own personal benefit."

"That is Nazi philosophy," said Witold.

"You're right, but not just theirs. Most people say and believe it. That's why we have this world, this war. I'm afraid that if we can't think of another meaning for life, we'll keep torturing and killing each other forever."

"You have thought of another meaning?" Witold smiled expectantly.

Pascale smiled back, suddenly nervous. "I've tried to. You see, I start with the fact of rational life. Morality is needed as soon as two people exist, since I have to have some way of dealing with that other person, relating myself to him...or her. I'd prefer to say her. The only thing I know about that other her is that she values her own life, for it's the one thing every living creature does—down to the fish that fights the hook or the wolf that gnaws its leg off in the trap."

"Animals sacrifice part of themselves from instinct alone," Witold objected. "They do not think."

"That's my point," Pascale said eagerly. "We'll sacrifice anything to live, cut off a hand to escape, trade freedom for food, because life is our single natural imperative. But we have no imperative to tell us how to behave to others. We have to use reason. My reason tells me there's no evidence that I'm worth more, objectively speaking, than that other person. She and I both live, so each of our lives, each of our selves, is equally valuable. And since I have no grounds on which to choose one over the other, I have to value her as much as I do myself." Pascale smiled in diffident triumph. "You can't escape it. Life gives meaning."

"If that other person does not think the same as you?"

"It doesn't have to be mutual. I have that responsibility whatever she believes."

Witold shook her head. "If that one were trying to kill you?"

"I'd defend myself," said Pascale. "I value my life. Though I could imagine the extreme: I might choose to die if that would help her. But I'm concerned more with those less dramatic daily choices that confront us, how we behave toward each other. I think the best way to act is always to think of her benefit. My actions should spring from valuing her."

Witold tipped her head, considering this. "Her needs are your ethics?"

Pascale hung breathless for a moment. "Exactly."

"You hold to all you have said?" asked Witold. "You would take responsibility for Nazis?"

"Yes. That's why I joined the Women's Army Corps. I had to help redeem ourselves from these iniquities."

"Take responsibility for both good and bad?" Witold's voice hovered on disbelief.

"Yes."

Witold glanced around. "Your companions also think this? It is what Americans believe?"

"No." Pascale grimaced. "They call me professor and consider me sunk in godless philosophy. They don't see why I can't accept heaven and hell and believe that good will prevail."

Witold said, "When you have fought with another starving person for the corpse of a dog, when you have killed for an overcoat, everything inside you dies. You cannot believe those comforting stories about goodness any more. You think to yourself at first, *This is what I must do to survive, I will become human again when this is over.* But when it is over you cannot rekindle faith in anything." She leaned forward. "Doing what you say would be to become human in a better way than believing in stories."

"I don't want anyone to believe in stories. I want them to test my reasoning and find it true."

"Even if it is not true, I could live as if it were."

Pascale's hand tightened on the edge of the seat. "I think—no, I'm sure, that's the only way we create morality."

"Acting, even while uncertain, makes morality, and morality makes you human?"

"Human in the best way."

Witold pondered this. "What you say is difficult to do."

"Yes, but I think it's necessary."

"Then it is necessary." Witold withdrew into herself and stared sightlessly toward the window, chin on her fist. Pascale contemplated her in wonder.

It was dark outside, a rain-shrouded evening. Soon they would reach Bremerstadt. Too soon. Pascale passionately did not want to put Witold out into the rain, into the dark, at Bremerstadt or anywhere else. She stared at Witold's reflection in the window, absorbing her: the way her hair sprang from her forehead, the straight lines of her brows, the scar at the side of her mouth. Witold met her eye in the glass and Pascale felt a rush of response from long-hidden depths.

"You must learn some English," she said to her urgently, wanting to say more, to give her more. "You'll be disadvantaged if you speak only Polish and German."

"And a little Russian."

"You mustn't say a single word in Russian from now on. One word could have you deported to the Soviet Union. You're in Allied-held Germany now. Learn *please* and *thank you, yes* and *no, excuse me* and *I do not understand.* Learn *I want to go to America.*"

"Aye vont t'gautoo Amaireeca," Witold repeated.

"I want to go to America," Pascale said again.

"Lord, honey, don't we all," said Velma. "But you're getting his hopes up, teaching him that."

"He's already decided."

"Better teach him to say, *I'm no Russian.*"

"Yes, that as well." Pascale turned back to Witold. "Say what I say. *Tak:* yes. *Nie:* no. *Nie rozumiem:* I do not understand."

Witold did, almost incomprehensibly. Pascale took her over and over them: *I am not a Russian, I am Polish, I want to go to America.*

"How about, *Give me liberty or give me death,* or the huddled masses stuff?" suggested Dot, distracted from her book. "Make some camp commandant's patriotic heart flutter and maybe our Mr. Rukowicz will be shipped express to dear old USA."

"The professor's trying to make herself feel better about throwing her Polish boy back into the water," said Marie.

"At least I rescued him from sharks," said Pascale, knowing Marie was right.

"Aye doo nut onderstond," said Witold.

"No, you don't," Dot laughed. "A good thing too, you poor beggar."

"I am saying it wrongly?" Witold asked Pascale.

"We knew what you were saying."

"Bremerstadt can't be far." Marie peered out the window.

"Yez. Naw," Witold practiced. "Excooz me. Aye vont too gau'too Amaireeca."

The compartment door slid open. Lieutenant Bergman stepped in, looking severe. Pascale's heart shrank. Her hand instinctively reached for Witold, who straightened her cap resolutely and said in German, "I am ready to go."

2

Maybe you are, my little *oyrech,*" said Francine. "But not yet." She switched to English. "Girls, we got a problem. We aren't stopping in Bremerstadt."

"Aren't stopping!" Marie yipped.

"The radio operator got a report that the UNRRA camp inmates are on the rampage. Nobody can spare time to chew the fat, so the general's decided to go straight through to Fontaine." Francine glanced at Pascale. "Looks like you'll be getting your pal clean across the border."

Pascale turned to Witold joyfully. "We're going directly to France."

Relief and calculation sped across Witold's face. "That is good." She stood and clipped a bow to Francine. "Dank yoo."

"Who's been teaching this pup new tricks?" asked Francine.

"Wait a minute," Marie complained. "Where are we going to put him? We're all women here. What are we going to do tonight?"

"We've got enough Yankee ingenuity to figure something out," said Jeeter.

"We won't reach Fontaine till midmorning," said Francine, "so you'd better do something with him. I'm sorry this whole damn mishmash has happened."

"It'll be fine, Lieutenant," Velma said confidently.

"And another thing: at chow time tonight, get those buns into your purses with a little less hooplah. Turner, got a cigarette?" Francine lit the one Velma passed and said to Pascale, "You'll be owing these gals a hell of a lot of favors by the time he's gone."

"I know," said Pascale.

"As long as you do." Francine closed the door behind her.

"I'm going to Captain Thorsby at once!" said Marie. "I'm not spending a night with a man!"

"What makes you think he wants to spend it with you?" asked Velma.

"It's immoral," Marie declared.

"Marie," said Velma, and whispered in her ear. Marie choked, blushed, and pulled away.

"How did you find out—?" She stopped, aware of the compartment's avid attention. "Very well. Out of loyalty to the unit I'll say nothing, but this is the last favor I do anyone."

"And the first," Binty muttered.

Pascale said to Witold, "We have to find a place where you can sleep tonight. There are only four berths in this compartment. These four share two and Velma and I have our own." She did not explain that Velma had this luxury because she was the sergeant, Pascale because no one cared to share a bed with her.

"I will sleep on the floor," said Witold.

"You can't do that."

"Why not? I sleep on the ground."

"You can't sleep in the same room as six women."

Witold looked confounded. Pascale, amused, felt for her.

"I will sleep in the corridor," Witold said finally.

"There's traffic to the lavatories as well as patrols along the train all night."

The others were discussing the problem.

"There's only one way," said Velma. "You four will bunk together as usual, I'll bunk with Pascale, and Mr. Rukowicz will get a bed to himself."

"I'm not going to sleep with a strange man only inches away!" Marie protested. "He could kill us all!"

"Shut it," said Velma. "We bunked with that artillery regiment near Haverstatten, didn't we? I don't think this boy has anything on his mind but food and sleep."

"Then I'm taking the inside of that upper berth," said Marie, "and I'm keeping my penknife with me."

"You girls agreeable?" Velma asked them all.

Having no other choice, they nodded. Pascale thanked Velma wryly; the sergeant was willing to share a bed with her now that she was interested in a man.

"It's only one night," said Binty. "There's more of us than there is of him. We can always scream and get a guard."

When she was told, Witold protested, "I will not take your bed."

"The only way we can be safe is to keep you hidden."

"*You* will be made safe, Pascale Tailland?"

"Yes."

"Very well." Witold touched her cap to the others. "Dank yoo."

Pascale went to dinner with them, leaving Witold with Dot, who smiled in a friendly way and began to drill her on her English phrases. When the others stayed in the smoking compartment to listen to the radio, Pascale returned to release Dot and to give Witold the hasty meal she had hidden.

"Fontaine will be better for you than Bremerstadt," she said as Witold ate her bread and butter. "I was posted there last fall. The camp has proper buildings, not tents. It's run by the army and is close enough to town for me to visit you."

"Fontaine is an army post?"

Pascale nodded. "It's a command station. That's why I won't be able to keep you out of the camp."

"You must teach me French words as well."

"To use when you've escaped?"

Witold grinned. "Do not tell me of camps. Tell me something interesting. Tell me of the town you are from. You have brothers and sisters?"

"I come from Boston. No brothers or sisters. I live in an apartment with a friend."

"Not with your mother and father? You must be rich."

"I work," said Pascale.

"What is Boston like?"

"It's an old city and can be beautiful. The harbor is full of ships from around the world. The rich people live on a hill; I live in the Back Bay, much lower down."

"What is your work?"

"I'm a translator for a publishing house. I grew up with Polish and French, then studied German and French literature at the university. That's another reason they call me professor: I translate academic books."

"You are an intellectual! Books, professional work, and an apartment in a city. You must have a wonderful life. What do you do, you and the friend who lives with you, when you are not working? You have a motor car? You go to the cinematograph?"

"I don't have a car. I'm not paid that much! My friends and I go to films, or to restaurants and clubs to dance, or we have outdoor parties in the park."

"If you do that you must be rich."

"I'm fortunate. Don't think that all Americans live this well. There are millions of poor people."

"I am not foolish enough to think America is paradise. I am going there because that is where you live."

"Why?"

Witold put her hands palm to palm. "This is the two of us. We are of the same mind. That is why you called me onto this train and why I came."

"We aren't the same. I'm different in a way you don't know. In a way you might despise."

"That cannot be," said Witold.

Pascale wanted to believe her. She heard Velma's voice in the corridor and said quickly, "You can't be certain until you know."

"Tell me."

Jeeter came in, arguing with Marie, "...and Carmen Miranda isn't what I mean by Latin music. Well, professor, let's shoo our boy out and get to bed."

"Where's she going to take him?" asked Binty. "It'll be a parade of toothbrushes up and down the corridor in a minute."

"I'll take him into the coupling space between the carriages," said Pascale. The next carriage, loaded with weapons, was sealed off to all traffic except the nightly patrols.

Velma nodded. "Fine. Okay, girls, make it snappy. Professor, you stay with him. Tell him to keep his clothes on tonight. All of them."

Checking the corridor, Pascale rushed Witold through the carriage exit. They stood shivering on the sliding connector plates, the cracked canvas walls that joined the two carriages giving no protection from the cold.

Pascale heard the train saying *tell her, tell her.* How could she tell her? Now, when it was so important, she could not face the light dying in Witold's eyes. But as she flinched from the thought, Pascale felt a curious uprush of confidence that nothing she could say would make Witold reject her. She looked at Witold, who was staring at the track as if counting off miles, and was sure. Was almost sure.

Eventually Velma knocked shave-and-a-haircut on the door. Witold's bunk, the lower one opposite Velma's, had its curtains drawn back. Witold prodded the mattress with a beatific smile and climbed on top of the blankets. Pascale closed the curtains for her and went to the washroom to bathe and change.

When she returned, Velma was tucked well to the inside of the bed looking at ease, but with her left arm firmly pinning the blankets along the open side. Pascale slipped in and turned her back, saying, "Good night."

"Enough room?" Velma asked neutrally.

"I'm fine," said Pascale, careful not to move until Velma was asleep.

It had been a long time since Pascale had heard breathing so close beside her. She put her fist against her mouth to stifle the remembrance of a woman's company, no comfort coming from the memory of Edie or those before her. Witold turned and punched her pillow. Pascale smiled in the dark. She knew by whose side she wanted to be.

She slept, then was wide awake, listening. It was dark. She lifted her head. Nothing. She knew from experience that she would sleep no more tonight. It felt about four in the morning. Reaching for her dressing gown and navigating her toes into her slippers, she slid through the curtains. Her ankles brushed a dark shape that moved. Biting off a cry, she bent and felt rough cloth. Something sharp, a knife, pressed itself to her ribs. Her heart skipped sideways more at its suddenness than with fear. The knife disappeared.

"Witold," she said in the softest of whispers. "What are you doing on the floor?"

"The bed is too soft. I am unaccustomed. I could not stay asleep."

"How long have you been down there?"

"A few hours only."

Velma turned and murmured in her sleep.

"I'm going out," said Pascale.

Witold rose soundlessly and slid open the door for her, whispering gallantly, "I will wait here until you return."

"I won't be back for a while. I can't sleep."

"Something is wrong?"

"No."

Witold hesitated, then followed her. "I cannot sleep while you cannot."

Pascale led her to the washroom and locked the door. Gesturing Pascale to the single stool, Witold sat between the sinks, her big boots incongruous against the polished wood of the cabinet. Pascale hugged her dressing gown around her knees. "Fontaine," she said. "There are two camps, one for men, one for women. An officer called Colonel Grove commands both. He won't let you be ill-treated."

"I am sure the camps are pleasant," said Witold. "I have escaped from more than one."

Pascale thought of the prisons she had seen, of their machine-gun towers, their dog runs. She thought of the endless years of war. "How did you manage?"

"That is without interest. I did what I had to do."

"It's interesting to me."

"You want to hear what is interesting about me? I grew up in a village near Siedlce. My aunt looked after us when my mother died. My father owned the inn. My oldest brother joined the army to fight the German invasion and was killed. The Russians came. My father was taken to a Russian labor farm. The Germans came. My older sister was taken to work in a German factory. My aunt grew sick from hunger and died. The Home Army sabotaged a bridge and our village was chosen by the Germans for their reprisal. My other two brothers were shot. I ran away with my sister Elzbieta. She was caught, raped, and killed. I got away. I hid. I evaded the Germans for a long time. I fought with the Home Army, I was made prisoner by the Russians, and I escaped. That is all there is to me."

Pascale could say nothing. In the silence Witold asked, "Tell me of you."

"What can I say that isn't ridiculous?"

"Then tell me of America. It has space still, for people? For me?"

Pascale could not refuse her. "Yes, there's space. We took millions in the past and could have taken millions more if fear and hatred of strangers hadn't closed the doors. When I walked through my first concentration camp I couldn't believe that we had refused entry to even one Jewish immigrant from the Reich."

"The purpose of countries is not to be moral," said Witold. "It is to swallow their neighbors for the glory of their leaders."

Remembering Manifest Destiny, Pascale could not disagree. She said, "America has given Poland to the Soviets."

"You think your government had that much power?" Witold scoffed. "No. This was never your war. The war was in Poland and Russia and the Ukraine. Where were you in 1939? 1940? By the time you came, our fate was decided. All you Americans have done is to accept the situation."

"The United States is the most powerful country on earth. We could defeat the Russians if we chose."

"You have not chosen to. You have chosen to help them."

"Until the war is over. If the Soviets keep Poland after that, we've failed."

Witold's smile was mocking, but she said gently, "To defeat the Germans is also a good thing."

"What's wrong for an individual to do is wrong for a country to do," said Pascale stubbornly.

Witold's expression softened. "How fortunate that responsibility is not mutual."

"It could be. It can be. Not between governments and citizens, but between individuals."

"You have experienced this?"

"No."

"No?" Witold was taken aback.

"Not yet," said Pascale, and Witold's gaze faltered. After a silence Pascale added, "It would take everything."

Witold looked up. "To say *everything* is to ask too much."

"Only if it's not mutual."

"And were it so?"

Pascale smiled slowly. "Could anything be—"

Steps approached from the corridor. Immediately Witold was at the door, knife bared. Pascale leapt to seize her arm. The door of the neighboring room opened and closed.

"One of the Wacs," Pascale breathed. "Put that away. If anyone finds it you'll be arrested, especially with the general so near."

"I am not interested in generals."

Pascale could feel Witold's arm like a bar of steel under her hand. The sound of running water came through the wall, then footsteps receding. Pascale looked down. "That's an SS dagger."

"A bequest from a sleepy officer." Witold put the knife away.

"You killed him?"

"How else does one inherit from Germans?"

They were standing against each other, whispering in case anyone else came by. Pascale felt she was exactly where she should be, her hand on Witold's arm and her lips close to her ear, yet she shivered as Witold turned to her.

"You are cold."

Witold took off her greatcoat and wrapped it around Pascale's shoulders. As Pascale breathed its warm scent, Witold took her by the waist and sat her on the counter to warm her hands and feet. Pascale was surprised at how easily Witold touched her, as if sure of Pascale's acceptance. She replied softly, "Now you'll get chilled."

"I am wearing more clothes than you," said Witold.

The train clattered and jolted over a series of points. Steadying herself, Witold unwittingly brushed Pascale's thigh. Pascale smothered a gasp and minutely withdrew. Witold, misunderstanding, leaned closer to her, head tipped as if listening, although Pascale did not speak. Pascale wondered at herself, how she could let Witold be this near and not reach out, gather her close. She clenched her hands together in her lap. Witold took them between her own, asking, "It is cold in Boston? You have snow?"

"Yes." Pascale concentrated on controlling herself. "It's much like northern Europe. I catch a streetcar in winter."

"Streetcars? I saw them in a city I was marched through, but they were bombed, not moving. The friend you live with, she works where you work?"

"Yes, but she'll be leaving my apartment when I return."

"Then you will have room," said Witold.

Pascale was conscious of her hands relaxing in Witold's. "You plan to stay there?"

"I will find a job and pay you," said Witold. "I could lift boxes where you work. I am strong. I could learn to drive a streetcar."

"The United States has tests for immigrants," said Pascale. "Education tests. Medical tests."

Witold smiled. "You think I have not faced such tests?"

"These will be impossible to evade." Pascale wanted to tell her that she would be stopped, either when her disguise was discovered or, if she dressed appropriately, because she was unskilled, unmarried, and alone. "Stowing away isn't easy, not to the States and not in wartime," she told her instead. "You'll be caught and shipped home."

"Then first I will escape to somewhere else. Mexico or Canada. South America. I know geography; I could walk to Boston from those places."

"Learn as much English as you can. Without it you're at the mercy of others."

"Teach me."

"We've no time. We'll be in Fontaine in the morning. I won't be able to see you often there, or perhaps not at all."

"You must try."

"Of course I'll try."

"If you do not come to me, I will come to you."

"Witold, you can't. You can't. You'll be in a well-guarded camp inside the Military Government Zone. If you escape you'll be recaptured. If you cause the army trouble you'll be deported to Poland without a hearing. I haven't the power to do anything for you once you're back there."

"I must stay inside the liberated parts of Europe." Witold nodded.

"That's not what I meant."

"I know what is best for me."

"I'll lose you."

"In a Military Government Zone?" Witold smiled again. "I will not be lost, no matter where I am. I will always be looking for you."

Suddenly breathless, Pascale stammered, "Witold, we—we've met by chance in a war. It doesn't mean—"

"Do not be foolish." Witold put two fingers to Pascale's lips. "We must be together."

It was hard to move away from her touch. "You don't understand."

Witold dropped her hand. "I am alone in my feelings?"

"No! But you need to be told—"

"I know enough."

Boots in the corridor. They paused. This was not a Wac. Pascale jumped as the military guard rapped the door. "Private Tailland," she told him, naming her unit.

"Sorry to disturb you, Ma'am." The guard went into the next carriage.

"I know little about you," Witold resumed coolly. "You know little about me. I do not need to know everything, just the one thing I do."

Pascale's pulse became heavy. "What is that one thing?"

"I am your necessity."

"My responsibility?" Pascale asked carefully, wanting to be sure, "or my need?"

"Have you not said they are the same?" Witold's smile was so tender that Pascale involuntarily leaned forward, but Witold, not seeing, had reached for the door. "We must go to our beds before that soldier returns."

Pascale subdued her clamorous heart with one hand as she led the way, Witold behind her like a shadow in the dark. She waited to hear Witold pull the curtains shut, then slipped in beside Velma.

She stared at the bottom of the upper bunk. What was she doing? What was she going to do? Witold was right, but that did not make things clearer. There was so much to say that could not be said until Witold confessed her disguise. And if she did? Pascale would have no defenses. With Edie, with the others, she had always had mansions in her heart that they had never reached, had never known. But Witold only had to knock and all would be opened to her.

Having lost her private self so completely should have been terrifying. Pascale found it otherwise. She fell asleep and woke only when Velma shook her shoulder.

"You're in the army now," said Velma.

"What time is it?"

"Reveille. Get your boyfriend off the premises till we're decent."

Pascale called. Witold pulled back the curtain, already awake. They stood again between the carriages until the women had dressed and had converted the compartment back to two rows of seats. Witold took her usual place. She gazed at Pascale as if seeing her anew in the morning's light. Pascale smiled at her and Witold turned, dazzled, to look out the window.

The train had left the dreary northern German plain behind in the night and was now threading its way through the border hills. Witold watched ploughed fields and blossoming orchards slip past with a neutral tip of her head.

"The war hardly seems to have touched here," said Pascale.

Witold nodded at a bombed church tower. "It touched everywhere."

The train began to slow. Witold sat up warily.

"Why are we stopping?" asked Marie.

"Hang on." Velma went to find out.

A small town suddenly appeared around them. The train hissed to a stop at the station. Its platform was crowded with refugees who had clearly spent the night within its inadequate shelter. Old women in scarves and shapeless coats, young women with children on their hips, old men in rag-bound boots were all staring silently at the train. Witold stared back, fists clenched on her knees.

A door must have opened, for the crowd surged forward. A man shouted in French, then in German, and their heads turned to him.

"That's Lieutenant Spelman," said Binty. "He's always stuck with telling them it's ix-nay on hitching a ride."

Velma came back. "The kitchen's loading eggs and milk for you-know-who's breakfast."

"I bet those folks are enjoying the sight," said Dot.

"Don't lean forward," Pascale warned Witold. "If they realize what you are, they'll riot to get aboard."

Witold pressed herself into the upholstery. The train whistled, blew steam, and pulled out, the refugees' dull eyes following.

"Those were Germans," said Witold. "Ten months ago they thought they were the conquerors of the world."

"Perhaps those ones never wanted the war," Pascale offered.

Witold snorted. "They wanted it when they thought they would win it. Once Hitler is captured, how overwhelmed we shall be at the number of Germans who had always hated the Nazis and always helped Jews."

"You're no champion of the common people."

"The decent, ordinary folk?" Witold sneered. "The ones who looted the houses of their arrested neighbours? Who dragged Jews from hiding? They have no special virtue. They are nothing."

"How can anyone have no value?" asked Pascale.

Witold's jaw hardened. "They have made themselves so. I will not be responsible for Germans. I will go to America and be responsible there."

"Is he still hep on America?" asked Velma, catching the word.

"He's determined," said Pascale.

"Amaireeca," said Witold. "Pleez. Aye vont too gau."

The women burst out laughing.

"That'll get him far," said Velma sympathetically.

"They are laughing at me?" Witold asked.

"They don't think you'll get to America."

Witold gave a half-smile. "Yesterday they did not think I would get to France."

The women went for breakfast in two stages. Pascale sat with Velma and Dot. She wished she could bring coffee back for Witold, but did manage two slices of bread filled with sausage inside her handkerchief.

"How's tricks?" asked Lieutenant Bergman, stepping over.

"All quiet on the eastern front," said Velma.

"We're reporting to Army Station as soon as we pull into Fontaine," Francine told them. "Sergeant, your unit has permission to deliver your package to the camp first."

One of the women of their company, overhearing from another table, asked, "What are you all dropping off?"

"Something we picked up at the last minute back in Gultenheim as a personal favor for the commandant," said Velma.

"Colonel Grove!" Norma sighed. "I surely wish I could do that man favors. What a dreamboat! Remember our last night in Fontaine? I got half a dance with him before that Binty Marriot cut me out."

"I bet the colonel enjoyed every minute," said Francine.

"At least I had the sense to be interested." Norma shot a glance at Pascale.

"Leave her alone," said Velma. "She's engaged to a Polish guy."

"You're joshing me!" Norma was startled.

Pascale squirmed. Having withstood their disgust and pity for two years, it was hard to sacrifice her defiance, even for Witold.

"They met just before we left Germany," Velma replied. "It was crazy romantic. Come on, troops, back to base."

They left Norma and the women at her table open-mouthed. Pascale could feel Francine's eyes on her all the way to the dining car door.

She found Witold angry and flustered. "What's been going on?" she asked the others.

"Marie's been trying to catch him out," said Jeeter disgustedly. "You know, springing German and Russian on him to see if he's fluent enough to be a national."

"Why don't you leave that to the refugee administrators in Fontaine?" Pascale asked Marie calmly. "They have people who'll make sure."

"I don't trust him," said Marie. "There's something fishy about him. I can feel it."

"Maybe it was something you ate," said Jeeter.

"That one!" Witold exploded to Pascale. "She reminds me of

Gestapo. Asking questions from the moment you left. She knows I have little German. I said so in English, I said *I doe nut onderstond*, but she goes on and on."

"She's suspicious of you," said Pascale. "She doesn't like people who are different from her."

"Different? The whole world is different from her. She has not seen? This is how I will be treated in the camp."

"They'll ask you questions, but they won't harm you." Pascale looked at her hopelessly. "I'll do all I can to prevent you from being repatriated."

"Tell them I killed Communists," said Witold.

"That's not enough to stop them sending you back." Pascale wrote in her notebook. "This might help: here's my name, number, and unit. You can find me through these. The one below is my address in Boston. This is how you say it." She made Witold repeat her words.

"Honey," said Velma kindly, "aren't you getting in a little deep? You hardly know the guy."

"He's using you," said Marie. "He'll batten on you for life."

"You're the one who announced our engagement," Pascale told Velma.

"I was sticking a firecracker under that Norma," said Velma. "You're going to get yourself in trouble over him."

"I'm already in trouble," said Pascale.

Witold was reading Pascale's Boston address. "I will be at this place," she said in wonder.

The sun broke from the clouds as the train descended into a valley. The orderly confusion of an army command station spread across the fields: a landing strip, rows of tanks, trucks, and tents, a fuel depot. Witold grew quiet as the two refugee camps, with their long wire perimeters and their streets of prefabricated buildings, came into view beyond the town.

Lieutenant Bergman put her head around the door. "Tailland, Turner, get that boy by the door. All of you stick close round him and hustle him through the station on the double. If you're questioned, Tailland, you're taking the full credit, am I right?"

"Yes, Ma'am," said Pascale.

"And don't ever pull a stunt like this again."

"No, Ma'am."

As the train began to slow, the women took up their coats, caps, and bags. Velma and Dot led the way, Binty shielding Witold at the front, Pascale and Jeeter flanking her, and Marie taking the rearguard.

"We ought to play for Notre Dame," said Dot.

Velma flung open the door as the train stopped. They were on the platform before any other compartment had stirred. Velma peeled away from formation to deal with the sentries at the exit while Dot led the rest into the street and quick-marched them across the town square, where they waited at attention on the corner.

"These are good soldiers," Witold smiled at Pascale.

Velma drove up in a jeep a minute later. "How about this, girls?" she said proudly.

"How do you do it?" asked Dot, climbing in.

The others followed, planting Witold in their midst. Velma fought the gears and they lurched through town.

Pascale saw Witold's face slowly close and set. "The guards won't hurt you," she told her.

"I am not afraid of soldiers. I do not want to be gone from you."

"We won't be apart a minute longer than I can help," said Pascale.

Witold looked at her with desperate concentration and began to speak. Pascale smiled reassuringly, but Witold dropped her eyes to her boots, mouth shut tight, a muscle jumping in her cheek. Pascale looked wistfully at her bent head.

The refugee camps began on the outskirts of Fontaine. A large farmhouse and the stone barn beside it had been transformed into headquarters and a hospital, each ringed with its own fence. Beyond were the detention areas.

Velma stopped at the main gate. "End of the line, troops."

The women squeezed aside to let Pascale and Witold descend. Velma stuck out her hand. "Mr. Rukowicz, this is good-bye."

Witold shook it.

"If you ever get to America, look me up," said Velma. "Akron, Ohio. Ladies' Dresses at Stedman's Department Store."

Pascale translated.

"Thenk yoo," said Witold.

Dot and Jeeter shook her hand. Binty patted her shoulder, saying, "It's kind of like losing your mascot." Marie nodded curtly.

"Go on," Velma said to Pascale.

Pascale turned to the gate, sick with reluctance. The sentries had already raised the bar and were swinging open one wing. A sergeant major approached from the sentry house inside the gate, asking, "One for us, sister?"

"His name is Witold Rukowicz," said Pascale. "He's Polish. He's a noncombatant and should be listed as going to America."

"They all want to go to America," said the sergeant major, eyeing Witold. "Come on, buddy."

"Let me say good-bye to him," said Pascale, and the sergeant major shrugged.

Pascale stepped closer to Witold. "You have the paper? My address?"

Witold tapped her pocket, nodding.

"I'm sorry I had to bring you here," said Pascale. "I'm sorry I couldn't—"

Witold shook her head. "Do not apologize, Pascale Tailland." She stooped and kissed Pascale's hand, hesitated, turned it and kissed the palm. Pascale felt fire flash to her heart.

"You see," said Witold, straightening, "you see. I must tell you—" Her eyes were on Pascale's lips.

"Witold." Pascale seized her by the lapels. "Witold!"

"I must—"

"I know you're a woman." Pascale flung herself into Witold's arms and kissed her. Witold's mouth went from uncertainty to certainty in an instant. Her arms tightened.

"Wait a goddamn minute!" The sergeant major jerked Witold away. "I'm not having some Polack pawing an American gal."

"Stupid fool!" Witold snapped, trying to wrench herself from his grasp.

"Sergeant Major—" Pascale's face was hot with fury and chagrin.

"You behave yourself, miss," said the sergeant major, hauling Witold back with one huge hand. "Don't let this Polack take advantage of your sweet nature."

Velma was out of the jeep. "Private Tailland, it's time we got to headquarters."

"Witold!" Pascale cried, but the sergeant major had already dragged her through the gate. Witold was shouting, "I am responsible! I am responsible for you!"

The gate closed. One of the sentries helped the sergeant major subdue Witold, who was struggling like an animal. Pascale stepped helplessly toward her.

"Let's go," Velma growled with friendly firmness, putting a hand on her arm. "You did the only thing you could, professor."

Witold was being manhandled into the sentry house. She was gone. Pascale turned away, eyes blank. Someone helped her into the jeep.

"Gee, I didn't think you'd got it so hard," said Jeeter.

"When they turn normal, they turn with a vengeance," Marie sniffed.

"Oh, shut up," said Dot.

At the old town hall, now headquarters for Army Station Fontaine, the women were ordered directly to the briefing room. They slipped into their seats in time to stand for the general.

Pascale did not hear his welcoming remarks, trying instead to think of a reason why Witold should be given U.S. immigrant status. She thought of Witold's lips on her hand. The general was thanking them for their past efforts. On her mouth. The general was discussing security. Pascale wondered if she could persuade her mother to claim Witold as a relative. Her mother might, if her father learned nothing of it. The general raised the need for translations. Or Pascale could have Witold released into her custody on a day-pass, drive her far from Fontaine with a map and money, and come back alone to take the consequences. The general named the destination, Chartres, and the embarkation time, 0830 hours Tuesday. Pascale jolted awake. Tuesday was tomorrow. They were leaving Fontaine tomorrow morning.

She pressed her fingers against the side seams of her skirt until the general finished his briefing on the Chartres Conference. The Wacs were marched to the offices upstairs, where stacks of documents in seven different languages waited by typewriters to be rendered into English.

"Velma," said Pascale as the others sank into their chairs with groans. "I have to talk to you."

"I can guess, honey."

"I told him I'd see him tomorrow. I can't leave him like this."

"You'll have to," said Velma. "We've got less than a week to deal with more than what's on these desks. We're going to be typing on the train, on round-the-clock shifts, in our sleep, until they're finished. You'll wish you never even heard of Polish. If you get a minute, which I doubt, you've got my permission to write him a letter. You know security: don't tell him where you're going, just wish him luck."

"But—"

"You've had your orders, soldier."

Pascale bit her lip to stay silent and went to her desk. She rolled a carbon and two sheets of paper from the top ream into her typewriter. First document: *War Crimes; Polish; Collaborators in.*

The discipline of concentration and the atrocities she was translating kept thoughts of Witold at bay. Around her, Pascale could hear the other women's typing falter and resume as they encountered details of torture and mass murder. They worked through the morning and, after a quick, subdued lunch, through the afternoon. Through the evening. In the sickly glow of the naked light bulbs they stared at each other's tired faces.

"That's all we can do," said Velma. "Let's get packed."

It was 2230. Witold would already be bunked down with a dozen, two dozen men in a camp hut. Anything might happen to her tonight.

"I need to see the lieutenant," Pascale said to Velma.

"About your Polish guy?" Velma yawned. "You don't give up, do you? I'll go check."

The others stood, flexing cramped shoulders.

"There's plenty of men better looking and more available," said Marie.

Velma came back. "You've got five minutes."

Pascale went past offices of men feverishly packing document boxes for the journey. She found Lieutenant Bergman and saluted.

"At ease," Francine said automatically without looking up.

Pascale waited. Francine added the memo to a heap, capped her pen, and said, "Yes?"

Pascale kept her eyes straight ahead. "It concerns the refugee we took to the camp this morning, Ma'am. I need to send a message to him. The sergeant said I could write a letter if I found the time, but there was no time. It's urgent."

"Send it through army mail," Francine said coldly.

"But it's important that I—"

"Private, hold it a goddamn minute. I don't think you got the picture. You smuggled a Polish national onto a train under military security. Serious offense. That refugee is now where he should be: a DP camp. Serious offense turned into good deed by the skin of your teeth. That's it. I won't indulge you any further."

"It's imperative that Witold shouldn't stay there."

"Soldier, I don't want you to think of anything, not a thing, but your work as of right now, you understand me?"

"Witold is a woman."

Francine's hand froze half-way to her pen. "That makes it imperative."

"I thought you might agree, Ma'am."

Francine sat back. "Have a seat, Tailland. I'll be damned. You sure?"

"I know it."

"I'll be damned." Francine lit a cigarette thoughtfully. "You had me fooled."

"I'm sorry. I had no way of telling you."

"Not telling has landed a girl in the men's DP camp. What were you using for brains?"

"I couldn't prevent it," said Pascale. "Once Velma and the others had taken her at her disguise, I didn't dare expose her. I had no right."

"That's mighty high-minded of you. Too bad for her." Francine smoked for a minute. "You can't do anything about it, Pascale. Work begins at 0600 hours, then we're on that train." She held up a hand against Pascale's protests. "I'll write to Colonel Grove myself. He'll think it's a hoot, but he'll sort something out."

"You mustn't tell him!"

"Use your noodle, girl. Grove's as nancy as they come. We're old pals. You can trust him; he'll get Witold out of the men's camp. Witold! What's her real name?"

"I don't know," said Pascale.

"Don't know? What do you know about her?"

"I know I have to get her to the States."

"What is this, love at first sight or something?"

"Yes," said Pascale.

Bron

3

Bronia lay on her bunk, hands laced behind her head, listening to the chords of snoring around her from the Lithuanians, Poles, and, in the corner, the two Russians who were passing themselves off as Latvian nationals. She had spent yesterday with the Poles. They had accepted with nods her almost-true account of how she had survived the war. Their war, she learned at length, had been as forced labor in a German shipyard.

"We were lucky to be put there," said Slawek, a man still coughing from the remains of a disease the American doctors had treated. "We could have been sent to the mines or the factories. At least we were outdoors. Twenty hours a day, but good clean sea air." He coughed again. "Our luck held to the end: we weren't freed by the British. I hear the food in their camps is terrible, and no cigarettes." He produced a tattered army magazine. "Look at this! Amazing. This is why the Americans won the war: they have the most money. See, every American has an automobile."

"Not all of them," said Bron.

"You know this, do you?" Andrzej asked. "You've been there?"

"I'm going."

"Indeed? The American army is flying you there specially?" Slawek sniffed.

"If they are, we'll join you," said Andrzej, taking a concentrated drag on his cigarette. "I'll go anywhere."

"Only Janusz wants to go back home," said Slawek. "That tells you a lot, doesn't it?"

"That Janusz is a fool," said Bron.

She studied the photographs in the magazine as Slawek turned the pages. Strange to see a street with its buildings intact.

"Roosevelt," Andrzej pointed. "He knows nothing of Poland. Or of Europe, I might add. He wants nothing but to bring his soldiers back to America, no matter what cost to us."

Slawek disagreed. Bron had spent most of the day listening to them argue. It reminded her of home. They bickered through dinner and in the washing rooms, were theatrically at odds about the future of the war and Poland in the latrines, allowing Bron to employ her usual stratagems, and were still at it in their beds until, to universal relief, *lights out* forced them to be silent.

In the Soviet prison farm she had escaped, the beds had been straw pallets and the latrines a ditch. Those had been difficult enough to deal with, but here American cleanliness and organization were going to defeat her. She would not be able to keep up her disguise, not with the compulsory washing sessions and medical checks that Slawek had described. Time to abandon her pretense and be transferred to the women's camp. Pascale would know where to look for her.

There. She had said the name. Alone with her thoughts amid the sleeping men, Bron finally allowed herself to think of Pascale.

She knew she did not feel this way about Pascale because of her disguise. It had nothing to do with trousers and tie. Pascale has seen past her disguise, perhaps from the first moment, had seen through it right into Bron's head. Into her heart. Being seen so clearly was like having a torrent of water rush through you, tearing away everything. Changing everything.

Pascale. Pascale would be here today. Today. Perhaps this morning. They would—Bron's breath tightened—kiss. She had to have Pascale's kiss. Had to have her arms around her, had to breathe the same air she breathed.

Bron was sure the hammering of her heart was loud enough to wake the sleeping men around her. She put her hands over it. Pascale must come soon before her heart exploded. She fell asleep protecting it.

Klaxons brayed into the quiet morning. The men rose, scratching and spitting as they pulled on their clothes. Bron waited to be the last up. It assured her the washing room to herself but made her the last into the dining tent. There was still food on the tables. She wedged herself onto a bench and piled a plate. So much! The tent was filled with an army of Poles, Czechs, Lithuanians, Danes, Ukrainians, Russians, Belgians, all waiting for the war to end while they lived off the generosity of the Americans. Would America accept any responsibility beyond feeding and deporting them? What did these men owe America for such a favor? She suspected Pascale would say that if anything was owed, it was not obedience.

Three guards paced the aisles, calling out names. One name was Bron's. Interrogation had finally arrived. She crammed a piece of bread into her mouth in case she would not be fed again for a long time. The guards took the summoned men through the inner gate to the farmhouse that served as the camp commandant's headquarters. She was separated from them and taken upstairs to a room with windows overlooking the camp. An officer was sitting behind the desk. In front of the desk, two nurses sat on either side of an empty chair. Bron saw no torture equipment. The guard nudged her toward the middle chair.

As she sat down, the officer smiled at her, shaking his head and saying something in English. The older nurse frowned. The younger nurse laughed.

"Your name?" the commandant asked Bron in reasonable German.

"Witold Grzegorz Rukowicz, sir," she replied in the same language.

He spoke in English to the younger nurse, who repeated it to Bron in clumsy Polish: "Colonel Grove has received a letter about you from a Lieutenant Bergman."

"Yes?" Bron said cautiously.

"Yes. He has decided that you can no longer be kept in the camp."

"I am to be set free?"

The younger nurse spoke to the commandant, who shook his head as he answered. The nurse told Bron, "Colonel Grove wants you to be a secret."

"Why?"

"I can't tell you that."

"Where am I going?"

Colonel Grove spoke again. The younger nurse said, "You will be kept in the hospital."

"I have no disease."

"Those are his orders."

"I am permitted a visitor?"

The younger nurse inquired. "Colonel Grove says you should be told that the Women's Army Corps unit that brought you to this camp has now left Fontaine."

Long schooled not to react to blows, Bron sat mutely. The colonel spoke with the older nurse, then looked kindly at Bron, saying in German, "Please go now."

"You are to come with us," said the younger nurse.

Bron stumbled after them.

The two nurses took her to a room at the back of the hospital. In a smaller side room was a wash basin and a toilet. The main room had a bed, a little table next to the bed, and a chair. The window faced the same direction as the colonel's, but this window had bars.

The younger nurse said, "You will stay here. Because I speak Polish, I'll be looking after you."

"For how long?" asked Bron.

"I don't know." The younger nurse smiled and left. A bolt shot home outside.

Bron sat on the chair. Pascale was gone.

After a while, Bron thought further. This must also have been a surprise for Pascale. Pascale would not have promised to visit Bron if she had known. Even surprised, she had managed to get Bron out of the men's camp; Bron knew who had prompted Lieutenant Bergman's letter. But what had the lieutenant's letter said to Colonel Grove? Why had he put her into this hospital? She could not think of an answer, so she gave up speculating and wondered instead if Pascale would write a letter to her. It must be permitted. If Pascale wrote to her from some place in Germany or France, Bron would have an address to go to when she escaped. It would be easier than going all the way to America.

Bron thought about Pascale. She thought of how Pascale had looked. Of what she had said. Of how close they had stood as they talked. Bron pounded her fists on her knees. All the time, all that time spent with Pascale, and she had been too wary to tell her the truth, afraid until almost too late. But it had been wrong to fear. Pascale would never have turned away from her. Pascale had known, had been the one to speak, had been the one to act. Pascale had kissed her. Bron put her palm to her lips, remembering it. Remembered Pascale in her arms.

When Bron finally opened her eyes, an hour had gone by. She stood and hung her greatcoat on the door. Tested the handle. The bolt was firm. She stood by the window. Another hour passed. She explored. In the smaller room was a tiled area with a drain in the floor and a spigot jutting from the wall. She turned the tap. Fine mist shot from the spigot. She jerked back, appalled for a second, though she knew that it would be only water. One finger tested it. The water was warm. At last she could wash. But the nurse might come back at any time. Not daring to take off her clothes, Bron contented herself with scrubbing her face and neck with the bar of soap.

She studied the camp again, her forehead against the glass. There were guards in the towers and pairs of soldiers patrolling the fences. The fences were high. But every place could be escaped from if you looked hard and thought like a mouse.

She had been hungry for some time when the bolt of the door slid back. The younger nurse who spoke Polish came in with a tray. Bron stood up. The nurse walked around her as if measuring her. Bron measured back. The nurse was wide and short, with hair the color of wheat and eyes like toasted wheat. Bron was close enough to read the tag on her impressive bosom: Lucia Jaarro.

"Hello again," said Lucia. "Mister Rukowicz. May I call you Witold? That's what you call yourself? Witold?"

"Yes," said Bron.

"As you can hear, my Polish isn't so good. I speak German much better. Do you speak any Finnish? That's what I speak best. No? Swedish, maybe? Too bad, it would have made things easier. Anything else?"

"Aye haf no Aingleesch," said Bron.

Lucia jumped. *"Sprechen sie Englisch?"*

"*Nein,*" said Bron. "*Ich kann ein wenig Deutsch sprechen.*"

"Then that's got to do. I've talked the whole war in one big hodgepodge," said Lucia in a mixture of German and Polish. "Can you understand me when I talk like this?"

"Yes," said Bron.

"Good, because it's the best you'll get." Lucia put the tray on the bedside table. "Here, eat your lunch."

Bron obeyed, then realized that Lucia was looking at her. "I am doing something wrong?"

"Not from where I'm standing," said Lucia. "You're doing just fine." When Bron had finished, she asked, "Can I get you anything?"

Bron considered. "Something to read. Please."

"I don't think we have a thing in Polish," said Lucia. "I'll try."

"I am to be interrogated?"

Lucia laughed. "We don't want to know anything more about you than we already do. You're unofficial and secret, and you won't be seeing anyone but me."

"Why?" asked Bron.

"That would be telling." Lucia laughed again as she left, bolting the door behind her.

Bron jammed the chair against the door handle to form an early warning, undressed, and stood under the shower spigot for half an hour. Finally clean, she was reluctant to wear her dirty clothes, so put soap to everything. She padded barefoot around the room, hanging her washing from the coat hooks and furniture. It felt strange to have no clothes on at all. When had been the last time? Years ago.

She sat on the bed and thought of Pascale. Perhaps Pascale was not in Europe any more. Perhaps she was already in America, writing Bron a letter. Bron would have to find work on a ship and get across the ocean. Were dirigibles still flying to America in spite of the war? She would like to be in one. There might be a job for her opening the valves.

She lay down. The room smelled of steaming wool. She scratched an old scar on her shoulder and wondered what a woman did with another woman. They had nothing to go inside. Pascale must not think it mattered. Perhaps you could do to another woman what you did to yourself. Bron thought of the friend Pascale had shared her apartment with, the one who had not been kind to her. Bron had seen it in Pascale's face. That friend would be leaving when Pascale got home. If she tried to stay, Bron would make her go. Having determined the matter, Bron went to sleep.

She woke with a flash of fear, her hand under the pillow grasping for her knife, in a room now dark. The scrape that had awakened her came again.

"Witold?" It was the nurse, Lucia. "What have you done to the door?"

"Wait, please," Bron called, groping for her clothes. They were still too wet to put on. Lucia shoved at the door. Finding her boots, Bron buttoned her greatcoat to the neck and pulled away the chair.

Lucia came in warily and turned on the light. She saw the wet clothing, Bron in greatcoat and boots, and giggled. "We've got a laundry service," she said, putting down her tray and drawing the curtains. "I could have sent your clothes out with the bundles this morning. Tell me next time and I will."

"I am happy to do it myself," said Bron.

"If it was up to me, you wouldn't be doing anything by yourself," Lucia said with a secretive smile.

Puzzled, Bron sat and put the dinner tray on her knees. "No, I am able to do much, although it is true that I cannot learn English by myself. Please, you will tell me the English names for these?"

"Spiking my guns, huh?" said Lucia. "Okay. That's corned beef. Beef is the meat, corned is what makes it that way. Potatoes. Cabbage. Milk."

Bron repeated them. Lucia continued, "Knife. Fork. Spoon. Plate. Cup. Tray."

As Bron ate, Lucia pointed around the room, naming the walls, floor, mirror, window.

"Thenk yoo," said Bron.

"Where did you learn English?" asked Lucia.

"Pascale," said Bron.

"Who's Pascale?"

"The woman who saved me."

"From the Germans?" asked Lucia.

"From the wolf."

"My Polish isn't good," said Lucia. "I don't understand."

Bron shrugged.

"Was she a soldier, the woman who saved you?" Lucia gestured at her lapels. "Women's Army Corps?"

"Yes."

"Do you like soldier girls?"

"I like her."

Lucia smirked.

"That is amusing?" asked Bron flatly.

"Not a bit." Lucia took away Bron's cleared tray. She came back later in the evening with a book and a set of light cotton clothing.

Bron threw the clothes on the floor. "No!"

"They're not prisoners' clothes," said Lucia, picking them up. "They're pajamas. For sleeping."

Bron remembered Pascale wearing them under her dressing gown, but said again, "No." She would not wear anything that doomed men had worn.

"You're stubborn as a mule." Lucia took them back and gave Bron the book. "Maybe you'll like this better."

Bron saw that it had pictures. "Thenk yoo."

"You're welcome," said Lucia.

"What?"

Lucia repeated it, adding *hello, how do you do, good morning, good night,* and *good-bye,* miming each one until Bron was chuckling. Lucia ruffled her hair, saying, "I see why your Pascale saved you."

Bron was abruptly serious.

"Oh, dear," said Lucia. "I can tell she's never a joking matter."

"Gud night," said Bron.

She had another shower before sleeping. Hot water at every hour! Americans were rich. She soaped herself thickly and let the water sluice her. No scrubbing. The feel of her own clean skin made her wonder what Pascale's would feel like naked and wet. Palms and forehead against the tiles, Bron endured a longing she could hardly bear as the shower pummeled her shoulders. By the time she had recovered, the water was cold.

Lucia's picture book was on the bed. It was in German and English and seemed to be telling the German people what their country was going to be like under American rule. Here was a map with flags. Her finger ticked off British, American, Communist. Poland had the Polish flag on it. The book's first lie. She looked at the pictures of bombed cities and, beside them, drawings of those cities reborn with tall buildings. They would still be filled with Germans.

She put the book aside and cleaned her teeth with the brush left for her in a glass cup. She went to bed, hugging her bare ribs until she was asleep.

Her clothes were dry in the morning. She got dressed and sat waiting. She wished the colonel would make her work. Waiting was worse even than field labor. It was nothingness that weighed like a chain. But now she could think about Pascale. She decided to remember the morning sun against Pascale's cheek. The way Pascale had looked at her. The shape of Pascale's mouth. Each image deserved hours to think about properly. A clatter made her glance around.

"Hello there." Lucia was putting down breakfast and a paper bundle. "You were a thousand miles away."

"I was thinking." Bron looked at the tray. "You have time to do this?"

"There aren't enough patients to keep us busy, not until the next shipment arrives," said Lucia. "For now, I'm going to wait on you hand and foot."

"Because you are the only nurse who can speak Polish?"

"That's one reason," Lucia said, her mouth primly naughty. "Let's say that there's nothing Colonel Grove doesn't know about his staff."

Bron, tired of riddles, raised her eyebrows politely, but Lucia said no more. Bron asked, "It is permitted to have a hairbrush? I have been given only a small one for teeth."

Lucia laughed. "It's here." She swung aside the washroom mirror to show her a brush and shaving equipment. "I've brought some other things for you."

"A letter?" Bron asked hopefully.

"From your soldier girl? The orderly didn't give me anything." Lucia unwrapped the bundle and gave Bron a pack of cigarettes, a bar of chocolate, chewing gum, a fine-toothed comb, and a mouth organ.

"Who has sent me these things?" asked Bron.

"The Red Cross. They send parcels to everyone."

"Everyone? Also Germans?"

"If they're prisoners, yes."

Bron snorted. "You should kill sick dogs, not give them bones."

"There are good Germans," said Lucia.

"You believe that?"

"I've seen it with my own eyes."

"Then you are—" Bron searched for a German word. "*Verrückt.* You are mad. I too have seen."

"Just because the Nazis in Poland were cruel doesn't make all Germans evil," said Lucia.

"Yes it does. Not only because of Poland."

Lucia shook her head. "You're all like this, you refugees. Full of hate."

"Sometimes one must be."

"The war's almost over. It's time to forgive. You've got to remember that people have to do what they're told. Look at me. Imagine if the United States was doing bad things, like, oh, invading Mexico or something. I'd still have to carry out my duties. It wouldn't make me bad. Don't be so hard on the Germans."

Bron wondered if Lucia was as foolish as she sounded.

"We're at the start of a brand new world," Lucia said stubbornly. "You'll have to learn to live in it."

"I will see if this new world is so different from the old," said Bron. "So far, the rules have not changed."

Lucia pointed to Bron's head. "You have to change what's in there first."

"I must have a better reason than your hope."

"Then you'll never change. Hope is what's going to make it happen."

"Hoping that a better world is true will make it so?" asked Bron.

Lucia nodded. "You've got to know what you're aiming for."

"Governments are not people."

"By the people and for the people, at least where I come from," said Lucia with a lift of the chin. "That's good enough for me."

After Lucia left, Bron tentatively blew on the Red Cross mouth organ. She thought about what Lucia had said. She did not think Lucia meant the same thing as Pascale. Hoping was not acting.

The mouth organ was a complicated instrument. She put it aside and watched the camp. Prisoners were moving listlessly from tent to tent, talking and smoking. Some hovered by the soldiers who guarded them, probably begging for favors. Fools. You did not get favors unless you did favors in return. What could they possibly offer an American soldier that he did not already have or could get a hundred times over? Bron looked down at her mouth organ. She had nothing to barter, nothing, and Pascale might be sailing across the sea this minute.

Lucia brought lunch but could not stay. A prisoner complaining of a sore toe had been found to have gangrene. Bron remembered finding a Russian dying of gangrene. She had not done anything to help him. A Russian was a Russian.

The next morning, she asked, "How is the man with the toe?"

"He has fewer toes now," said Lucia. She took a clothbound book from her pocket. "You asked for this."

"Thenk yoo. A letter for me?"

Lucia shook her head. "Sorry."

Bron thumbed through the book. "A lexicon! Polish and English." She looked in the front. "It tells me how to pronounce Polish, and I know this."

"I'll teach you the English sounds," Lucia offered.

"Why?" asked Bron. "You have been ordered to help me learn?"

"I've had three orders from Colonel Grove: to look after you, to keep my mouth as shut about you as I have about everything else, and to stop you from making trouble."

"What trouble can I cause, locked in here?"

"You're trouble just breathing. Mac—MacIntyre, the chief nurse, you met her—isn't a bit happy about you living in the hospital, but

Colonel Grove thinks you might cause havoc anywhere else."

"Why does he think that?"

"I'm not supposed to discuss any of this," said Lucia. "After lunch you'll go for a walk. You're to get an hour's exercise every day."

"My health is of concern to the colonel?"

"Of course we're concerned. Americans aren't like the Nazis. We believe in our moral duty. There are international rules for keeping prisoners, you know."

"Yes, for captured Allied soldiers," said Bron. "When Polish soldiers are caught, they are not given exercise and Red Cross parcels."

"Were you a prisoner of the Nazis?"

"For a few days. Enough to know."

"How long were you on the run?"

"From when the Germans invaded until now."

"That's a long time. I was still a kid when the war in Europe began."

"So was I."

Lucia's eyes fell. "Then you've spent your whole grown-up life as a refugee."

"Until the Americans came I was not a refugee," said Bron, "I was scum, *untermensch*."

"That's one thing you'll never be now. Not with us."

"No, with you I am a problem."

Lucia flushed. "We don't want to keep you any longer than we've got to, but you know it's not safe to be out there on your own." She pointed to the tray. "At least we give you three meals a day. That's oatmeal. Bread. Peaches."

"Americans have good food."

"We have the best of everything," said Lucia proudly.

"You have the most."

"Most is best."

When Lucia delivered lunch, she had an overcoat draped across her arm. "We'll go on that walk in the yard once you're done."

"They are concerned with your health as well?" Bron was amused by Lucia's galoshes.

"They want me with you at all times," said Lucia. "I'm happy to obey orders like that."

"Why? You need exercise also?"

"Not the kind we're going to get outside."

"What is your kind? We would need rubber shoes?"

Lucia giggled. "That'd be something new."

Bron's room was next to a bolted door that led to a fenced-off area behind the hospital. One dead apple tree did its best to ornament the empty space.

"We hope to set out chairs and benches this summer for convalescents," said Lucia.

"That will cheer them," said Bron, looking at the tree. "May I go other places than here?"

Lucia glanced at Colonel Grove's window. "No. This is it."

They began to walk in a circle. Bron considered Lucia out of the corner of her eye. It was time to see what responsibilities Lucia thought she held. Bron said to her, "I want to go to America. Will you help me?"

"Nix!" said Lucia, startled. "That's definitely not my department. I'm just a nurse. Allocations are up to the administration. Only Colonel Grove has the power to decide, and he has policy to follow. You've got to be able to offer grounds for consideration."

"I have no family and no home. Where could Colonel Grove send me? I have nothing to return to. These are not grounds? Why can I not be set free? There is no need for me to be here."

Lucia shook her head. "Forget it. The colonel can't let you go—and he won't, for another reason. We had a ruckus a few months back during the first repatriations. The colonel didn't want to send any prisoners home, so when the gates were pushed open he let as many of the men escape as he could before he had to close them. It got him into big trouble. They sent a team of MPs to investigate. He won't be so nice again, not even for you." Lucia sighed. "Don't you want to go back? Aren't you homesick for Poland? I'm tired of the war and I miss the States like crazy. The army was an adventure, but now it's just work and boredom. I've been away too long."

"You have a man waiting for you? A family?"

Lucia stopped, her hands on her hips. "My, you are an innocent. Do I seem like the kind of girl who has a man?"

"How can I know? You are pretty."

"Thank you," Lucia lowered her eyes demurely.

"That is why you are here? Because you have no man?"

"Something like that," said Lucia. "The army got me out of my hometown."

"Hometown?"

"Where I was born. I wanted to get to the big city."

"Boston!"

Lucia shook her head. "Buffalo."

"Is that near Boston?"

"Nearer Boston than Texas."

None the wiser, Bron asked, "What is the best way to get to Boston?"

"I'm not going to talk about that. I think it falls under *sedition, encouragement of.* I've told you I can't help you."

Bron took out her lexicon. "But you will help me with this?"

"I think that's encouragement, too." Lucia encountered Bron's look. "Okay, okay, I promised. Give it here."

She went though the vowels, Bron repeating them. "Do you understand?"

"Yez," said Bron. "Onderstond."

"It slays me when you say English words."

"Pascale taught me many, and her friends a few."

"What else did she teach you?" Lucia's voice held an odd note.

"How to be alive."

Lucia groaned. "There's no competing with that."

Bron spent the afternoon looking up words in her lexicon: *freighter, job, to go, going.* She had another lesson in pronunciation from Lucia over supper, but Lucia was distracted.

"What is wrong?" asked Bron.

"We're getting a shipment pretty soon. Men from the liberated German camps. That means a lot of work to prepare for them and even more work when they get here. They come in terrible condition."

"Yet there are good Germans."

"Nazis aren't the same as Germans."

Bron smiled politely.

"You're going to have to get used to living with Germany," said

Lucia. "The Allies aren't going to stay around forever."

"Give us guns and we will deal with the Germans."

"Not on your tintype! Look how you Europeans messed things up. If we hadn't come, heaven knows where everything would be."

"Worse," Bron admitted.

"Don't forget it," said Lucia.

"I am sure we will not be able to."

"While you're making cracks at Uncle Sam, remember who's feeding and taking care of you."

"You are," said Bron.

Lucia smiled reluctantly. "I shouldn't talk to you about anything."

The next morning saw no letter from Pascale.

"Seems like your soldier girl has loved you and left you," said Lucia with alert neutrality.

Bron did not look up from her breakfast. "That is not true."

"It's none of my business, of course, but I think you could do better."

Bron shook her head.

"She knows where you are. What's stopping her?" Lucia pursed her lips as Bron remained silent. "I'd think about my future if I were you. Greener pastures."

Unperturbed, Bron watched Lucia pack up the tray. She knew what her future was. Anything could stop a letter. In the garden that afternoon, she asked Lucia about the camp, hiding her probes within questions about English names of things, asking, *"Das Tor?* Gate. How do you say many? How many gates? One, two. Is there another? I say two gates. Yes, two gates. One door. One fence. One tree. Two gates. Soldiers? Not soldiers? Military Police? What is the difference? Same guns?"

By the end of the exercise period she was satisfied that she knew the extent of the camp's security, but she needed more than information. She needed a door unlocked, a gate unguarded. She could not see how she would get them, not from these Americans who wanted for nothing.

The afternoon was unprofitably spent trying to learn the mouth organ. Once on the road again, she might earn money by playing tunes. That evening she asked Lucia, "Teach me this."

Lucia shook her head. "The only thing I know is 'The Streets of Laredo.'" She took the mouth organ and played a sad melody.

"How do you make one note come out alone?" asked Bron.

"Like this." Lucia put the tip of her tongue against one of the holes. "You cover what you don't want."

Bron leaned forward to see. Lucia reddened and thrust the mouth organ at her, giggling, "You try."

Bron attempted to tongue off notes. "It is not easy to do."

"No," said Lucia a little breathlessly, watching her mouth. "It takes practice."

"I have time."

"You'll have even more soon. I've got a day off tomorrow, but after that I won't be able to spend as much time with you as I've been doing."

"I am sorry."

"Me, too," said Lucia, "but duty calls."

The next day a male orderly brought Bron her meals. She asked, but there was no letter. The orderly did not take her outside. She spent time with the dictionary and by evening had mastered twenty words she hoped would be useful, including *ticket* and *voyage.* After supper she managed to pick out a song on the mouth organ. She remembered her father's customers singing it in the taproom, remembered her brother, not yet tall enough to reach the top barrels, singing treble.

Thoughts like these were not useful. She decided to go to bed and had taken off her boots and a sock when someone rapped on the door.

"It's Lucia."

"Why are you here?"

"I have a surprise."

Bron considered. A bad surprise would be interrogation, but Lucia would not then be snuffling with laughter.

"The lock is on your side," Bron reminded her.

Lucia came in with a swift, backward glance and shut the door. She held up a half-empty bottle and two cups. "Bourbon!"

"What is bourbon?" asked Bron.

Lucia sat on the bed. "Alcohol."

"Ah."

"It's Lillian's, but she's past needing it."

"It is like brandy?"

"Much, much better." Lucia poured two generous cupfuls.

Bron could see that Lucia had already drunk a quantity of this bourbon or another liquor: her cheeks were flushed and her eyes bold but unfocused. Bron sipped her bourbon. It was smoke-flavored like whiskey.

"Well, that's my liberty day gone," said Lucia. "Been and done. What's the point? All you can do is go into Fontaine. It's full of soldiers. Nothing there for a girl like me."

"What do you prefer? Books?"

Lucia giggled. "Books? Me? Not unless I've got to. How's your English?"

Bron recited her words.

"No mystery what you're aiming for," said Lucia. "D'you think you can wait for your soldier girl?"

"Of course," said Bron, puzzled.

"Even though you haven't heard a peep from her since you got here? How long are you gonna wait for her to remember you exist?"

"I can wait."

"Isn't that sweet? I'd be fed up. Fed up and climbing the walls." Lucia stretched her arms, her uniform straining at every curve. "I *am* climbing the walls, and you're the new kid in town. What d'you think about that?" She leaned closer.

"That this bourbon is nice, but it leads to foolish talk," said Bron, finishing the glass. "You should not be here so late in the evening."

"I've always said your type are the only real gentlemen." Lucia did not move away.

"I must insist."

"Okay, okay." Lucia slid off the bed, revealing her stocking tops. "I'm not so drunk that I don't take a brush-off. Guess I'll finish this bottle by myself."

"You should not," said Bron.

"Don't you worry 'bout me, honeybun." Lucia winked and closed the door behind her.

Bron loosened her tie. Something knocked. She jumped; it was the radiator. She pulled the curtains back. The camp was lit by rows of electric lights. Smoke drifted from pipes where paraffin oil heaters warmed the cold huts. She went to bed.

She woke with hot, alcohol-laden breath against her face. Thrusting the attacker away with one hand, she tore under her pillow for her knife.

"Witold!" said Lucia indignantly.

"What are you doing here, and very drunk?"

"What'm I doing here? Don't pretend."

"I am not pretending anything."

"That's how you drive me crazy."

Lucia bent over her. Bron, suddenly aware that Lucia was naked beneath her robe, lay still. Lucia came closer, lips against Bron's cheek, lips brushing her mouth. Bron jerked away. "You are not Pascale."

"Dead right, but she's not here, is she?"

"No, but—"

Lucia ran a finger down Bron's cheek. "C'mon, it's plain as day she's dumped you."

"I do not understand."

"Poor kid, you just don't want to admit it, do you? But you don't need to be sad anymore, 'cause you got me to take care of you." Lucia kissed her again. "If you want me to stop, you'd better tell me now 'cause, brother, I won't be able to in a minute."

"You must stop," Bron said desperately. "I am not a man."

Lucia laughed. "Of course you aren't!"

"You know this?"

"Do I know? I know, Mac knows, the colonel knows."

Bron retreated. "All of you?"

"That's why you're in queer quarantine, silly. Colonel Grove couldn't leave you in the men's camp, and he didn't dare put you with the women, so here you are at my tender mercies." Lucia's hand stroked the blanket over Bron's breast and Bron jumped at the sensation.

"Amen," said Lucia, shrugging off her dressing gown.

4

Bron could see Lucia's body milky in the camp's light. The room swayed. She felt sick. This terribleness should not be happening. She held the blankets tightly, aware that Lucia's hand was still on her.

"Don't you want me?" asked Lucia.

"I, ah—"

"Forget your soldier girl for an hour." Lucia slid onto the bed.

"This is not right to do!"

"What's not right is someone like you spending your nights alone when I'm willing and able to keep you company." Lucia swung up her legs to lie full length beside Bron. "Why don't you lower your guard? You can't be scared of me."

Pinned by Lucia's weight, Bron realized feverishly that here, that finally, she had a favor she could do for one of her captors. In the past, she would have been delighted to have something so easy to offer and would have offered it without a qualm. But Pascale. Pascale had made her know what she was offering.

Lucia snuggled closer and managed to get one foot beneath the blankets. "Mmm, nice," she said, running her toes along Bron's calf.

"C'mon, honey, you need cheering up. Nobody's worth being lonely for."

Bron recoiled. "You do not understand."

"Understand the torch you're carrying? Sure I do." Lucia put a finger on Bron's chin, turning her head to her. "It's better to live in the here and now, believe me. Haven't I helped you? Haven't I been nice to you? This is just a bit of fun. It doesn't mean more than that. C'mon, honey, kiss me."

Bron fought herself. To do this would be to put Lucia in her debt. To do this would get her out of prison. It would free her to find Pascale. Nothing else was important. To do this was simply necessary. Bron lifted her head and kissed Lucia on the mouth.

Lucia made a sound in her throat and wrapped her arms around Bron's neck. After a hesitation, Bron embraced her.

"That's right." Lucia squeezed her hard. "You like me, don't you?" She pulled the blankets from between them. "Let me show you what you're going to do to me."

Her mouth met Bron's again in sloppy kisses. Bron panicked and snatched for air. Everything was happening too fast. Lucia was sliding on top of her like a happy puppy, kissing her, moving her breasts with her hands. Bron exhaled sharply at the strangeness of this.

"Thought I'd get you going," said Lucia.

She slid further down, kissing Bron's stomach, her hands stroking Bron's hips and thighs. Bron could not stop herself from reacting, flinching and gasping at Lucia's touch. Lucia impatiently straddled her, thrust her legs apart, and dropped her head. Bron yelped, heaved, was locked between Lucia's heavy thighs, not sure what Lucia's mouth was doing, but twisting and groaning in helpless dismay as her body slowly made a fool of her. Soon she had no choice, she had to give way to it. She hid behind her locked arms, face wet with tears and sweat, grunting and lurching in involuntary response until, at last, she came with a sobbing clench, grinding her fists against her skull.

The sheet, pulled from its surgical neatness, was like corrugated iron under her. Lucia lay moist and breathless across her belly, kissing her lightly on the inside of one thigh. Bron bared her teeth in the dark, desperate for something to say. Lucia moved to stretch beside her, running her fingers up to Bron's breast. Bron shivered in spite of herself. "All—all of that—" she gulped as Lucia kissed her ear, "that is what American women like you do?"

"Perhaps not so well as me," said Lucia smugly. "I've had a lot of practice."

"You need to practice?"

Lucia chuckled. "Practice makes perfect, honey."

"There are so many to practice with?"

"If you know where to look." Lucia kissed her.

Bron smelled her own scent on Lucia's mouth. Lucia's breathing was still uneven, and Bron realized that it was not over. After a moment, she swallowed and asked, "I should do to you what you did to me?"

"Or use your imagination," said Lucia, her breath quickening.

Bron followed her example, kissing her mouth and her breasts. She must be doing the right things, for Lucia moved against her in a ripple like a physical purr. This was not unpleasant. Lucia's body had a soft meatiness and her skin was clean. Bron moved further down, daunted but determined. Lucia hissed, "C'mon, honey, c'mon!"

Bron touched Lucia with her fingers, then as Lucia had done, with her mouth. Lucia began to moan. Her hips rose and fell. Bron moved her tongue gently. It was strange to have her face in this wet, warm place. Bron wrapped her arms around Lucia's hips and explored delicately, uncertainly, not wanting to hurt her, but Lucia's fingers forked through her hair, urging her mouth and tongue harder, harder. Bron began to wonder if she would ever be freed when Lucia finally shuddered, jerked, and slumped languid in Bron's arms. Bron lifted her wet face for air.

So. That was that. Another bodily function, like eating or scratching. There was no mystery to this, no meaning beyond sensation.

"Come here, lover girl," said Lucia.

Disquieted by her discovery, Bron crawled up to lie in Lucia's embrace.

"You've been practicing, too," said Lucia.

Bron brushed the side of Lucia's breast with her fingers. "No. I must learn it all."

"Not from where I'm standing, honey. I can tell when a girl knows her way 'round."

Bron shook her head.

"What do you mean?"

"That I do not know anything."

"What d'you—oh, God!" Lucia jolted upright. "Don't tell me—is this?—this can't be your first time!"

Bron was silent.

Lucia said something reverential in English, then giggled, "Makes me the lucky one! I feel a whole lot better about cutting out—do you mind?"

"No," said Bron. "I am glad." Glad to have learned the emptiness of this in a stranger's arms.

"Well, aren't you a sweet thing? C'mon, kiss me."

Bron did.

Lucia sighed. "I do believe some women are just born naturals. Mmm, that's right, snuggle up, I like the feel of you."

Lucia's kisses grew fainter and fainter. She fell asleep. Bron propped herself on one elbow. Since she had decided to do this, she should be honest: though it was without meaning, it was quite pleasant, and even interesting. She had been partly right. Women did please other women as they pleased themselves, but two women together could do much more.

The bed was narrow and filled with Lucia. Bron grimaced. However interesting, she had had enough. She slid to the floor. The darkness seemed to press down on her. Would this truly be what she would have with Pascale? Bron remembered Pascale's kiss. Surely between them it would be more. It had to be more. If this was all she would have with Pascale she would die. Bron covered herself with Lucia's discarded robe and lay her cheek against the cold linoleum.

"Wake up."

It was still dark. Bron blinked against a faceful of hair. Lucia was leaning over the side of the bed. "Wondered where you'd got to," she said, running a hand along Bron's body. "Come on up here, honey, I'm raring to go."

She lay Bron on the bed and made love to her, slowly this time, until Bron thought that waiting for Russian tanks was easier to bear.

Lucia relented and brought her to a speedy release. Bron went to sleep at once as if slammed on the side of the head with a rifle butt. She woke in the early dawn to find Lucia still beside her, faintly snoring. Bron woke her in turn and spent longer this time learning what Lucia liked, lying across her to pin down her tossing hips. Again Lucia rose, jerked, and relaxed, then fell asleep. She roused at last, squinting at the pale sky and saying with a yawn, "I'd better get to my own bed, lover girl. I'm on duty at 0700."

"When will you come back?"

"With your breakfast, little prince, as usual." Lucia kissed her and locked the door as she left.

Bron rubbed her head reflectively. She should be pleased that she had created this debt, but she felt flat like mud. Best not to think too much about it now. She tried to straighten the blankets. It was too hard. It was all too hard. She gave up and went to sleep.

Two hours later Lucia, bright as a tin can, came in with a tray before Bron had time to slip from the shower. Bron instinctively grabbed her towel, seeking a retreat, then set her jaw and stood her ground.

Lucia only half-pretended to go weak at the knees. "Don't tempt me, darling." She set down the tray and grabbed her. "I haven't got a minute to spare."

"Not one?" asked Bron, improving on her night's work by unbuttoning the top of Lucia's uniform and bending to kiss her breasts.

"Not even for this," said Lucia after a pause, re-buttoning herself. "If you make me late, Mac will complain to the colonel and I'll be in trouble."

"Does she know what you do?"

"Boy, how she wishes she didn't! Now you know why Colonel Grove put me in charge of you. Mac doesn't like it, but thank goodness orders are orders." Lucia crossed her arms. "No more of that, greedy. Eat your breakfast. I can't go until you're finished. I'm not allowed to leave you alone with dangerous cutlery."

"Who might I want to hurt?" asked Bron, licking maple syrup from her knife.

Lucia, transfixed, said, "You just stop that, you naughty flirt!"

"That was flirting?" asked Bron. Something she should remember to do. Bron could not imagine Pascale being a flirt. But she could not imagine Pascale's life at all. "Tell me about this," she asked. "About being this."

"About the Life? What's to tell? Some women like men, some like women, just the same way that some men like men. The women who like men are called normal. We're called deviants. They can talk about it, we can't. In the Army Nurse Corps or the WAC, it gets you a dishonorable discharge. That's not going to happen to me."

"Why is it then that you came to me last night? You might have been found here."

"I know my way around this hospital pretty well," Lucia sniggered. "We all keep our mouths shut. It's a code of honor. If you try to tell anyone about this, I'll deny it till I'm blue and my pals will back me up."

"Who would I tell?" asked Bron. "I see no one but you."

"That's the way I like it," said Lucia.

"This is against the law in America?"

"Of course, though it's harder to be caught in civvie street than in the service."

Bron remembered Pascale's friend. "You can live together?"

"If that takes your fancy," said Lucia. "Some like to settle down, some like a little fun."

"You like fun," Bron guessed.

"With so many yummy women in the world? Sure I do."

"And men do this with men?"

"Men are different. There's more of them and it's more accepted. No, not on the street, but secretly. Look at Colonel Grove."

"The colonel?" Bron was taken aback.

"Especially him."

"I have seen men raping men. I thought it was for degrading them."

"Probably was," said Lucia soberly.

"Do women like you hate men?"

"The word is *lesbian,* lover girl. No, I don't hate men. Why should I? I don't have to share my bed with them."

"Lesbian," Bron repeated slowly. She thought of Soviet soldiers, of Wehrmacht officers. "But I do hate men."

"I find your kind usually do."

"What kind?"

"The kind who naturally wear the trousers." Lucia took the empty cup from Bron's hand.

Bron wanted to ask her if there was a letter from Pascale. She wondered if, after last night, Lucia would tell her. She asked instead, "You will have time for me today?"

"I'll be pretty busy with incoming tuberculosis and malnutrition cases, but I haven't been reassigned," said Lucia. "I'll see you at lunch. Before you say a word, your exercise has to be outside."

As they put on their coats that afternoon, Bron asked, "Why do you still speak to me as a man?"

"Am I?" Lucia considered her own word endings. "Guess I'm used to it. You were signed into camp as a male and the colonel wants it that way, so I'll stick with it. Does it bother you?"

"I am accustomed."

They walked around the garden. Bron stayed close to the fence to watch the guards herd the arrivals into the camp. With heavy innuendo, Lucia gave Bron more English words: *investigation, search, inspect.*

"It is unfair to say such things," said Bron, deciding that the time had come for flirting. "You make me want to take hold of you."

"Later, lover girl. No, don't come closer. The colonel might be looking out of his window."

"He would not be shocked."

"I'd lose my Good Conduct medal. Nobody's going to make me do that."

"Good conduct for what?" Bron asked, and Lucia giggled.

Once back in her room, Bron stopped Lucia as she was leaving and kissed her. "When is later?" she demanded. "Tonight?"

"If I can," said Lucia.

"Try."

"You know I'll try."

She did, creeping in after midnight, shivering with cold. Bron wrapped her in the blankets and began to do the things she had planned that afternoon, demanding the English names of everything, to which Lucia replied breathlessly, *labia, vulva, clitoris.*

"You sound like a priest," said Bron.

"I could tell you other words, but I was raised to be a lady," said Lucia. "Don't stop."

Bron chuckled and kept on.

After Lucia had arched and sighed in what she named *orgasm,* she said dreamily, "You are one fast learner. You're better at this than you are at English."

"I am not so good with English?"

"You need more time. Lots more time."

"I do not want time. I want to get out."

"You'll get out when the Germans are whipped. The whole bunch of you are being sent home just as soon as Hitler surrenders."

"You could let me out now."

"Oh, no, lover girl, I couldn't." Lucia rolled over and kissed her lightly. "Why would I want to, anyway, when I could keep you here?"

"Would you?"

"It's not up to me," said Lucia.

Bron was unsettled. When Lucia had slipped away, she tucked her hands behind her head and stared at the ceiling. Did Lucia not understand the rules of collaboration? Did she think Bron was giving sex for nothing, in spite of the bars on the window? Lucia had to be made aware of her obligations.

But Lucia had little time to be convinced during the following days. Bron could hear the newly arrived refugees' coughing and quavering voices in the hospital's corridors. More prefabricated huts were being erected in the camp. Lucia still came to her after dark, though less eager now for sex than for sleep. Bron knew the load had finally lifted when Lucia stayed awake most of the night, but each time Bron tried to talk with her she managed to doze off, yawning apologies.

Returning with breakfast one morning, Lucia said, "Oh, my aching back! We've got to sort out this shipment before the next one comes and two of the nurses are down with the flu. The French will be sent home soon, lucky things. The rest have to be questioned to find out which ones are German before we release them into the camp."

"You have let Nazis in with their victims?" Bron was outraged.

"If there are any here, you can bet they're keeping their lips buttoned," said Lucia.

"I hope you will discover them quickly."

"Of course we will. Our translators can pinpoint a man's dialect to his street."

"Pascale is a translator."

"What was she like?" asked Lucia.

Bron stared at her, not knowing how to answer.

"Can't remember?" Lucia smirked. "Too bad."

"I remember," said Bron.

"She hasn't remembered you. And she won't be coming back. None of the WAC units sent to the Chartres Conference have come back."

"What is this?"

"Chartres Conference. Like Yalta or—well, you don't hear a lot of news, do you? It's when politicians or generals get together to organize the world. They finished one in Chartres about a week ago."

"Chartres? This is in France?"

"A long way away." Lucia removed the tray from Bron's knees and slid onto her lap. "And I'm right here."

Why had Lucia not spoken before of this Chartres? Bron wanted to throw her on the floor. Instead, she tugged up Lucia's skirt and ran her fingers across Lucia's thighs between stocking top and girdle. "Why must you wear these foolish corsets?"

"I haven't time for—no, no, I can't."

But she did, splayed in Bron's lap, her face against Bron's shoulder, leaving a trail of bite marks as she stifled her cries in Bron's shirt. Within a minute of orgasm she rose shakily and rushed to the sink to restore order.

"I'm going to have to feed you through the keyhole," she said. "You're dangerous. Don't kiss me, I've just put on more lipstick."

She left with the tray, but Bron pushed open the door before she could bolt it. "No."

"I have to," said Lucia. "Orders."

"Do not lock me in. Please. I am not a wild animal."

Lucia hesitated. "Okay, okay. It's not like you've got anywhere to go. Just don't get me into trouble."

"I will behave."

Bron did not touch the door and was ostentatiously sitting by the window when Lucia came to her room that night. Lucia's eyes were red.

"What has happened?" asked Bron.

"The president is dead."

"Killed?"

"He was ill and he died."

"Who is your leader now?"

"The vice president. That's how our government works. Roosevelt didn't even get to see victory." Lucia began to cry.

Irritated by her grief, Bron looked away. Leaders were loved because people enjoyed propaganda. You had only to see how happily they worshipped Stalin or Hitler. She managed to say, "I am sorry for you Americans."

Lucia sighed. "He was a great man. I can't stay tonight, I'm too upset, but I thought you'd like to know."

The next day the chaplain came with Lucia to ask Bron if she would like to attend a memorial service for the president. Bron politely agreed and was taken, with several patients, to the men's camp. A photograph of an old man in a bow tie hung on the back wall of the dining tent. She was placed with Andrzej, Slawek, and the other Poles.

"Hello, young one," said Andrzej. "I didn't know you were still here."

"I live in the hospital now."

"What's the matter with you?" Andrzej and Slawek edged away. "You have a disease? Typhus?"

She shook her head. "They think I'm someone else. They're observing me."

"They suspect maybe you're Hans Frank?" Slawek snorted.

While they waited for the American officers to join them, Bron said casually, "It's too bad about Roosevelt. We might have appealed to him for help."

"What do you mean?" asked Andrzej.

"I hear gossip in the hospital. It's back to Poland for the lot of us the day after the Allies win."

Slawek and Andrzej looked glum.

"Are you sure?" said Slawek.

"That's what I've heard." Bron shrugged. "Perhaps it's not true."

"Perhaps it is," said Slawek.

As she returned to the hospital after the service, Bron looked at the guard towers, the lights, the gates. She saw how thinly placed the military guard had become since the expansion of the camp.

That night, satisfied that Lucia was not coming, she left her room. The corridor stretched empty to the front entrance. The guard formerly stationed there was gone. She slipped from the back door. The dead apple tree was silhouetted against the lights of the men's camp. She moved along the hospital wall, staying in the shadows.

She could see the camp's main entrance. It was there that she had been taken from Pascale. The sentry house was on the right. There had been four guards then. They had dragged her inside and had hit her to make her be quiet. The gate was flanked by two guards now. She waited.

Two trucks arrived at the entrance as the sun rose over the hills. Bron had listened to their clanking and grinding every morning since she had arrived. The sentries swung open the wings of the gate and the trucks rolled toward the hospital. Bron ghosted back behind a row of big metal garbage canisters. One of the sentries opened the gate to the hospital precinct. The trucks pulled up at a loading bay. Bron watched orderlies unload clean hospital linen from the first truck and load it with bags of what she guessed to be laundry. The second truck delivered boxes of supplies. The sentry, waiting for the trucks at the inner gate, shut it behind them and followed to close the main gate.

Having seen enough, Bron crept back to her room. As she closed the door she smiled sardonically to herself: Americans could learn much from the Germans about security.

Lucia was busy for the next few days with two groups of Ukrainians who had decided to beat each other to death. During her hasty delivery of meal trays, she had time to tell Bron only the latest war news. A week after the president died, Leipzig fell. Bron was interested to hear that the Second Polish Army had taken Rothenburg, wherever that was. She was impatient with Lucia's quick kisses and promises to try to come that night or the next. During one afternoon walk, Lucia excitedly told her that a Polish woman from the other camp had given birth to a boy in the hospital. Had she heard him crying? And she would never believe this: his mother had named him Witold!

"It's a new generation. He'll help make a better world," Lucia sighed, gazing at the hills. Daffodils shone thickly at the edge of the camp.

Bron looked at the barbed wire and said, "You think the world will be made better? The children born now will be wiser than their parents?"

"We'll never have a worldwide war again, not after this."

"They said the same thing a generation ago."

"This time it'll be different. The United States is in charge now."

Bron stared at her in caustic wonder. "Americans can resist the temptation to rule the world?"

"We don't want that. We want democracy for everybody."

"Except for us in this camp. We have no choice about what you do to us. I have no choice."

"There's more to this war than what you want or don't want," said Lucia. "We can't have you all wandering around. We've got to protect you."

"Like the Soviet invaders protected us from the German invaders," said Bron.

"It's not like that and you know it!" said Lucia.

"Show me how you Americans are different."

"I'm not going to let you rub me up the wrong way." Lucia stomped mud off her galoshes. "I think you do it on purpose. Why? Don't you like me?"

"You will come to me tonight?"

"I don't know," said Lucia. "You're not answering me."

The next morning Bron set aside Lucia's tray, closed the door, and backed her against the wall. "Now," said Bron, "I will have you now," half-undressing Lucia as she kissed her lips, her throat, her breasts.

Lucia struggled, mostly for the pleasure of the effect, and clutched

Bron's head as Bron worked her way down. Bron forced her to stay upright and Lucia sagged against the wall, her hands on Bron's shoulders as Bron knelt to put her mouth on her. Eyes closed, Lucia moaned and rocked, finally toppling in orgasm. Bron caught her and carried her to the bed to recover.

Bron ate breakfast as Lucia rose shakily and adjusted her uniform.

"You're a brute."

Bron put down her coffee cup. "I would have stopped if you had told me."

"Am I that irresistible?"

"Of course."

Lucia preened. "I've never had any complaints."

"You have a lover in America?"

"Plenty. In the hospital where I worked I once had four on the go at the same time."

"It was enjoyable?"

"A little busy," Lucia said sleekly. "I can't resist the strong silent type."

"Come to me tonight."

"I sure will, lover girl," said Lucia, and later that evening she did, saying, "How can I have been too busy for this?" as she flung aside her dressing gown and nestled into Bron's arms.

Having seen how roughness excited Lucia, Bron put firm hands on her, was masterful with her mouth, and finally clamped one arm across Lucia's frenzied hips, forcing her to concentrate, until Lucia came with a piping squeal that Bron worried would fetch the guard. A few minutes later Lucia whispered, "You little thug, you're spoiling me for other girls. I'm going to have to sneak you home in a suitcase."

"I am being returned to Poland with baby Witold and the rest."

"What a waste."

"Not many lesbians back there, I think," said Bron. "Not with the Communists in charge."

"No," said Lucia thoughtfully.

The next day Lucia brought her news that the Russians had reached the area around Berlin. "Only days to go," she said with a happy nod. "They'll capture Hitler and the Germans will surrender."

"Then come to me tonight. We have little time left."

"Aren't you glad about the news?"

"Glad that the Germans are being defeated? You can ask that?"

"You really don't want to go home, do you?" Lucia said slowly.

"What is for me there? I fought Communists. For that they will put me in a labor camp, or kill me."

"But you're a woman," said Lucia.

"I have seen women stood against walls and shot. I have seen women raped to death."

"I couldn't bear you being hurt like that."

"Help me. Help me get out."

"I can't!"

"You can."

"I should have kept your door locked. You've been sneaking from your room, haven't you?"

"You have said yourself there is nowhere to go."

"You've been doing something."

"You will inform on me?"

Lucia turned away. "I don't know. I'm in the service. I have my duty."

"What would the army do if we were found together?" asked Bron.

Lucia hunched her shoulders. Bron said, "I need to be free of here."

"You want me to smuggle you out," said Lucia unhappily.

"No. I want you to see nothing of what I do. I want you to say nothing of what you see. I want you to do nothing."

"You've already got a plan, don't you?" Lucia asked. "I don't want to know about this. Why are you telling me? I probably wouldn't have guessed."

"I must tell you. It is my responsibility. I do not want to betray you."

Lucia's mouth twisted. "I don't want you to go."

"I am going eventually. I would rather go west than east."

"It would be dereliction to help you." Lucia left with a troubled frown, but did not lock Bron's door. That night she slipped into her bed, saying nothing beyond words of desire. The following night she did not come to her. In the morning, delivering breakfast, she asked, "Do you hate me?"

"Why should I hate you?" asked Bron.

"You think I'm a coward because I won't help you escape."

"I think you are not Pascale," said Bron.

"Pascale! Was she such a heroine, this girl who never writes to you?"

"Yes."

"If you escaped, would you try to find her?"

"Yes."

Lucia chewed her lip. "You're kind of gone on her, aren't you?"

"Yes."

"Damn. Damn." Lucia crossed her arms, hands in fists. "I won't. I can't."

"I am not arguing."

"I know, and it's not fair. Finish your breakfast, or I'll talk myself around."

During lunch and their walk, Lucia firmly discussed the latest victories. Bron asked her for more English words. Lucia refused. "It's part of your escape plan."

The next day she brought the news that the Russians had finally reached Berlin.

"Red Army soldiers are ferocious," said Bron. "I know what will happen."

"Will it be terrible?" Lucia asked.

"Do you care?"

"Yes, I do. I don't want a massacre."

Bron could not stop herself laughing. "You know so little."

"You despise me. You'll never make love to me again."

"No, I would like to. I am available any night."

Lucia smiled, but did not come that evening or the next, and Bron feared that she had lost her gamble. Lucia's ideals were no more than words. On Friday Lucia told her of Mussolini's execution. On Saturday the Italians surrendered.

"That means the Allied armies in Italy can come here to fight the

Germans," Bron nodded. "Good."

Lucia continued to keep herself at arm's length. Bron spent her nights alone, wakeful with worry and wild to be gone. The Germans, Lucia told her over supper one evening, had surrendered in the Netherlands and throughout northern Germany. Bron slammed her fist into her pillow that night: she was going to be trapped in this camp by peace and a pigeon-hearted girl.

The news that Hans Frank, the Nazi governor general of Poland, had been captured, reached the men's camp. Bron and Lucia stood in the garden to listen to the singing of the Poles.

"Frank enslaved Poland for the Nazis," said Bron. "I hope he will be shot."

"I'm sure he'll be put into prison," said Lucia.

"He should not have the privilege of breathing," said Bron. "They should all die."

"We can't kill the whole Nazi high command," said Lucia. "That would be criminal."

Bron laughed shortly. "Let some Polish or Lithuanian prisoners at them. I could accept their notion of justice."

Two days later she was sitting puffing on her mouth organ when she heard whoops and cheers in the corridor outside. Her door was flung open by a patient. *"La paix!"* he shouted at her. *"La paix!"*

She went into the corridor. Nurses, doctors, and patients were thronging from doors.

"Who heard it?" someone demanded in German.

A doctor emerged, radio blaring behind him. "The Nazis have surrendered. It's to be announced officially the day after tomorrow."

Bron looked at a group of nurses dancing together. Lucia was one of them. Seeing her with her colleagues made her suddenly distant, a member of a huge foreign organization whose duty was done. Bron went back to her room.

Lucia stopped at her door later. "You heard! There's going to be a celebration in the camp. Do you want to come? The whole staff's going."

"Yes, I want to be there," said Bron.

Lucia threw her arms around her and kissed her. "We can go home! At last, at last."

Bron, as many patients as could walk, and a dozen nurses, doctors, and orderlies, went into the camp that evening to join the guards and the inmates for prayers and a party. Crates of beer bottles were stacked by one wall. The dining tent was full of people, the air thick with languages, the men solemn, excited, earnest, crying. Lucia stayed with the other nurses. Bron squirmed through the crowd, looking for the biggest gathering of Poles. She had enough warning to put an arm across her breasts as Andrzej grabbed her from behind in a bear hug.

"Little Witold!" he shouted in her ear. "The Nazis are finished. Hitler's dead!"

"The Russians shot him?"

"Suicide, I heard. Dog coward."

"The Nazis are finished," said another Pole. "I can't believe the words I'm saying!"

"Now we've only the Communists," said Slawek.

"Better learn to like them," said Bron. "We'll be seeing them soon."

"What do you mean?" asked Andrzej.

"It's as I said. We're going to be handed over to the Russian army."

"What have you heard?" A man shook her by the shoulders. "When?"

"I'm not sure," said Bron. "Perhaps before the end of the week."

"They haven't told us," said the man.

"Would you announce it to a prison of this size before you had to?" asked Bron. "The last time repatriations were carried out at this camp everyone rioted. Some even escaped."

"Some escaped?" Slawek repeated, one bright eye on her.

Bron shrugged. "The colonel looked the other way, so I'm told. He's a compassionate man."

"What do you say, Andrzej? Jósef?" said Slawek. "We'd better talk to the others."

"Remember that the Americans want to go home," said Bron. "They'll be rid of us as soon as they can."

She eased her way from the huddle of Polish men and found the nurses. "Miss Jaarro," she said to Lucia. "I am unwell. May I be taken back to the hospital?"

Lucia's smile faded as she turned to her. "Witold."

"Miss Jaarro," Bron took off her cap. "Please."

Lucia said something to the others and led Bron to the entrance. "It's tonight, isn't it?"

Bron said nothing.

Lucia gave orders in English to one of the guards at the door. Eyes down, she muttered, "Tom will escort you back."

"Good-bye," said Bron.

Lucia did not look up.

Bron followed the guard across the camp. At the inner gate, she paused to glance back. Lucia was silhouetted against the tent's brightness, watching her.

The guard took Bron to her room. He did not bolt the door. That had to be Lucia's order. Bron smiled.

She took a last shower and went to bed, telling herself to wake in six hours. She did, and listened to the lack of sound around her as she dressed. The party had ended. She put her lexicon in one jacket pocket, her mouth organ in the other, and left the room, easing out the garden door. Cold rain blew against her face. She edged around the corner of the hospital and crouched behind the metal garbage canisters. It was cold. She had forgotten how cold the night could be.

An hour later, half-dozing where she crouched, she saw the dawn rise on the hills. The first day after the war. The rain had stopped. Birds were singing on tent poles and fence wire. Hearing the grinding gears of trucks, she hunkered as close as she could to the loading doors, wrapping her greatcoat around herself to turn into another brown and grey lump among the rubbish.

The first truck came around the corner and backed in. The men laughed and spoke to each other as they unloaded and loaded laundry bags. The first truck pulled away and the second took its place. She could hear the dragging screech of crates across metal and stone. She waited as the two loaders returned to the cab. The hospital doors shut.

Scrabbling on all fours as the engine fired, she hoisted herself inside the truck as it pulled away. Its cold metal shocked her hands. The truck passed the first gate and stopped. She muffled her panting against her sleeve. The drivers called their good mornings to the sentries. The truck started again. She saw barbed wire pass overhead and behind her. The truck lurched as it changed gears. She lifted her head.

Already the houses of Fontaine surrounded her. She swung a leg over the tailgate and waited. The truck turned a bend. She let its acceleration fling her off, hit the mud with a grunt, and rolled. Something hurt. She fished out the mouth organ, smashed flat by her fall. She scrambled over a stone wall and buried it under a pile of last year's leaves, then worked along the backs of gardens away from the direction of town. The gardens petered out. She slipped through an unwalled orchard until it, too, ended, and emerged onto a cart track.

It led up a hill. She followed it and found herself on the summit of the northern ridge of the valley. Below her lay the camps, bright cities asleep in the dark. Or not asleep: the population of the men's camp was pouring into the streets, darker movement under the lights. There came a faint blare of klaxons.

She turned west. The far valleys were filled with mist. The ridge track she was on stretched in front of her past a farm and trees to fields and emptiness as far ahead as she could see. She started walking.

Nell

The woman at the next table was one of the most beautiful she had ever seen, a Byrne Jones madonna: oval face, full mouth, grey eyes, dark hair smoothed back beneath her regulation cap. A madonna in uniform. Knowing herself a fool, Nell asked, "Got a light?" as she shook a cigarette from her pack.

The woman gathered herself into awareness and smiled enough to reveal to Nell that she was worth some trouble. "I'm sorry, no."

"Clean living, huh?" Nell signaled the waiter, who lit it for her.

"Not my particular vice," said the madonna. She asked the waiter for another cup of *gaseuz.*

"Would you get me one as well? I don't speak much French," said Nell. "With the place overrun by Yanks, I don't need to." She leaned across, extending her hand. "Nell Tulliver of the *Baltimore Morning Mail, Storace's* magazine, and the Transamerican Broadcasting Company, in no particular order of importance."

"Helen Tulliver? I listen to your broadcasts on the European Forces station every week. I'm Pascale Tailland. I enjoyed your talk on women in the army last month. It was nice to be treated seriously."

"You Wacs ought to be." Nell looked at Pascale's insignia. "You're attached to the unit that was in Germany right after the Ardennes bustle, aren't you? The unit involved with the interviews of captured Nazis? Mind me asking what it was like?"

"I translated what our officers asked and what the Germans replied," said Pascale.

"Were the first to hear their answers, in other words."

"We spent most of our time translating captured documents. We also dealt with refugees."

"Didn't you work in the concentration camps?"

"For a little while," said Pascale in such a way that Nell asked instead, "What was it like coming in contact with those Nazi generals? I sat in a room with one once, but you know war correspondents aren't allowed to interview prisoners of war. How did the generals justify themselves, or didn't they? What's the worst excuse you heard? Did you have any trouble with them? What was the *esprit de corps* like in your unit?"

"Which would you like me to answer?" Pascale smiled. "Is this how you get your stories, by barraging people with questions?"

"Something like that," said Nell. "I like to know. What was the funniest thing that's happened to you in the service?"

"That would be Binty's apples," Pascale said at once.

"Binty's apples. Sounds promising. Spill."

"I don't think she'd mind. She bought a string bag of apples the day we were posted into Germany. It was crowded in the carriage, so Binty hung the bag out the window. She didn't realize that the apples were mashing through the net bag and ending up as applesauce on the windows of the general's carriage. He thought angry locals were throwing fruit at him and wouldn't stop the train for his scheduled parade of honor at the next town. When we heard his aides fulminating about ungrateful natives, we faded Binty quietly away."

"Your officer never found out?" asked Nell.

"I'm sure she knew, but she has a genius for turning a blind eye."

"That's a good story. Too bad I can't use it, at least until your pal Binty's out of uniform. Can I buy you something other than that muck? I'd kill for real coffee."

"You'll hurt the waiter's feelings; he's pretending so well that we enjoy *gaseuz.* May I ask you a question?"

"Shoot," said Nell, shifting her chair to share Pascale's table.

Pascale turned her coffee spoon over a few times, then said, "Could you find someone? I promised to help a person and I failed."

"What's the pressure?" asked Nell, intrigued.

"I'm afraid he's going to be repatriated to Poland any day, if he hasn't been already. He mustn't go back. I told him I'd help him. Last time I saw him, he was in a camp near the German border, but I can't find out if he's still there or where he is."

"How do you know him?" Nell sipped her ersatz coffee.

"I smuggled him out of Germany. He'd got himself across the Red Army frontier and I took him into France on the general's train."

"Done it to me again, haven't you?" Nell grinned. "A story I can't print until you or the general's in civvies. Especially the general."

Pascale laughed. "I didn't think of it turning into a story."

"Imagine the copy! *Intrepid Young Wac Rescues Polish Refugee*—how old is he?"

"Early twenties."

"Okay. Wac rescues brave Polish boy from clutches of...hmm, can't say the Commie devils while we're still allies...say, clutches of the last desperate Nazi hoodlums. Intrepid et cetera smuggles brave Polish et cetera under general's nose to freedom and safety in France. End of story, and a good one."

"If he's already been repatriated, he's probably in a Russian prison now. Not a good ending."

"Rough," said Nell sympathetically, "but there's nothing you can do. He's only one of millions of poor bastards."

"He's my one. I have to do something. I promised."

Nell was at once interested and deflated. "You're sweet on this guy?"

"I am."

"Pretty romantic. Was he a soldier?"

"For a while, in Poland."

"Fine. Intrepid Wac rescues brave Polish Resistance fighter only to lose him to heartless bureaucracy. If I omit the stuff involving the general's train, I could still use it, maybe to jump-start one of my wee homilies on the need for human decency in victory."

"Don't belittle your broadcasts," said Pascale quickly. "They're good."

"A story like that could help find him," said Nell. "Every army clerk in every DP camp would comb the files for your boy's name. Polish-American associations back home would flood the top brass with letters. You can bet that'd get things moving."

"There are complications," said Pascale. "I'd like to think about it."

"Here's my card." Nell fished in her jacket pocket. "I'm staying at the Hôtel Scribe, opposite the Opéra." She wrote on the back of the card. "That number'll fetch me. Reuss magazines' headquarters or TBC will get me during the day. You can leave a message, but don't say what it's about. I want my scoop."

"Thank you." Pascale took the card. "I'm off duty again tomorrow afternoon. I'll call then."

"Looking forward to it." Nell shook hands with her, caught a faint whiff of perfume, and thought, *What a waste.* She watched Pascale cross the square in front of the church of St. Germain des Prés. A damned waste.

Nell put Pascale's rear view from her mind and considered the story. Refugees were becoming less interesting for the folks back home as they increasingly became a problem to be dealt with. It was time to remind those by the home fires about *give me your poor, your homeless,* and a girl-meets-boy story would be dandy bait. Nell hoped Pascale would want to meet again to talk about it. Hell, there was no harm in looking.

She tossed money into the saucer and went to her hotel. She had a room to herself, a spacious but airless box on the top floor, one flight above the bath. The bed was narrow, with the hardest bolster Nell had laid her head against, but the tiny sink gave water for her whiskey and the big table looked onto a postcard view of leaded mansard roofs, trees, and the Eiffel Tower poking up at the right. Nell lifted the cover off her typewriter, ran in a sheet of paper, and glanced over the notes of her recent trip through the starving French provinces. She poured whiskey into an inch of water by sound alone and started her column for the next issue of *Storace's.*

Two whiskeys and four cigarettes later, she put the final version in her pocket and went to the Reuss building to have her copy teletyped.

"Nell." Roland, the bureau chief, waved her into his office. "The boss says enough suffering civilian stories. Folks are getting depressed. He wants something upbeat."

"I thought I was upbeat," said Nell. "They're alive, aren't they? Cheerful in spite of having to eat sawdust while their American liberators chow down on meat and gravy."

"You've got a funny attitude," said Roland.

"I might be able to make the boss happy." Nell mimed thoughtfulness. "I don't know...it'll take a little work. Haven't got an ending yet. Who has contacts with DP camp staffs?"

"A refugee story?" Roland looked interested. "Something first person I-was-there? No faceless masses stuff."

"Definitely not masses. I've got a lead but I don't know how long the string is."

"Lonny's in Germany right now. He could help. Donald's still in Italy. Any particular DP camp?"

"I wasn't told, but from clues dropped, this canny sleuth has deduced that it's either the big camp at Fontaine or the one across the border from Dortbrucken."

"Fergal isn't a million miles away from either."

Nell considered. "Okay, let's cast a few crumbs. Ask him to find out what's happening at both camps. Have the DPs there been repatriated yet? Could he locate a particular person once I get a name?"

Roland made a note. "I'll contact him."

Her work done for the day, Nell hailed a jeepful of Canadians for a lift to the Pigalle district. They dropped her there with friendly warnings.

The night crowds were drifting into the area: laborers with their tough girlfriends, prostitutes with stiff hair rolls and bright lipstick, brilliantined young men in waisted coats loitering by the entrances of *hommes seulement* clubs, black market dealers opening their delivery vans for business, bigger crime bosses rolling by in dark cars. It was like a Warner Brothers set for a movie of the mean streets. Nell, crossing the Boulevard de Clichy, paused to make a note.

The Club Sevastopol's green light was on. A large Turkish man sat inside the door.

"Howdy, partner," she said to him as she always did.

"Howdy," Ahmoud replied solemnly, half his American vocabulary depleted.

She paid her entrance fee and went inside. Too early for action. Most of the booths were in shadow, half the tables were empty, and the dance floor was unlit. Behind the bar, Blanche was cleaning glasses.

"*Bonsoir.*" Blanche nodded as Nell climbed onto a stool, sliding a glass of black market whiskey in front of her. Nell added a splash of water from the carafe and lit a cigarette.

"That's bad for you, honey." A slender hand took it from Nell's lips. Its owner had a drag and handed it back.

"I spend my life in clichés," Nell complained to the air. "What do you want, Angelique?"

"A big strong woman like you to take care of me."

"Blanche, a brandy for Angel," Nell sighed.

Angelique grabbed what she had played for and scuttled to her regular booth. Nell picked up the dropped cigarette. On her first visit to the club, she had unwittingly been Angelique's final victim of the evening, not knowing that buying Angelique's last drink won the dubious reward of Angelique herself for the rest of the night. Nell made sure she was never last again.

Flicking off an inch of ash, she glanced around the room, checking what talent she could see in the booths. Angelique was near the front door, eyeballing the newcomers. In the next, a British nurse Nell half-recognized, a regular like herself. Two French women talking with their heads close together. Pascale. Nell stiffened. Hell and lightning. What did this mean? She ambled over at Pascale's gesture. "Okay, I'm surprised. Mind if I sit down?"

"Please," Pascale smiled.

"How did you know?"

"I surmised, though I didn't expect to see you so soon. I only learned about this club today. Eavesdropping in the cloakroom, I'm afraid."

Nell settled beside her in the booth. "What's that story you were pitching me about the brave Polish Resistance fighter you lost your heart to?"

"Exactly what I said, except for the complication that now ceases to be one. My Polish boy is a girl. She was disguised as a man. I try to keep the secret."

"Hell." Nell took a long pull on her cigarette. "Thanks for nothing. What a story, and how can I run it? *Intrepid Wac Falls for Polish Girl Fighter in Drag.* I don't think it will warm the hearts of the folks back home. I need another drink."

Martine, the waitress, came at her signal. "Another—and make it *vite,*" said Nell.

"I suppose you'll want the details," Pascale offered.

"To quench my curiosity?"

"To help me find her."

"Why would I do that?" asked Nell.

"Because you can."

"Is that how you think the world works? People help because they can? What convent were you raised in? Do I look like an altruist?"

"Aren't you?"

Nell grimaced. "This is like having a seraph ask why you ain't on the side of the angels. I might help, on one condition."

"What is it?" Pascale asked. Nell saw the flicker in her eyes and said, "Not that; I'm not such a bitch. Though I wish. No, it's that we do a deal on this story."

"You said you couldn't use it."

"I might be able to salvage something. You pick up a Polish boy—"

"I knew Witold was a woman from the start."

"She's that obvious?"

"Not at all. My officer, who's one of us, was fooled, though I knew almost at once."

"So you rescue this boy-girl, get her into France and take her to—?"

"The men's displaced persons camp at Fontaine."

"Interesting." Nell raised a brow. "She'll have been found out: a routine medical, delousing, one of those."

"My officer told the camp's commandant about her secret."

"The camp commandant knows? Lord almighty! Why aren't you and this girl both in jail?"

"The commandant had a particular reason for helping us."

"Must have been a hell of a good one. Let's take it from the top. You saw this—what's her name?"

"She's using the name Witold Rukowicz."

"Rukowicz. You picked her up where?"

Pascale told the story. Nell smoked and listened, watching Pascale's face kindle as she described Witold, watching her become stern with herself as she explained why she had not saved her from internment.

"If it hadn't been for my lieutenant," Pascale concluded, "Witold would have been in a terrible position. As it is, I assume that at some point she was removed from the men's camp. I've tried to find out. I've written to friends at the army station in Fontaine, I've written to the camp, but my friends didn't answer, perhaps couldn't, and my letters to the camp were returned by the commandant's office. I tried the Red Cross. They're too busy to help. I tried to go back to Fontaine during my leave, but Captain Thorsby denied me permission. I've tried everything I could."

"Now you're trying me."

"I'll do anything."

"Lucky Witold," said Nell.

"I'm the lucky one. I had twenty-four hours with her."

"You don't look crazy. How can you be so damn sure? Don't answer that—I'm too old to hear about True Love, especially in Paris." Nell smoked until the ash warmed her fingers. "Okay," she said, crushing the stub. "I'll put out feelers to my pals in high places. If I can figure an angle on the story, can I have it?"

"As long as Witold's safety isn't compromised. And she permits it."

"If we find her, I'll get her to sign a release. You want another drink?"

"I wish I could buy you one as a small thank you."

"Are you kidding me? If I buy for you, nobody'll raise an eyebrow. If you buy for me, we'll be an item."

"I know. Lesbian tribal laws rule here as well."

"Biggest universal secret society after the boys and the Masons," Nell agreed, ordering drinks.

They moved by unspoken agreement to other matters, eventually exhausting Parisian and army gossip and turning to the war.

"If we whip them on Okinawa, they'll have to surrender," said Nell. "It takes a lot of money to win a war, and Uncle Sam has more than Tojo."

"Witold would agree with you."

Nell winced theatrically. "We managed two whole hours without that intrepid Pole's name."

Pascale laughed. "I see how you get your stories. Do you flirt with everyone?"

"Was that flirting? I thought it was a cry from the heart." Nell looked at her watch. "You have a curfew, don't you? Where are you based? May I see you home? The sooner we leave the sooner the bees here can start humming."

"About what?"

"You haven't been in the Life long, have you?" asked Nell, one corner of her mouth lifting.

"Since I was eighteen," said Pascale. "But I took myself out of circulation for three years. Then I signed up."

"What happened to the little woman back home? She Dear Jill you?"

"Yes," said Pascale.

"She's crazy. You grab this Pole on the rebound?"

"I was long past that."

"I'm not going to shake your conviction that Witold's the one and only, am I?"

"You haven't a chance," Pascale laughed. "But you're not serious."

"Me, serious? Give me air," said Nell, not entirely certain.

Nell accompanied Pascale to her quarters, then walked to her own hotel. She was waylaid on the first landing by Drina and Andy, a husband-and-wife team working for the Griffin Photo Agency.

"Want a drink?" asked Drina.

"Does a cactus love rain?"

Inside, other newshounds were draped on the chairs and floor. Janet and Jerry were making scrambled eggs over a gas ring, and someone was playing a ukelele.

"Who here has a buddy on the French-German border?" Nell

asked, accepting a coffee mug of red wine.

"You're looking at one," said George, European bureau chief of the Colored Americans Press. "My man Frederick's doing a piece on the clean-up. He'll be in the Fontaine area sometime soon."

"Oh? Swell! I'd appreciate it if he'd find out what's happening in the refugee camps there. I'm looking for a fellow called Rukowicz."

"I'll do that." George made a note. "What's the story?"

"Can DPs learn to bebop," said Nell. "What do you think?"

"That you're holding out on us, and it isn't pretty."

Nell grinned. "Human interest story. If I pull it off, Drina, want an exclusive on the photogravure?"

"Deal," said Drina, and shook on it.

They ate and drank, catcalled their friends on TBC's European Forces Radio, and compared notes on the army's public relations officers. Nell finally staggered to her room in the early hours, glad to have had a dose of the real world after Pascale's fairy tale.

The next day, squinting through a hangover, she sat at her desk writing to every contact she had in the news and photographic agencies who might still be in western Germany. Cast your bread upon the waters, she thought, wondering if all this work would be worth it.

Nell received a note from Pascale the following week asking if they might meet again. She went to SHAEF headquarters, where Pascale was stationed.

Pascale was waiting at reception. "Would you like to meet my colleagues? They'd love to see you. You've clearance, haven't you?"

"Sure," said Nell unenthusiastically. She followed Pascale upstairs to a far wing.

"My friends believe I'm in love with a man called Witold," Pascale warned her. "You'll see how acceptable it's made me."

"Made you? You mean they knew about you before? The truth?"

"I didn't lie about it. The only time I've ever lied is hiding Witold's secret."

"Being a self-confessed lesbian must have made life fun. How'd you get into the WAC?"

"I didn't answer what they didn't ask me."

"What's worse, your pals knowing you're lesbian or them thinking you've gone straight?" Nell grinned.

"The latter, by far," said Pascale seriously. "Here's my office."

Nell was plunged into excited introductions, shaking hands with a Marie, a Dot, a Jeeter—"Jeanie Peter, Miss Tulliver, but I'm called Jeeter"—and Binty of the famous apples. Nell found them like all Wacs: overworked, undervalued, dedicated, bright. She loved the company of women and entertained them with her best stories. Women from other offices came to discover the reason for the clamor, and Nell found an hour had passed by the time the sergeant called her staff back to duty. Nell parted with them cordially.

"Nice bunch of gals," she said as Pascale fetched her shoulder bag and hat.

They caught a ride in a British staff car to the Left Bank, then walked to the same café on the rue Bonaparte where they had first met. Only when their *gaseux* had been placed before them did Pascale ask, "Have you heard anything?"

"Not a peep," said Nell. "It's too soon. My contacts have to shoehorn my request into their own work."

"I'm selfish, expecting all these people to help me," said Pascale. "And you. But I don't care."

"The ruthlessness of young love," laughed Nell. "What will you do with your Polish girl once you find her?"

A startling flash of longing transformed Pascale's face. She smiled to banish it. "Aside from the obvious, I'm going to take her to the States. I'm not sure how, but I will."

"Is that what Witold hopes?" Nell's voice was flat with cynicism.

"You think she's using me to get to America. No. She had no such thought when she met me."

"Just a lucky break for her that you're a Yank."

Pascale was unoffended. "I know Witold. If I decided to emigrate to Argentina, so would she."

"You got damn well acquainted in a day."

"It was different from any feelings I'd ever had. It wasn't a crush. I've had those, and I've been in love, too, but no one, not even the woman I lived with, ever fitted with me as completely as she did, and at once."

"Can you be so sure?"

Pascale smiled. "I am."

"I hope you're not wrong," said Nell. "If you do get Witold across the Atlantic, and I'm not betting you do, what then?"

"What do you mean?"

"Are you going to support her? Build a love nest for two?"

"You don't need to protect me from Witold," said Pascale.

Nell looked at her cigarette. "I hate anyone to be taken for a ride. I did a story on war brides, remember. I met a lot of them and I figure maybe half were the genuine article. The rest just wanted out. I've also met my share of refugees and prisoners of war. They were all hunting an angle on Uncle Sam."

"When Witold got on my train, she expected no more than to gain a few hundred miles. She's used to looking after herself."

"Sez you," Nell grunted.

Pascale put a hand on her arm. "You're a nice woman, Nell Tulliver. You're worried about me, but I know what I'm doing."

Like the lady who married the ax-murderer, thought Nell. "Sure," she said.

They strolled to the Seine's embankment. The sun appeared from time to time, lighting the buildings across the river. A strong, hot wind rattled the cables on the barges.

Pascale asked, "Do you like Paris?"

"I'm pretty fond of it," said Nell. "I was here before the war, back in the twenties. It was lively then. Being occupied has done zilch for the Parisian character. They're all trying to pretend they were never humiliated. Our Yankee presence irritates them because it makes that pretence harder. Once we go, they'll revert to their usual charming arrogance."

"You've been all over the world, haven't you?"

"Here and there." Nell began to walk toward the Pont de la Concorde. "London and Berlin before the war. Rome. Spain, during their Civil War. The Levant. Shanghai."

"It must have been difficult being a woman reporter in those places."

"No worse than investigating the Chicago meat-packing plants. You're tolerated if you can do your job."

"Do you want to remain a foreign correspondent?"

"Damn right I do. I wouldn't mind staying in Paris, as long as I'm not expected to cover the fashion houses."

Pascale glanced at Nell's baggy uniform, her scuffed shoes. "You don't think there's much danger in that, do you?"

Nell laughed. "You think my editor's crazy?"

"What do you prefer to write?"

"The things I do. My as-yet-unpatented chocolate rivet technique: a sweet human interest story wrapped around a hard truth that will stick in their minds. That's what I could do with this Witold business. The folks back home have to be shown what forced repatriation means. Not that they'll care, but at least they'll know what they're ignoring. I despair of them sometimes. If America acted on its rhetoric, it would be the country it claims to be." Nell laughed at herself. "I sound like a sermonizing grandma."

"You're hardly old enough for that," Pascale protested.

"I hope not," said Nell fervently.

They had reached the foot of the Champs d'Elysées. Traffic, most of it American military cars and trucks, spun round the Place de la Concorde.

"Do you want to walk up?" asked Nell.

"I'd love to, but I can't," said Pascale regretfully. "I only have this afternoon and I need to write letters. I swapped evenings with Dot. You met her. Her fiancé's in town unexpectedly."

"That's mighty accommodating of you."

"She helped to hide Witold."

"Lots of people have helped Witold," said Nell. "Not bad for a self-sufficient gal."

"She shouldn't have to be," said Pascale. "You're helping her, too."

"I haven't done anything so far," said Nell, but Pascale took one hand in both her own and smiled. "You're my best hope. I've complete confidence in you."

As Pascale hurried away, Nell lit a cigarette to hide the fatuous smile on her face.

The afternoon her own, she strolled up the Champs d'Elysées. She remembered the Allied victory parade here. She had been, let's see, in that building there, crouched behind two Arkansas sharpshooters, listening to their walkie-talkie as they hunkered in the small attic room and let her watch the parade between their shoulders.

The memory of her vigil with the sharpshooters made her ponder the Nazi sympathizers still lurking in this city. Collaborators were generally assumed to have supported Hitler's New European Order out of self-interest. What of those who had worked with the Nazis by conviction? It wouldn't be a bad story: *The Nazis the Nazis Left Behind.* Her French friends might not like it, but Americans ought to know that winning a war didn't bury ideas. Nell pulled out a notebook and began jotting thoughts. It would make a good radio talk. She went to the Gare de l'Est to pump one of her sources.

The program went well. Her broadcast engineer gave her the thumbs-up, the light went off, and she eased her damp waistband. No matter how many of these damned things she did, she was still as nervous as a puppy in a wiener factory. She took the engineer's offered cigarette.

"I hate to think of those Nazi-loving bastards out there," he said.

"Like the Confederates, they're nursing their grievances."

He choked. "I'm glad you didn't draw that parallel on air."

"It's true, and it leaves the same bad taste in my mouth," said Nell. "Those letters for me?"

"Yes. One of your *Baltimore Morning Mail* pals dropped them off."

"Thanks." Nell sorted through them. "Holy Joe!"

"Good or bad?"

"Something I didn't think would happen." She stuffed her V-mail into her pocket and suppressed the impulse to go straight to Pascale's office. She went back to her hotel, poured herself a drink, and stretched out on the bed to read the miniaturized letters properly.

Fergal Calhain, from her own paper, had answered, as had Frederick Lyle from the Colored Americans Press and Eric, an old press photographer friend.

Fontaine's camps, wrote Fergal, were almost empty now. The refugees had been sent to their respective homelands in May and June. No news about a man named Witold Rukowicz.

So much for Fergal. Nell picked up Frederick Lyle's letter. She vaguely remembered him, a tall, serious man who had won an award for his reportage in the deep South.

The camps at Fontaine, wrote Frederick, were closing down. He had spoken to the remaining Americans in the town. A riot in May was well remembered. It had lasted three days. Colonel Grove had gone in with a revolver but had managed to quell the men without violence. A Witold Rukowicz had been held in close detention before the uprising, but Frederick regretted that he could not trace the man past the riot. An army clerk at HQ thought that Rukowicz might have been part of the first repatriated shipment. So sorry, said Frederick, that he could not be of more use.

Darling Nelly, Eric began. *Isn't it yours truly who's supposed to chase the men? Do you know Charles Grove, the camp commandant at Fontaine? To keep the dear censors reading this letter happy, let's just say that the colonel belongs to the same club as thee and me. His special chum is a fellow in admin, a sweet little guy named Arthur. When Arthur heard, and I quote, it was that battle-ax Tulliver doing the asking, he split his sides. Your fame precedes you, sweetie. This Witold Rukowicz, you probably already knew that he isn't what he seems, right? No, it wasn't a well-known fact. A couple of nurses and Colonel Grove knew. And Arthur, of course. He had orders to return all letters sent to this Witold. Seems our colonel wanted to keep his guest a deep, dark secret. Witold, whose real name no one found out, went on the lam during the V-E Day celebrations. Nobody knew he'd gone because the nurse looking after him pretended for a whole week that he was still there. She was dipped in the usual boiling oil. Colonel Grove tried to locate Witold, but the only sightings of someone answering the description were in France. The same nurse was persuaded to 'fess that Witold might have aimed for Chartres. Fan of the Gothic, your wee Pole, or what's the lure? You know, don't you, Nelly? Have you got a little scoop you ain't sharing with your Uncle Eric? Do tell—I promise I won't breathe a word. Yours with love and kisses, Eric Camberwell.*

Nell rested her hands on the letters in her lap. Now she had something she could tell Pascale. What a pity that Witold hadn't got herself repatriated. Nell made a moue of distaste at herself as she admitted that she would have been happy to learn that Witold was permanently removed from the picture. But Witold was still in it, tramping around France, needing to be dealt with. Nell would have to find out if Pascale had been at the Chartres Conference in April. If she had, Nell might be able to cut Witold's trail somewhere between Fontaine and Chartres.

She wrote to her contacts in France, then a note to Pascale, who telephoned to say that she had no free time until the following week. On that Wednesday Nell found her already at their café, anxiously watching. Pascale waved with an eagerness that caused Nell a pang; she wished it were for more than the news she brought.

"You've heard something," said Pascale, jumping up to take her hand. "You're splendid. Tell me everything."

"Can't a gal get a drink?" Nell grumbled, giving Pascale a written summary of Frederick's and Eric's letters.

"Ah," Pascale devoured the page. "Yes." She looked up. "Detention in the hospital? That means Colonel Grove did rescue her."

"So it seems, though he suppressed your letters. Probably didn't want a diplomatic fracas. One of the nurses covered up Witold's escape."

"I'm in her debt," said Pascale. "She saved Witold from a Soviet prison. Or worse."

"Does this Witold of yours speak anything but Polish?"

"So-so German. Half a dozen phrases in English."

"That's not going to get her far."

"She's resourceful."

"I don't doubt it. You were at the Chartres Conference, weren't you?"

"Yes." Pascale re-read the summary. "Witold went straight there."

"She headed west," said Nell dampeningly. "Chartres is a surmise."

"She has my regimental details. She'll have asked at Chartres for me."

"I'm checking on that," said Nell.

Pascale smiled warmly. "I knew you wouldn't let it rest there."

"You've got a lot of faith in my reporter's curiosity," said Nell.

"Aren't you curious?"

"In the girl-meets-boy, girl-dumps-boy-in-refugee-camp, girl-finds-boy story? That I can use. But if I manage to arrange a happy ending, all the news agencies in the States will be chasing you. I can see the anniversary follow-ups in five years' time: *Where are they now? Wartime lovebirds find happiness in Boston, cradle of liberty. Vot a place, says new citizen.* What are you going to do when reporters want a photo shoot and all you can offer them is me-and-my-gal?"

"I hadn't considered," said Pascale unhappily. "You can't write this story, I see that. And of course you mustn't trouble yourself over this anymore. I'm extremely grateful, but I know you're a busy woman—"

Nell dismissed this with a gesture. "I've sent out my second round of queries, so we might as well see what they produce. If we find Witold, I'm going to pump her for generic stuff: days in a DP camp; my life as a Resistance fighter; Heinie horror; a Pole speaks for his fatherland; that kind of thing."

Pascale was laughing. "You don't write like that!"

"I have to fight my natural instincts," said Nell.

"Witold is a good person to write about. You won't find braver. She lost everything, survived Soviets and Germans, fought as a soldier. She never surrendered. She's dauntless."

"There are plenty who dodged the bad guys for the duration. It's you who's remarkable."

"No," said Pascale instantly.

"You, openly lesbian in a place like banned-in-Boston? Joining the WAC in spite of it? Serving close to the front line in Hürtgen and Germany? Smuggling a refugee from the war zone, risking arrest and court-martial if Witold had been found out? Not bad."

"That's paltry."

"You think so? I don't."

"Then you're easily impressed, which I don't for a minute believe. You're Nell Tulliver, the only woman reporter at Pearl Harbor! The first woman war correspondent in Paris! I should be in awe of you."

"But you aren't," said Nell with a crooked smile.

"I like you too much," said Pascale. "You can't be in awe of your friends."

"You can't respect your friends because you know too much about them," Nell quipped.

"How sad if that were true."

Nell sighed at Pascale's earnestness. "You don't make friends in my business; you make buddies, pals, contacts. If you're a lesbian, you keep even the best of them at arm's length."

"It was like that in my own unit. Some avoided me, the others were civil but distant. Until Witold, of course. Now that they think I'm one of them I've been included in all the gossip: boyfriends, husbands, yens for the cute corporal at the door, everything."

"How do you stay awake?"

"I like them. Even if I didn't, I'd still call them friends out of gratitude."

"For Witold's sake?"

Pascale nodded.

"My, my." Nell ordered more *gaseuz.*

"Have you ever been in love?" Pascale asked after a silence.

"Sure, plenty of times. Death-us-do-part stuff."

"I mean seriously."

"So did I. Each time. Unfortunately."

"Why didn't it last?"

"They got bored, or I did. A cottage built for two isn't my style. I was always steaming off on assignment. When I got back they usually weren't there."

"Knowing it would end didn't stop you from starting."

"I'm a sucker for that first fine careless rapture."

Pascale looked at her levelly. "What are you hoping for now?"

"Nothing but your girlish gratitude."

"Nell, I'm neither insensible nor a fool."

"No, though damn plain-spoken," Nell complained, shifting uncomfortably. "Are you really holding out for this Witold?"

"It's not about exclusive rights. I'm not being chaste for her sake."

"But you wouldn't consider a mutual arrangement?" Nell asked more harshly than she meant.

"Why are you pretending it would be that sort of exchange?" asked Pascale.

"Okay," said Nell. "Cards on the table. I'd be delighted to drop Witold into a mine shaft—and then sweep you off your feet. I figure I could do it, and I want to. But I'd also be delighted to present her to you on a silver platter. What does that make me? I'll tell you: stupid."

Pascale laid a hand on her arm. "No, it makes you breathtaking."

"You haven't traveled much, have you?" Nell snorted, lighting a cigarette and feeling as if she had run a marathon. "Are you always this brazen with your elders and betters?"

"Entirely my better," said Pascale. "You make it difficult to refuse you."

"Kind of hard on me, aren't you?"

Pascale's gaze did not waver. "We should end this now if it is."

"Raising the ante?"

"I don't want to lose you as a friend, but not at the price of the Little Mermaid."

"Smiling, though each step cuts?" Nell grimaced. "I'm a tough old bird; I can handle anything you dish out. You better hope you can do the same. How did Witold manage?"

"She idolized me."

Nell choked on a lungful of cigarette smoke. "Sez you!"

"I adore *her,*" Pascale shrugged.

"Am I in a bad play?" Nell fanned the air.

"It's not something I wanted. It just is. For Witold, too."

"You think."

"She wouldn't have gone west into France if I hadn't been at Chartres. She's putting herself in danger to find me."

"Maybe she figured France was safer."

"In what way? She's more easily identifiable and hasn't the protection of the language. France is full of officials sending refugees home."

"I'm not convinced," said Nell.

"You're still looking for her," Pascale pointed out.

"I want to find out where she is and what she's doing. If it turns out she isn't looking for you, I'll consider all bets off."

"Fair enough," said Pascale. "But if she is?"

"I hope she's what you want when you meet her again."

Pascale smiled. "You're a good woman."

"I'm a chump," said Nell.

6

That night, with a blank sheet of paper wilting in her typewriter and a tumbler of whiskey in hand, Nell stared at her slice of Paris and tried to convince herself that it was simply lust. Of course she wanted to fuck Pascale stupid; any lesbian laying eyes on her would. Nell had never confused desire and infatuation. What she felt now was something new, something she could not name, a—she groped for words—a kind of brooding care. Nell tapped ash from her cigarette. She was getting dopey in her old age.

By the end of June she began to lose hope in her contacts. With so many refugees roaming France, another poor starveling Polish boy was both unremarkable and unnoticed. She met Pascale every week at their café to report her lack of news, and spent the occasional evening with her at the Club Sevastopol.

Entering the club one night, Nell was mortified to feel her heart lurch as she caught sight of Pascale sharing a table with a patrician redhead.

"Nell!" Pascale beamed as she approached. "This is Captain West. Corinne West. She works on the floor above me. She was sorry not to have met you when you came to our office. Do you mind?"

"Of course not," said Nell.

Corinne West smiled briefly and held out a hand. "It's an honor to meet you, Miss Tulliver. I've been a faithful follower of yours for years."

Nell could not imagine anyone less like a fan. "Mighty gratifying," she said, sitting down.

"My father read your column aloud to me every week," said Corinne.

Nell winced. "While he dandled you on his knee?"

Corinne flashed a smile. "I'm glad I look that young. No, he enjoyed instructing his family, being, as it were, an autocrat at the breakfast table. He had ambitions for me and hoped that your column would educate me on world events."

"Are you the wiser?"

"I like to think so." Corinne smiled coolly.

"You wouldn't be one of the Wests of the Chicago, Denver, and Pacific Railroad, would you?" asked Nell, snagging a memory.

"I'm Vernon West's daughter."

Nell whistled. "Why aren't you in Palm Springs?"

"Because my French is flawless, Miss Tulliver. Ah, there's my date." Corinne lifted a hand to a dashing British WAAF. "I've enjoyed meeting you."

"Entirely mine," said Nell gallantly.

After Corinne left, Nell turned to Pascale. "What was that about?"

"She overheard me say I was seeing you tonight and asked if she could presume an introduction. When I said we would be at the Club Sevastopol she said only that she rather preferred the Café Verneuil."

"A cool customer," said Nell.

"I never knew she was a lesbian, but then she's a captain and in a different company. I hope you don't mind."

"Mind such effusive admiration as that? How could I?"

Pascale laughed. "Corinne's certain of her worth, but I think she's steel rather than starch."

Nell, uninterested in Captain West and wanting to get past her usual announcement, said, "No news of Witold, natch. I don't think she ever reached Chartres."

"I'm afraid you're right," said Pascale. "If she had, she would have asked for me and been told where I was."

"I could get a car for the day," Nell offered. "We could scout the vicinity and ask a few questions. She might have gotten close but then been steered wrong. It's the logical place to search."

"Yes." Pascale brightened. "When?"

"Next week, if I can wangle expenses. I'll have to write a story to justify the trip. What will it be?"

"The ancient cathedral looks down on the dawn of a new age?" Pascale suggested.

"I don't write that kind of—oh, okay, you got me. I'll have to inspire myself on the way there."

Madame Grevaniski, owner of the club, had with sadness permitted inside its doors an ancient Victrola. Between serving customers, Blanche and Martine took turns keeping it cranked. A few couples self-consciously jived on the dance floor. Nell saw Angelique working hard on a square-jawed army nurse for the same pleasure.

"In the late twenties," Nell told Pascale, "Madame Grevaniski had a small band playing at the back, two colored girls from Texas and an Algerian. Talk about hot jazz! They added a horn player from Sweden who damn near blew off the front of the building. Fun times."

"Let's dance," said Pascale, as Blanche switched from Miller to Dorsey.

"That's the stuff," said Nell over "Fools Rush In," leading her onto the dance floor.

Pascale stepped into her arms. Nell thought, *This is plain tiresome,* as desire surged through her. Pascale seemed fitted for her embrace. Hell and lightning. Why couldn't Witold get herself shot? It happened all the time.

Blanche put on "Imagination." Without hesitation, Pascale stepped into Nell's slower dance. Nell held her close, then closer still, until they were rocking gently to the music, dipping around the dance floor as if skating on ice.

The record scratched to its end. Pascale sighed, straightened, and stepped back.

"Don't you dare tell me you were thinking of Witold," Nell

growled lightly, the corner of her mouth tugging down.

"A little. I was also thinking of you. How could I help it? What do you want from your life, Nell?"

Nell walked back to their booth, giving herself time before replying, "Fame, fortune, you, and a comfortable old age. What you're asking me is do I want to find a nice girl and stick with her, or play the field until I'm too old to be enthralled with anything but my bunions?"

"I hate to think of you wasting yourself in clubs and bars. Back in Boston, my friends slept around until they were desperate, then settled for the first woman they could tolerate. That's not good enough for you."

"You want me in a cottage for two? Like what you'll have with Witold?"

"I don't know what we'll have," said Pascale. "I don't know what will happen. I don't think I'll have the sort of life I had with Edie."

"From what you tell me, Witold's going to need house-training first."

"She took the *wilczy bilet*," Pascale agreed.

"Decode, soldier."

"Took the wolf's ticket. It means roaming like a hunted animal, every man's hand against you. Witold's been living in a wilderness for six years. That's why I don't know how we'll be together."

"Like I said, needs house-training."

"In a way, it's how you live your life, too. I don't think one ever fully tames a wolf."

"My bark's worse than my bite," said Nell, gratified.

"I hope the woman who's meant for you finds you," said Pascale. "She's out there somewhere."

"Probably in Bolivia." Nell lit a cigarette dismissively.

At the end of the evening, Nell accompanied Pascale to her quarters, asking at the door, "You think you can get leave for a trip to Chartres?"

"Yes, if you can, I'd love to. We'll make a day of it." Pascale stood on her toes and kissed Nell's cheek.

"What's that for? We haven't found Witold yet."

"It's not for Witold," said Pascale, going in.

Nell thrust her hands in her jacket pockets and strolled moodily through the dark streets, ignoring the occasional mutters of passing men. Despite Pascale's kiss, Nell could not dispel the feeling that she was not going to be lucky.

Her plan to take Pascale to Chartres was interrupted by the sudden illness of Ed Picket, *Storace's* political reporter. Nell argued hard and got his assignment to cover the Potsdam Conference. It was infinitely better than reporting the trial of that cretin, Pétain. She wrote a hasty note to Pascale explaining her absence and caught an air force plane to Germany. In Potsdam she ran across Eric Camberwell.

"Nelly!" He hugged her hard. "So you browbeat poor Roland into letting you come."

"By the skin of my teeth. Thanks for digging up the information on that Polish refugee."

"My pleasure. What a giggle! When are you going to tell me what it was about?"

"If and when I know the outcome. Here's hoping for a happy ending."

"Oh dear," said Eric. "Not another notch on the bedpost?"

Nell laughed. "Entirely not that at all."

"You interest me strangely," said Eric. "Oh look, there's Nigel of the *Times.* Too ravishing. What's going to happen if the British voters toss Churchill out on his ear?"

"His replacement will carry on, like Truman did," said Nell. "The Brits are a democracy, you know."

"Barely," Eric sniffed.

The word *democracy,* thought Nell as the conference progressed, was not high on the list of the three leaders. It looked as if Poland and half a dozen other eastern European countries were going to be left holding the short straw. No wonder Witold did not want to go back.

Nell returned to Paris in time to hear the news of the bombing of Hiroshima. She frantically rewrote her broadcast as news of Nagasaki came down the wire, then was told by her New York producer that, until further notice, her slots were to be given to Tom Shane in Manila. Nell was not displeased, exhausted by Potsdam and sick of the war. She asked Roland about a car.

"Go ahead," he said. "Nobody's paying Europe any attention. The whole place is slack. What d'you think? Will the Japs surrender unconditionally or hold out for the Emperor?"

"I'm betting the first," said Nell. "I'll be back in a day or so."

"Fine, fine." He waved her away, his eyes on the teletype machine.

Nervous after a month's absence, Nell telephoned SHAEF headquarters. Pascale's unfeigned gladness threatened her self-command.

"I wish I could see you tonight, but I'm on evening duty," said Pascale. "Tomorrow?"

Nell smiled at the telephone receiver. "I feel like something frivolously Parisian after all that Teutonic grim. Have you ever been to the Café Verneuil? No? Okay, I'll see you at 7:30."

Sorting her notes at her table to begin her series of essays for *Storace's*, Nell became aware that she was humming. She did not hum. What the hell. She usually didn't make a fool of herself, either, so why not have one with the other?

The streets were hot as she walked south with Pascale. They paused on the Pont du Carrousel, looking at the Seine lying still as cellophane under its bands of bridges.

"Saint Denis sure looked after his city," said Nell. "There's nothing left of Europe east of here. It's obliterated."

"Will they recover? Do we want the Germans to recover?"

Nell laughed without humor. "Of course we do. You want de Gaulle's France to be top dog?"

They threaded their way into the heart of the Left Bank. Pascale said, "I have the feeling that too many deals are being brokered for the good of Europe."

"Truer words were ne'er spoke. We've said good-bye to everything east of Berlin. What remains needs a big strong friend, and that means Uncle Sam for Lord knows how long. Here we are." Nell led her through the ranks of outside tables to Café Verneuil's smoky interior.

A waiter, discreetly made up, found a table and handed them a menu with most of the choices crossed out.

"Horse, cat, or boiled shoe?" Nell asked Pascale.

"Shoe," Pascale replied. "I'm fond of horses and cats."

"Two shoes," Nell ordered gravely in English. Pascale translated without a tremor for the waiter, who bowed and left. Pascale took her hand. "I've been looking forward to seeing you again."

"I've been looking forward to you."

Pascale smiled, but said, "Tell me about the conference. I knew my service days were numbered when my unit wasn't ordered to Potsdam as part of the translating team."

"You're being shipped back?" asked Nell, her heart dropping through her body.

"The scuttlebutt is that they'll have us home by the end of September."

"Lordy," said Nell. "That doesn't leave us a hell of a lot of time. I mean, to find Witold."

"You won't be in Europe much longer yourself, will you?"

"Don't suppose I will."

"Potsdam," Pascale reminded her as Nell stared, abstracted, at the candle's flame. "What's your opinion of the political settlements?"

"I thought they stunk to heaven. What with Uncle Joe getting hurt feelings when anyone questioned his integrity, and Churchill so worried about the glory-that-was-Greece that he gave away the whole damned Balkans, it looks like Europe's in for a bumpy ride."

"Witold can't possibly be sent back to Poland now."

Nell's laugh held an edge. "I'm talking about the fate of the world and your angle is how it affects Witold."

"I think of war and I think of her. I think of peace and I think of her. I can't help myself. I'm not a crusader like you; I can let the world spin without my attention."

"You think I'm a crusader?"

"Of course you are." Pascale smiled at her. "You're an idealist. That's why you're still looking for her."

"Is that the reason?"

"Yes," said Pascale.

Nell leaned back to let the waiter serve their gelatinous meal. "Now you can be my trusty assistant. Remember I said that we ought to hunt around Chartres? If you could play hooky for a couple of days, I've got the okay for a car."

"I'd like that," Pascale smiled, the candlelight teasing her mouth with kissable shadows.

Nell looked down. "This sheep lived a rich, full, athletic life, somewhere steep."

"So did this cabbage," said Pascale.

Nell was aware of someone at her elbow.

"Miss Tulliver? Pascale? How pleasant to see you both again." It was the redhead. Nell reached into her memory and said, "Captain West," half-rising and gesturing to a chair. "Will you join us?"

"Thank you, no, I'm otherwise engaged," said Corinne, and Nell could see a plump, well-dressed French woman looking daggers at their table. "I thought I'd say hello. You were at Potsdam, weren't you, Miss Tulliver?"

"Yes, for my sins," said Nell, adding with as welcoming a note as she could, "would your friend like to join us?"

Corinne glanced over, then back at Nell with a quirk of laughter. "My companion didn't enjoy your article on aristocratic dabblers in the black market."

"I don't think her name came up," said Nell blandly.

"If she dabbled," Pascale pointed out, "she wouldn't have to eat here."

"Exonerated," Corinne smiled.

"I hope your coming over won't cause a rift," said Nell.

"It will be worth it. Shall I wish you luck with your meal?" Corinne returned to her table.

"If it weren't for people like Madame over there, Paris wouldn't be beggared by illegal marketeering," Nell growled softly.

"Corinne wouldn't be interested in someone like that," said Pascale.

"I think she's regretting it in any case." Nell poured more wine. "What about our foray?"

"Chartres? Yes, I've a day's leave and Jeeter owes me another. How soon can we go?"

"I'll pick you up tomorrow morning. Bring a coat in case we come back after dark."

"I like driving in the dark," said Pascale.

"Then I'll make a point of it."

Nell got up early enough to snag the big Citroën from the Reuss magazines' car pool, rolled down its top, and jauntily greeted Pascale wearing a pair of dark glasses.

"Here's the map," she said. "You're navigator. I'm not hot on reading French while I'm driving."

"I should have opted for the aerial photo and map reading course," said Pascale, but she had them out of the Parisian suburbs and past Versailles by mid-morning. The roads were still rutted from the tank convoys of last summer.

"I hope your training covered basic engine repairs." Nell steered over the scarps and ripples.

"Once they heard me speak German and Polish, I was doomed never to be near an engine. Actually, I'd hoped to do cryptography."

"Secret codes, cloak-and-dagger? Doesn't sound like you," said Nell.

"An odious necessity in war," said Pascale solemnly, then spoiled the effect by adding, "I love puzzles and word games. That's why I like translating."

"Have you worked on any of the Surrealists?"

Pascale nodded. "Péret. Now, there was a puzzle."

The hot midday air rushed past them, teasing loose wisps of Pascale's hair and flushing her cheeks. Nell glanced at her appreciatively from time to time. Despite her uniform, Pascale looked like a French woman: chic, poised, intelligent.

"When did your folks go to America?" Nell asked.

"My paternal line is as ancient as you can get in the New World," said Pascale. "They emigrated to Quebec before the Pilgrim Fathers had set sail. My father went south to the States as a young man. My mother's family is newer: they came from Poland after the last war. My grandfather was a scholar from Gdansk. He lived with us and spoke to me in German. My mother and her sister spoke Polish in rebellion against him. My father and I used French as our secret language. I was a polyglot from the cradle."

"Do they know about you?"

"Yes," said Pascale unhappily. "My mother prays for me constantly. Proof of the inefficacy of prayer. My father says nothing. My Aunt Maria once took me aside and said she was glad I'd never know the beastliness of men."

They drove between a long avenue of trees. Nell glanced up as they emerged and said, "Look."

"Oh!" Pascale breathed. The spires of Chartres cathedral rose through the rippling heat of the plain. "How beautiful it is."

"A mirage of faith," said Nell, still moved.

They drove into Chartres and, after receiving directions from passers-by, reached the square in front of the cathedral.

"Do you want to go inside?" asked Nell.

"I must," said Pascale, and they wandered in the cool blue light of its windows, speaking quietly.

Nell had the happy thought of asking one of the priests for assistance. They were passed to Father Luc, who had dealt with many refugees, but who did not recall a young Polish man. The Sisters of Our Lady of Mercy, he told them, had been running a hostel for displaced persons since Liberation; perhaps the two ladies would try there.

The convent was a big nineteenth-century building in the lower part of town. Pascale was taken to the mother superior while Nell, itching for a cigarette, stood in the vestibule looking at a lithograph of the Sacred Heart and a lachrymose Crucifixion. Was it comforting to believe in a God who had shared the pain of the world? Could anyone accept the burden of that much obligation?

Pascale returned. Judging from her expression Nell guessed, "You've got something."

"Yes."

"Let's eat. You can tell me then."

"But we ought—yes, of course," said Pascale, clearly curbing herself. Not until the soup had been removed did she say, "Reverend Mother didn't remember Witold, and their records aren't complete, but they had a number of men from eastern Europe with them in the spring. The Sisters found places for them as laborers on nearby farms. She gave me the names and directions of the most likely."

Nell looked at the list and the sketched map. "Nicely dispersed for inconvenience," she said. "Let's skip dessert."

An hour later they were speaking to Monsieur Brevard. He stood in a sea of chickens and thought back, his arms crossed. Nell could almost see him squeezing his memory like a hen producing an egg.

"No, I'm sorry," he said at last. "No one like that. Dutch, yes. Good workers, but hungry. No Polish boys." He gave them directions to the farm of Monsieur Chesainne.

Monsieur Chesainne had had one Polish man working for him, a poor soul with half his right hand shot off. Age? Monsieur Chesainne thought no younger than forty. He directed them to Monsieur Bosquet, but Monsieur Bosquet had employed neither Polish nor Russian men and suggested Monsieur Montleon.

Monsieur Montleon was with the harvesters. Madame Montleon said, "No, no, we never took anyone but French lads. Nobody but French. You can't trust anyone else. Have you tried Monsieur Brevard? Yes? Then Monsieur Vayenne might be the next choice. He has a foreign wife—Provençal—so he might have taken a Pole. Yes, try Vayenne."

They drove back to the main road and stopped to consult the map.

"The Vayenne farm must be near here." Pascale put her finger west of Chartres. "By the time we arrive it will be too late to call." Her voice was weary with discouragement.

"Vayenne, Robichoux, and Fabré are close together." Nell consulted the list. "If we get an early start tomorrow, we can see them all. The trail's pretty cold, but it won't get colder in one day."

Nell drove back toward Paris by a route that would take them through a village she remembered. She hoped the hotel was still standing.

In the long amber evening light, Grospont-Ste. Madeleine glowed like the incarnation of a perfect French village. Nell drove through slowly. Was that the same man letting his cat in? The same horse waiting for the farmer to ride it home? The church tolled evening mass and a few women crossed the square. On the outskirts of town stood a small, early nineteenth-century inn. If custom held, tables would be set outside in its walled garden for dinner. Nell parked.

"I was here over twenty years ago," she said.

"With someone?"

"Lordy, yes. A painter who'd taken a fancy to me. I had a weakness for incredibly rich and sophisticated women. Made life easier."

"You don't seem to have retained that predilection," said Pascale, getting out.

"I'm trying to live it down."

"Was she nice?"

"I was crazy about her. No, she wasn't nice, but she was pretty close to being a genius."

"Did she hurt you?" Pascale's tone was combative.

"Probably. Or I hurt her. It was a long time ago. I do remember the time we spent here. I remember the smell of linseed oil on her hands."

A middle-aged man greeted them. Dinner was indeed being served, but they must appreciate that he had a limited range to offer. Nell asked, in her halting French, if they might eat in the garden.

"You know of it, madame?" he asked, surprised.

"I was here a long time ago."

He frowned at Nell. "Long ago? I do not—ah! Ah! The young American reporter! With the famous painter. It was when my father was still alive. Well! We had the honor of your friend's patronage many times."

Nell made a face at Pascale, who grinned and shook hands with Monsieur Ramponneau. Nell remembered him as a slim young man waiting tables. Now he was thickset, lined, looking like his father. He gestured them into the garden, where five tables stood on a stone terrace and a cat stalked a butterfly. Trees around the wall dappled the grass with sunset light.

"Thank you for bringing me here," said Pascale as she sat and looked around.

"I'm glad you like it," said Nell. "It was magical to me then."

Monsieur Ramponneau emerged with two brandies, compliments to an old friend and, dared he presume, a young one. Had they heard the verdict of Pétain's trial? The gentleman had been found guilty. That, he suggested, deserved a toast. At Nell's request to join them, he went inside for another glass. He was gone for some time. The church bell of Ste. Madeleine began to ring again. Monsieur Ramponneau burst through the doors.

"Mademoiselles! The Japanese war is over!"

"What?" Nell and Pascale looked at each other.

"The Japanese have surrendered! My friend Monsieur Evrard heard it on his radio from London and has come to tell me. Unconditional surrender! Peace begins tomorrow morning."

Nell did a mental chronology. "That means the Pacific's at peace right now. Lord Almighty! What a time and place to hear this! The war's over."

With Madame Ramponneau, who emerged from the kitchen, and their friend Evrard, Monsieur Ramponneau, Nell, and Pascale toasted the victory and the peace.

"How about that," said Nell in English.

"How about that," said Pascale softly.

Monsieur Evrard rushed to fetch his radio on his bicycle, bringing back Madame Evrard, his children, the mayor, the priest, and neighbors. Trestles were assembled to accommodate everyone. The radio, perched on a chair in a window, was a gabble of speeches and news. Nell and Pascale withdrew to their own table, talking quietly over their meal until called to a toast.

"Our noble American allies!" The mayor was bowing to them.

"Our gallant French allies," Nell replied, raising her glass, and was caught in a string of toasts to the valiant British, the stalwart Canadians, the brave Poles, the doughty Russians, the...er...Chinese, the Greeks, and the Americans again. Nell's head was buzzing by the time she sat. Pascale struggled with giggles.

"So much for a quiet supper," said Nell.

"But memorable."

One of the young men, by appearance Ramponneau junior, cleared their table. More brandy was served. The radio's talk changed to music and Nell sat listening, looking at how the lights around the garden wall cast tree and flower silhouettes. Moths batted the lamps above their table. She looked at Pascale, who was eavesdropping on the villagers' talk as she sipped her brandy. Nell thought that time could stop right here.

"On a night like this," said Pascale, "one might almost believe a better world is begun. After what we've been through, after all that pain and death, who would dare to repeat them?"

"You don't believe it, do you?" asked Nell.

"I've never had faith in such things," said Pascale, "but it's nice to pretend on so beautiful a night."

Nell said nothing, secure in her own belief that Witold would never be found.

Husbands waltzed with their wives on the terrace. A young man gallantly asked Nell to dance. She did, but it was clear on her return that he had asked the older woman from courtesy and now the younger one by choice. Pascale came back at the end of the song and said to Nell, "I'd rather be dancing with you."

Nell nodded to a door in the garden wall. They slipped through and found themselves on a patch of grass by an orchard. Light from the open door lit the tree trunks. Nell shielded her eyes and looked at the stars, the radio's music more distant than the constellations. Suddenly the strains of "Long Ago and Far Away" drifted through the doorway. Pascale turned to her and they were dancing in the dark, taking small steps in the grass. Nell slipped into an unthinking dream, letting the wine and the night and Pascale be everything.

The music slowed and stopped. Pascale reached up, tipped Nell's head down, and kissed her.

Nell pulled back. "What about Witold?"

"Witold isn't now," Pascale said so lightly that Nell almost missed the despair in her voice. "You are."

"Now," said Nell. This must still be the dreaming moment. Pascale was kissing her again, kissing her until Nell was desperate. "Pascale—" she gasped, "what am I going to do?"

"Find out if we can afford a room," said Pascale practically. "It's late, we're too drunk to reach Paris tonight, and I want to make love to you."

Nell almost repeated *Witold?* but realized that, for once, for now, Witold was none of her business.

Monsieur Ramponneau was delighted that his dear friends were doing him the honor of staying the night. Madame Ramponneau showed them the best room.

"I can't afford it," said Nell.

"For our friends on this night, I am sure this room can be given at our lowest price," cried Madame.

"How kind," said Pascale, taking the key.

She locked the door and came to Nell, who was standing uncertainly in the center of the room, feeling the double bed beside her looming like a continent.

Pascale's arms, Pascale's mouth banished her apprehension. Their kisses were tender, exploring, ardent. Nell hurried off Pascale's uniform, her own clothes, and they tumbled onto the bed in the sweet shock of nakedness. With an impatient gesture Pascale pulled out her hair pins; a flood of silky dark hair poured across Nell's arm and breast.

"My God," said Nell, "you're flawless."

Pascale stopped her mouth with kisses, made love to her with the grace of experience and desire. Pascale's mouth on her was bliss, was torment. Nell wondered if she could bear Pascale's finesse. She gasped and choked like one drowning as Pascale kissed her breasts, kissed down her body, was on her. She cried endearments and curses, tensed and built into exquisite pressure, was jolted into a single moment of release that peaked, dissolved from heat to warmth, to the warmth of Pascale's arms, to sparks becoming the church bells at midnight.

She turned to Pascale, muffling the words she could not stop herself saying against Pascale's moist skin. She thought herself exhausted, but the sweetness of Pascale against her lips, the fragrance of her, Pascale's faint trembling, fired her again.

She eased over Pascale, not meeting her eyes—that was expecting too much of herself—but kissing her, stroking her skin, mumbling her lips against each soft place: the base of her throat, her wrist, the sweet length of her back. Pascale reacted with a faint laughing wonder that made Nell light-headed and, when Nell became serious, abandoned herself in animal delight to Nell's hands and mouth. Nell made love to her with every skill and nuance she could summon, with every feeling in her heart. She would have this go on forever, but Pascale was insistent and Nell obeyed, bringing her to climax. Pascale caught her breath, sighed, and was still.

Nell held her close and considered how imperfection made this bearable. Perfection required Pascale to be in love with her. The fact of Witold kept things in proportion, and Nell was bitter and glad.

She woke with the morning light in her eyes. Pascale had risen to fold back the shutters. Nell looked at her glowing in the sun and held out her arms. Pascale came to her. They made love again, the sun hot on their backs and legs. Finally they lay together, overcome.

Nell wondered if she had enough money for another night. Pascale said, "We should get up and see Monsieur Vayenne."

Nell blinked. "Oh. Yes. No time like the present," and began to move.

"Wait." Pascale put a restraining arm over her. "I've never lied to you. What you mean to me will never change. Witold is my life, but you are my dearest."

"I'm in love with you," said Nell.

"No, I'm one of your hopeless passions. Dearest Nell, kindest Nell, you deserve better."

"Who's that?" Nell glinted.

"Not Pascale Tailland, even if I were free. It wouldn't last. You know it wouldn't. I want you to have a splendid woman who's your equal."

"That's you."

"Oh, Nell, it's not!"

"How the hell would you know?" Nell demanded, kissing her, moving a leg across her to pin her down. They looked at each other and Nell felt as if she were seeing the rim of the world. She made love to her, concentrating, memorizing, tenderly adding sensation to sensation, wanting Pascale to remember this morning forever. When it was over, when she had stroked her to quietness, had kissed her, Nell turned away and stood up. Through the window she could see a mower moving in the wheat fields.

"Thank you," said Pascale from the bed.

"Thank you, my dear," said Nell.

They bathed, dressed, had breakfast, and said farewell to Monsieur Ramponneau, who held the car doors for them.

"I am glad you returned, Mademoiselle Tulliver," he said. "I will always remember that you were our guest on the last night of the war." He waved until they were through the village.

"Monsieur Ramponneau's hotel might merit a line in a guidebook one day," said Pascale.

"Helen Tulliver slept here? I doubt it," said Nell. "Where's that map?"

They went to the farm of Monsieur Vayenne. His son did not remember any Polish man sent by the Sisters, just three shiftless

Czechs.

"There's still Robichoux and Fabré," said Nell as they drove away.

"Only two left," said Pascale, unable to hide her hopelessness.

The Robichoux farm was to the south. Nell put on her dark glasses. Behind them she snatched glances at Pascale, acutely aware of Pascale's body under the uniform, acutely aware that Pascale's attention was elsewhere.

For the first time, Nell longed to find Witold. Then Pascale would realize—might finally realize—that this damned Polish girl was not the one for her. Nell determined to be at their rendezvous, just in case.

"The next left turn," said Pascale.

They bounced along a rutted track to an old farmhouse. A dog yapped. Nell stepped from the car, one eye on it.

"Mesdames?" A large woman came to the back door. "May I help you?"

"Madame Robichoux?" asked Pascale.

"I am."

"Good morning. My friend and I are searching for a young man, a Polish refugee, who might have been sent to you by the Sisters of Our Lady of Mercy."

"Yes, we have taken a few. We have only Tomasz still with us."

"The man we are looking for is young, fair, and not tall. His name is Witold Rukowicz."

Madame Robichoux nodded.

"He was here?" Pascale asked faintly.

"Yes, briefly. He was with us in June. A good worker, if not as strong as Tomasz. Kept himself to himself, as they say. We would have been happy if he'd stayed."

"He's no longer here?" Pascale asked.

"Unfortunately, no. He came to us saying that he would remain as long as it took him to get well. Such a terrible cough. He worked not so hard then, but later, when he was better, twice as hard, to make up. Then he was off to Normandy."

"He was ill?" asked Pascale, and Nell could see her knuckles whiten against the door handle.

"Influenza. He got better, I assure you. May I ask if you are a friend of his, mademoiselle?"

"Yes, a good friend. I had promised to help him, but I was sent to Chartres."

"I understand now," said Madame Robichoux. "Come in, please, both of you."

They followed her into the farmhouse, to a parlor filled with horsehair furniture and clusters of family photographs. Over a glass of pear brandy Madame explained, "Witold told us that he came to Chartres to find an American soldier. You must understand, he had not ten words of French, and my husband and I not five words of German, but we made ourselves understood. He had been told in Chartres that the soldiers attending the conference had been shipped back to America. Poor boy, he was devastated. Clearly his information was not true, for here you sit before me, mademoiselle. Witold was determined to go north to find a ship."

"I see," said Pascale. "May I ask when he left you, madame?"

"At the beginning of August."

"August!" Pascale looked at Nell. "He might still be in France."

"That I cannot say." Madame Robichoux shook her head. "He was a good boy. I'd like to think that he's come to no harm. Mademoiselle, if you find him, please let us know and give him our kind wishes."

"Of course I shall," said Pascale. "I'll translate anything Witold wants to write to you."

"He could speak simple sentences by the time he left," said Madame. "He has a quick brain and a nimble tongue."

"Has he?" asked Pascale, amused.

On the drive back to Paris, Nell felt a new tightly strung quality in Pascale's silence. She said to her, "I'm going to need an early lunch to counteract that pear brandy. Is there a town on this road, or do you want us to head straight for Normandy?"

Pascale laughed self-consciously. "My first impulse. Poor Witold! She has so little information, and most of it wrong. When I get back, I'll telegraph my family and my landlady in case she's already crossed the Atlantic. She might be sitting on the steps of my apartment this minute."

"I don't think Witold's anywhere but France," said Nell. "The coast is still in navy hands and they don't let just anyone stow away on their ships. If she's unlucky, the navy might even have tossed her on a train bound for Poland."

"No," said Pascale. "That can't happen."

They lunched at a roadside inn and reached Paris by mid-afternoon. Nell, not bothering to suggest her hotel, dropped Pascale at her quarters.

"You hang tight," said Nell, getting back into the car. "I'll contact my pals in Normandy."

Pascale leaned over and kissed her. "Dear Nell. I owe you my happiness."

"Wait till she's found," said Nell. "Tell me then."

She returned the car and went to the Reuss building.

"Great timing," said Roland. "You missed V-J Day."

"How could I miss it? There's a big world out there, pal. They actually read the papers and listen to the radio."

"You got a column for me?"

"Sure. The world born anew. The eternal rhythm of the harvest witnesses the birth of a new era."

"Mood piece, huh? Okay, let's see it tomorrow."

"By the way," asked Nell, "who've we got in Normandy?"

"A few stringers."

"I'm still on the trail of that Polish refugee."

Roland perked up. "Normandy now? Heading for the States?"

"Hole in one," said Nell.

TBC had left a message at her hotel to say that the Tuesday broadcast slots were hers again. Drina greeted her on the landing. "Nell! Did you hear the news?"

"V-J Day. Yes, I heard."

"Jerry's been posted home. There's a stash of gin for his send-off. You're coming, of course."

"Sure. Call me when he gets here." Nell went to her room. It was stiflingly hot. She heaved up the window. The faucet gave a trickle of brown water. She poured herself neat warm whiskey and took the cover off her typewriter.

"Today," she typed, "I want to talk about the lost ones. Now that our men and women in the services are coming home, now that our thoughts are of our loved ones returning, I want to speak of those who cannot return, who have no homes, no families to go to. I'm speaking about the displaced persons of Europe and the world. For example, I know of a young man from a village in Poland, a village that no longer exists. He's lucky: he's met an American girl who loves him and who is looking for him. Before I speak of the less lucky ones, the ones in the camps, the ones sheltering in bombed ruins, the ones barely existing, let me ask Witold Rukowicz, if he is listening, to come to Paris, where his girl is waiting for him. Witold Rukowicz, please make contact. I hope you find her. But the others also need our help. If you could see the devastation throughout Europe you might think that no amount of work and money could rebuild these people's lives—but we can, and I'll tell you why we should."

Nell sipped her whiskey, lit a cigarette, and kept typing.

Sibylle

7

The safest way home was behind the bombed factory and along the road, keeping close to the trees. Sibylle clutched her string bag to her chest. It held old bread, but a whole loaf, a piece of cheese, and a bundle of dandelion leaves plucked near the stream.

A man was waiting on the steps of her house. Sibylle steadied herself. Gilles. Gilles, come to—but no, not the right size. This was a stranger.

"Pardon," said the man in a thick accent, rising as she approached. "I want work, please, if have, or to..." He ran out of words.

"German?" she asked impatiently.

"*Non. Polonais.*"

"There's nothing for you here," she told him, then saw darkness on his shirt. "Are you hurt?"

He looked down. "A little. Not important. Work?"

"I've none for you," she answered. "Go away."

He eyed her bread as he moved from the door. "Pardon, mademoiselle."

She hesitated. "Do you have any money? *Das Geld?*"

"A little," he answered in German.

"I do nothing for free," Sibylle said in the same language. "Do you understand? I'll help you for money."

"I understand. I will pay."

Sibylle unlocked her door carefully in case her neighbors had pushed another unpleasant surprise under it. "Come in," she gestured. "Sit."

He took the one chair, looking around her single room.

"What did you expect?" she asked.

He shrugged. "*C'est* okay."

"You speak English?"

"Little." He pulled out a small book. "*Regardez.*" It was a two-language dictionary. "See? Polish, English. Also I have some German. My French you hear."

"I do," said Sibylle. "Where's your money?"

He took out one copper coin at a time, pausing to look at her with each, expecting her to indicate when it was enough. Trusting fool. Two more coins. Sibylle held up her hand.

"That'll do." She swept them away. "Show me your wound."

"No, I do it. I need water."

Sibylle heated water in her single saucepan. He took the piece of rag she gave him, turned his back, undid his shirt, and, wincing, swabbed the wound.

"What is it?" she asked. "A bullet?"

"No. Scratch only, from a broken bottle."

"In a fight?"

"Yes." He finished, rebuttoning his shirt and vest.

"What did you do to the other man?" she asked.

"Stopped him from hurting me."

"I'll feed you tonight. Tomorrow you find your own food."

His eyes weighed her small loaf, the smaller piece of cheese.

"It'll have to do," she said. "I don't cook, and I won't for you. Do you drink coffee? I have to mix it with chicory; you probably won't like it."

They sat at the table, Sibylle on the chair, the stranger on the edge of the bed. He concentrated on his half of the loaf and cheese and drank the chicory-coffee mixture without distaste.

"I suppose you want to stay here tonight," Sibylle said.

"If you permit, mademoiselle."

"Sibylle. My name is Sibylle. You'll have to sleep back there." She indicated the half-destroyed rooms at the rear of the house. "Or pay more."

He looked at her uncertainly.

"That's how I make money."

He smiled, enlightened. "Whore."

"Yes. How nice of you not to have guessed."

"I will sleep in the back. Then you can earn money."

"What a thoughtful boy!" Sibylle said sardonically. "Unless you want to watch?"

He frowned. "No."

"My customers will start coming in an hour."

"Okay." He gestured at the room. "This is your house?"

"It was the Clicards'. An American shell fell on the back. They were sheltering there."

"No more Clicards."

"No one to complain when I moved in."

"Whoring makes poor money." He looked at the broken glass in the window, the tumbled ruin of the rear of the house.

"It's better than starving."

"You look nice enough to make better money. Though your hair is very short."

"It's short because Germans were my customers. *Collaboration horizontale*," Sibylle quoted bitterly.

"Sleeping with Germans has earned you little except punishment, unless your money was taken from you as part of it."

"Money? I wasn't trying to get rich, I was staying alive. You don't know what it's like to be a woman alone. I was a whore before the Occupation. Nothing changed. What difference if the man was a German pig or a French pig?"

"You talk this way to all men?"

"Of course I don't. You haven't hurt me yet and you don't want to fuck me, so I don't have to be nice to you."

"No, you are not," he agreed. "I see why you earn little."

"I'm given what they choose to give me. I've no pimp, nobody to raise a hand if I'm robbed or beaten. The police don't care. I'm lucky to get what I get."

"You do not leave? Go somewhere else?"

"With my hair this short? Everyone in France knows what that means."

"You cannot blame them."

"I can. I do. Monsieur LeBrun cozied up to the Germans, but he's rich, so you don't see him cropped and beaten. Madame Hébert wasn't dragged through the streets, though Commander Ströengel went to her musical salons every week. No, they punish me, the poorest of the poor, to make themselves feel better for having done nothing."

"I am a Pole. You expect me to feel sorry for you?"

"I don't care what you think of me."

"You say you collaborated as necessity. I know about these two things. If necessary, then there is no shame, and it is you who punish yourself with misery."

"Easy for you to—"

"Yes, yes, I cannot know what it was like." He looked tired. "I do not care what you did, mademoiselle. I have given you money. I will sleep now."

Sibylle stripped one of the blankets from her bed. "Take this. Included in the price. I'll charge you more if you watch."

He stood slowly. "You are safe with me."

"Are you a sodomite?"

"I am interested only in sleep."

"Sleep, then. Tomorrow you go. I don't need to give a room to someone who despises me."

"Someone other than you?" He took the blanket and left the room.

She could hear him pushing rubble from the middle of the back room. She went to his door. He had spread his greatcoat on the floor and was wrapped in the blanket.

"What's your name?"

"Witold Rukowicz."

"Don't come out, Witold," she said, lifting his cracked door to close it.

She changed into her work clothes, a thin blouse and tight skirt, high-heeled shoes instead of her wooden-soled *semelles de bois.* Turning on her radio, she stood in front of the shard of mirror to make up her face with the bottle of rouge she had been nursing for months. The light from the single electric bulb made her look cadaverous.

A knock.

"Sibylle," said Michel, the banker's clerk, through the door.

She opened it and he wedged himself in, urgent not to be seen. "Ei, Sibylle," he said, unbuttoning his trousers.

She knelt, wishing she had not wasted rouge on her lips. It was soon over; she automatically closed her throat and her mouth filled and overflowed. She rose, not wiping her mouth and chin, knowing that he liked to see the glistening evidence of her distaste. He tossed a coin on the table, leaving with a nod.

She wondered why he came all this way for that. At least he always paid something. She rinsed her mouth with cold coffee and re-rouged her lips.

Later Edouard rapped on the door and called. She knew what he liked, so threw open the door with one hip thrust forward.

"Edouard! I've been wanting you, needing you, since the last time. Be quick, be quick."

He pulled off her clothes like the tough sailor he wanted to be and knocked her onto the bed. It was easy to sustain the patter and clutch at his shirt and bite his shoulder and gasp and squeak and pound her hips and sigh in fulfillment exactly as he ejaculated. The difficult part was cajoling him afterward, pretending he was her lover who could be teased for a gift.

"You're a naughty wanton," he said, pinching her cheek and pressing coins into her palm. She could feel that it was not enough. "Here's a little token, my dear. Buy yourself something pretty."

Teeth gritted, she cooed her thanks as he left. A few centimes for a complete fuck! Less than half the rate he'd have been charged by Clothilde, who worked up the hill, less even than Monette, who did it against the wall in an alley behind the church. Bastard.

She douched herself with warm water from the saucepan and dressed. Two more hours passed. No one else came. It was a windy, damp night; they would not care to leave the bar or their hearths for the long walk to the edge of town. She stripped for a shivering sponge bath in her tin tub and went to bed.

Not a movement or a noise had come from the back room. She would have heard the door move, but still she raised herself on one elbow to look. The door was as she had left it. She slipped from her bed and peeked through the crack. Moonlight showed Witold sleeping as purposefully as a cat. She went back to bed.

She woke in daylight, certain of being watched. His door was open. "You!" she hissed. "Come out, you pig."

No answer. She quickly pulled on her day frock and went to his room. The greatcoat was hanging from a nail. The blanket was folded. He was gone. Not before having a thorough peep at her, she was sure.

Good riddance, she thought, starting breakfast. She could sell the coat. The saucepan was coming to a boil when she saw him approaching the house from the back.

"Good morning." He emerged dustily from the hallway, cradling four eggs and half a loaf of bread.

"What are you doing?" she snapped, angry that he had confounded her.

"Making breakfast. You have lard? I will fry these."

"None."

"Boiled is also good."

"You stole them."

"Your neighbors will not miss these few. The bread was discarded. I see nothing wrong with it." He filled her frying pan with water from the standpipe. "If you grind your coffee beans between a brick and that marble slab, you will make it better."

"Why are you doing this?" she asked.

"The brick dust will settle to the bottom of the pan."

"If you feel sorry for me, you can leave right now."

"I feel sorry for myself, having to get my own breakfast when I paid you. The world is unjust."

"You're laughing at me! You're a pantywaist, I can tell. With your dainty ways, making your bed, fussing with coffee beans, you're a pervert."

"Because I am not ravishing you?"

"A runaway monk, then, afraid of women."

"You assume that I have considered you at all. People who live alone think too much about themselves."

"Why shouldn't I? No one else thinks of me. I might as well not exist for all anyone cares."

"Those electric cables were rigged for you." Witold nodded to the wires running from the stove and the overhead bulb.

"A soldier named Aaron. He boarded up the back of the house and built this kitchen. You can see the stove is American army. He was in the Quartermaster Corps."

"He does not sound like a man who took advantage of you."

"He was a Negro. I wanted him to stay, but he had a wife and children and aunts in America. He gave me the radio."

Witold brought breakfast to the table. "I could do things for you, as Aaron did, if you let me stay. I would prefer to be out of sight until I am sure nobody seeks me. The Italian I fought might be dead from my knife."

"Are you heading anywhere, or just on the run?"

"I am going to America."

"How are you going to do that? Sprout wings?"

"I do not yet know. I must find new clothes. If I look unrespectable, I will get no work."

"You look like a German."

"I do not," he said unamiably.

"Blond hair, blue eyes? Completely Master Race. Do you think they'll let you into America?"

"You make it hard to help you."

"Help me? I'm no charity. Are you a priest, with this do-gooder talk?"

He laughed. "Not priest, monk, or pervert. Eat your eggs before they cool."

"Are you a virgin?"

His smile twisted. "No."

"You sleep with women but you won't sleep with me. You're too good for me."

"It is because I do not like you. I go to America to be with someone."

"You're a faithful lover!" Sibylle crowed. "How sweet. Does she know you're coming? Or are you hoping she'll remember you? I don't believe you have a woman."

"I do not have her. She has me."

"Why is she in America? Is she Polish?"

"She is an American soldier."

"A woman soldier? A man who cooks and a woman soldier."

"She translates many languages."

"Does she need a chef? You're going to be surprised when you find her; she'll have a husband and children and she'll get the police to arrest you."

He shook his head. "None of those." He finished his breakfast and rinsed his plate at the standpipe. "I could build a shelf for this."

"If I had a hammer and nails."

"If you had this, if you had that, if your hair was longer, if people were not so unkind. Take responsibility for yourself."

"I don't need your sermons. I need money."

He took all he had from his pockets. "How much do you need?"

"That's nothing. It'll take more than that to get away from here."

"Who runs this town?"

"Monsieur Albert, the mayor."

"No, I mean who brings in the liquor and meat and perfume."

"Who runs the black market? Gilles Roche. He works from a barge on the river." Sibylle's voice flattened as she said his name.

Witold looked at her. "He comes to you?"

"Sometimes. He knows I can't complain."

"I might get work with him."

"You won't last a day. You're too little."

Witold put a finger to his head. "I am smart."

"If he finds where you're staying, he'll think you're my pimp."

Witold laughed. "That will amuse Pascale."

"Who's she?"

"My American soldier."

"You'd tell her?" Sibylle stared at him. "You're not a pervert or priest, you're crazy."

Witold grinned and fetched his cap. "I cannot say when I will return."

"Are you really going to see Gilles Roche?"

"I speak no French, so I overhear nothing. I have no local connections, so have no reason to betray him. I will get work. I have done it before."

"It doesn't bother you to work for a criminal?"

"I do not answer for him or for his customers."

Sibylle snorted. "You think like a Jesuit."

"If you are listening to news reports, attend for a murder south of Rennes. That is where I disagreed with the Italian."

Sibylle went to the kitchen and turned on her radio.

"What is that?" he asked, appalled at the trumpets and percussion.

"American music. It's wonderful. Aaron and I used to dance right here." She laughed as he winced and left, then stepped out the door to watch him climb the hill into town.

Why was he staying? Perhaps he had secretly fallen in love with her. Perhaps he would murder her tonight. She went to his room and searched the pockets of his greatcoat. He had only his lexicon and a handkerchief, brown with dried blood. She washed it and hung it over the broken glass in the kitchen window. Looking out, she could see a dancing haze of insects above the wilderness that had been Madame Clicard's garden. Aaron had wanted her to plant vegetables: *You can't live on Spam and K rations forever, Sib.* He had been transferred before he could make her do it.

Witold did not come back that evening. A fool after all. Pierre came, then the lawyer's clerk Monsieur Duvas, and finally Raymond. Raymond stayed most of the night. He drove a truck and always left at dawn for his first run. Sibylle was bathing when a face flashed at the window. She had one moment of terror until she recognized Witold.

"I am sorry," he said from the hallway. "When you are dressed, tell me."

"You were spying!" Sibylle jerked on her frock. "Now I'm ready."

He came in and slumped on the chair. "I was checking in case a man was still here with you." One side of his face was dark with bruises.

"What happened?" she asked sharply.

"Your Gilles Roche is a bully."

Sibylle curled her lip. "He got a taste for it under the Germans."

"Apart from that," said Witold, "he is a good businessman. What he brings up the river! Oysters, lobsters, fancy seafood to sell in Paris. I spent all night carrying boxes to his trucks."

"Where were you all the day before that?"

"Proving I was tough enough and stupid enough to carry boxes."

Sibylle filled the saucepan with water. "Why don't you get honest work?"

"There is no work for a Pole, not with the French prisoners of war back home. I worked on a farm in the spring, but that was charity."

Sibylle was silent. It had been June when the interned men of Balmoigne returned. It was then that the good citizens had come to her with their shears, their sticks, their placards. Sibylle had stared at the emaciated faces of the freed prisoners in the crowd, angry that anyone thought her hurt and shame could be restitution for them.

"You're going back to Gilles tomorrow?" she asked.

Witold showed her a handful of coins. "For this much money? Yes." He drank the chicory-coffee she gave him as if the inside of his mouth hurt.

"You won't be much use as a pimp if we're both working at night," said Sibylle.

"Gilles laughed when he heard where I was staying. He thinks you took me in because I look German."

"I hate Germans. I hate men."

"So do I," said Witold. He dragged himself to his room. She heard the clump of his boots as he took them off. Irritated with herself for listening to him, paying any attention at all to him, she rinsed his cup and went to bed. His money lay on the table.

It was still there when she woke the next morning. She kept the radio low so as not to wake him and listened to the French announcer. No news of a murdered man. Had Witold killed anyone? She went to his door. He was sprawled out, his dirty bare feet exposed. He was younger than she had realized: no beard, or one so blond that it was invisible in this light. If he kept working for Gilles he would not get much older. He would end facedown in the river.

Witold shifted and blinked, saw her at the door, and grabbed his blanket.

"I need some of your money for food," said Sibylle.

"Okay." He rubbed his head muzzily. "Take what you need."

Sibylle put on her hat and went by the back streets to Madame Perronet's dingy greengrocer shop. There was nothing of quality, but Madame Perronet would sell to anyone.

"Business must be picking up," Madame Perronet sniffed as Sibylle gave her Witold's money.

Sibylle took her bag without a word and went to the baker. He made his usual joke of sliding the baguette back and forth through his cupped hand as he gave it to her.

From the top of the street she could see the wharves and brickyards on the other side of the river. That big rusty barge next to the bridge was Gilles Roche's. Witold must look like a sparrow on its deck.

The house was empty when she returned. She saw that Witold had had a bath. She was unpacking her bag when he came from the hallway with an armload of bricks.

"What are you doing?" she asked.

He piled the bricks next to the standpipe. "I am making that shelf."

Sibylle put a hand against his cheek as he walked past her. "How old are you?"

He backed away as if burned. "Why?"

"You're just a boy."

"How old are you?"

"Twenty-three."

"You said you whored before the war."

"Monsieur Danon began to pay me when I turned sixteen. What are you? Sixteen? Seventeen?"

"Older than that."

"Don't you know?"

"It does not matter."

He ferried half a dozen armloads of bricks and stacked them in an unmortared bond around the standpipe and drain until the brick box was at knee height. He found a piece of board and a dented tin pail, laid the board across the top of the bricks, and put the pail under the tap. "No more bending," he said, and went to make a twig broom to sweep away the brick dust. He continued around the room, cleaning the cobwebs from the ceiling and the dust from under the bed.

"What a treasure you'll make your soldier," said Sibylle. "But you must learn more English." She turned on the radio and found the European Forces station.

"I will learn little from that," said Witold above the music.

"It's jazz."

He went to the garden to dust himself off. The radio moved from music to talk as he returned and he stood listening to it, head tipped.

"It's about Japan," Sibylle explained. "They've dropped another bomb on it."

"There was a first?"

"This is a new kind. One destroys a whole city."

"One bomb! I am glad the Germans and Communists did not have it."

"I'm a communist myself," said Sibylle.

"Why?"

"Because," Sibylle said vaguely. "Because the lowest have nothing and do everything and the rich live off our labor."

"The laboring men in town think you are one of them?"

"This is work." Sibylle's voice was harsh.

"Why not do something more profitable?"

"I can't sew, I can't cook, I can't add in my head. When I was young I went with older men because it was fun. Once I got money for it I didn't fancy working in a shop or a fish-canning factory for less than half what I could earn on my back. Now that I'm a prostitute, no one will give me a job anyway, not even gutting fish."

"Start again somewhere else. I could take you to the next town."

"What would I do there? I've no clothes and no money. I'd have to go on the game. How much do you think the local women would like the competition? There's no such thing as starting over when you're at the bottom."

"The bottom is when you are starving in a ditch," said Witold. "Bottom is when you eat rats."

Sibylle hunched a shoulder. "You don't know what it's like to be considered garbage."

"What do you think the Germans called the Poles?"

"Are you saying we're equal?"

"We are not. I am going to America and you are going to rot here." He went to the garden again for scrap wood and wire.

Sibylle watched him settle on the floor to make a stool. "Why do you stay if you think so poorly of me?"

"To see what I can do with you."

"Do with me? I wouldn't take a million francs to touch you!"

"That is not what I mean. I mean this, how you live. If you are going to whore, do it because it gives you a chance to succeed."

"Better myself as a prostitute?" Sibylle had to laugh. "Live in luxury and retire to a chateau? Do you believe that?"

He shrugged, grinning. "Save your money, buy property, live off the rents."

"You don't understand," she said.

"Tell me what it is I do not understand."

"You're a man. You can never understand."

He began to speak, deliberated, and said, "Now I know how Pascale felt."

"If anyone's ignorant, it's you, thinking that a few nights or weeks with an American woman will lead to anything."

"Perhaps," he conceded, unruffled, and Sibylle was left without the satisfaction of hurting him.

He slept through the rest of the afternoon, waking in time to hear the American news on the radio. "That was Poland," he said, catching a word.

"Your government," she agreed.

"Not mine. The one in Poland is Russian-made and all traitors."

"We had Pétain." Sibylle turned to the French news. "He's on trial in Paris."

"I would not try him, I would shoot him." Witold put on his jacket. "I am going to see if Gilles wants loaders again tonight."

"Have something to eat first." She served him bread and cheese. "Tonight I have Marcel. He leaves after breakfast, so don't come back early."

Marcel was preceded by a man she had not had before. He smelled of beer, but was clean and wanted nothing nasty. He was happy with what she did, saying *bonsoir* as he tossed his money onto the blanket covering her. She douched and was dressed in time for Marcel. He liked the light on all night. After he fell asleep, she watched the moths swarm the naked bulb.

Marcel finished the last of her bread and coffee in the morning. She bathed and counted her money after he was gone. Witold did not return. She foraged at the back of the house and found two stiff burlap bags, went into the garden and filled them with grass, tearing up clumps until the creases of her hands were green. She put them in Witold's room as a mattress.

It was noon before he came home, grey with exhaustion. He filled the bucket and washed his face. Two fingers were bound with the handkerchief she had laundered for him. "I was nearly at the sea last night," he said. "We loaded stolen machine oil. Military."

"What happened to your hand?"

"Caught between two oil drums."

"You'll be in pieces if you stay with Gilles."

"I will not be there long. He dislikes me."

"He'll kill you."

"I will not let him." Witold saw the mattress in his room. "Thank you," he said, shutting the door.

Sibylle went to the shops, buying what she could afford for him: carrots, onions, a chicken, needles and thread to mend his torn shirt, a handful of coffee beans, bread. She hurried home, feeling strange to have a man to go home to, a good man.

Witold was at the back of the house with the radio turned loud when she let herself in.

"What are you doing?" she called.

"There are useful things back here. You could sell them. Garden tools, pots. I have found a bed frame hardly broken."

He emerged with a dented wheelbarrow full of salvage to sort while he drank coffee and listened to the talk of the American broadcasters.

"What is that?" he asked with every new program.

"This man's on every week," said Sibylle. "He tells funny stories about soldiers. There's a woman who's serious, but she hasn't been on since they dropped the bombs in Japan. This man is describing a game soldiers play. *Baseboll. Pitchur...bat....* I don't know the words."

Witold polished a heap of rusted bolts. "I will ask one of Gilles' men tonight where I can sell these."

Sibylle switched to the French news. No reports of a wounded Italian in their area or of a police hunt.

"Neither of you is important enough," said Sibylle, making supper.

He grinned as she chopped vegetables. "You said you did not cook."

"Anyone can boil a hen."

He parked the wheelbarrow outside the front door while she turned the dial back for the American music program. She tapped her feet where she sat. "This is what it was like when the Germans were here. Not this music, of course, but dancing and fun."

"You did not worry about the consequences to come after the war?"

"The war was over for us. I never thought the Germans would leave."

"You did not try to fight? Join the Resistance?"

"The Resistance! Now that the Germans are gone, every second man and his pigeon were part of the Resistance. Let me tell you: the brave citizens of Balmoigne didn't fight too hard."

"You really thought it was no different to fuck Germans?"

"Of course there was a difference. They paid better."

He smiled at her. "Are you so tough, Sibylle?"

"Yes." She stood defiantly. "Dance with me."

"I do not know how."

"Then give me your hand."

He did, and she used it as a launching post for high kicks and jitterbugging. "Aaron taught me," she said breathlessly, whirling her skirt around her hips. She spun toward him in the last crescendo, winding into his embrace, and would have come flat against him had he not barred her with his other arm.

"Can this soldier of yours be worth it?" Sibylle asked, her lips close to his ear.

"It is nothing to do with her."

Sibylle stepped back. "I disgust you."

"Not yourself. All those men—I could not follow so many men."

"I'm not giving up whoring to please you."

He turned down the radio. "I do not ask it, though you would get more money scrubbing floors."

"No one would let me into their precious house."

"Two hundred kilometers from Balmoigne, who will know you? Change your name and, if you want respectability, get a ring and call yourself a widow. Make yourself new."

"I can't." Sibylle paused. "Do you think I could?"

"Of course."

He left for work. She bathed and dressed. The evening was not busy. Michel came, then a man she had seen once before, then François. The chief of police, Yves Ponty, slipped through her door at midnight. He slapped her to arouse himself, crushed her breasts in his hands as he heaved inside her, and left her with a derisory scatter of copper coins. She cooled her face and breasts with cold water, thinking of Witold. Knowing that someone would be coming home to her made this less desolate.

Witold was back before dawn, sodden and shivering.

"Witold!" She leapt out of bed. "God, you're half drowned."

He peeled off his jacket. "I was pushed into the river."

"Why?"

"Gilles Roche no longer wants me working for him." Witold's feet parted from his boots with sucking sounds. "I spent all night shoveling fish guts from the bottom of his barge. He did not pay me."

"Why has he turned against you? You haven't been cheating him, have you?"

"No. He finds me intolerable."

"The nerve! He stinks like a hog."

"You will smell me, too. I fell into the fish guts I had shoveled into the river and my swim has not washed them off." A pool of water collected across the floor.

"I'll heat you a bath," said Sibylle. "You'll catch your death if you stay in those clothes."

"Wait, Sibylle," he said. "I have to tell you this first: I am a woman."

"What?"

Witold looked at her steadily. "I am a woman."

"Don't be crazy! What are you, a pervert? Do you want to be fucked by Gilles? That doesn't make you a woman. Is that what you're saying to me?"

"I am saying that before I strip for that bath, you should know that I am a woman. Female. My mother's second daughter."

"You're sick."

Witold skinned off his vest and flattened the wet shirt against his body.

"Lots of men have little breasts, even strong men." Sibylle backed away.

"I have all the other parts, too."

"Were you born that way?"

"Sibylle, listen to me! I am a woman disguised. A good disguise. I am not deformed or insane."

"But your soldier—but Pascale! You said—"

"That is true."

"She knows?"

"Of course."

"You lied to me!" Sibylle's voice soared to shrillness. "You said you were a man, but you're a pervert! A woman pervert! You made a fool of me. Get out. Get out!" She flew at Witold with flailing fists, trying to hurt her, to drive her from the house. Witold caught her wrists and would not let the blows land.

"Sibylle," she said.

"Don't," Sibylle sobbed, enraged. "Don't lay a finger on me." She tore free, ran through to the garden, blundered against the pear tree and clung to it, hysterical with shame and fury.

Played for a fool, laughed at, by a little Polish pervert, a girl queer, a pussy-licker. Sibylle tore the tree's bark with her nails. After all her hopes. She felt humiliated to the center of her bones.

After a while she sat down against the tree, gazing drearily at the house. She would never get away from it. None of it. She plucked grass stems. So much for her dream of a good man. That would teach her.

Time passed. It was too damp to be sitting here on the grass in her shift, but she could not, would not, go back into the house until that liar was gone. She heard water being poured. The bitch was bathing in her tub. Sibylle could wait her out.

Witold emerged wearing her greatcoat and carrying two cups of coffee. "Sibylle, you will be ill if you stay here."

"I want you out of my garden. Out of my house."

"Have your coffee." Witold squatted beside her. The aroma made Sibylle desperate, but she did not take the cup Witold set by her hand. Furious again, she spat, "How could you do this to me?"

"I have done nothing except keep myself safe."

"You used me."

"I paid you."

"You made a fool of me."

"How?"

"Letting me talk to you as if you were a man."

"This is the worst thing that has ever happened to you?" Witold raised a brow.

"You know what I mean."

Witold sipped her coffee.

"Where did you learn to be a pervert?" asked Sibylle. "From Pascale?"

"I am not a pervert."

"Yes you are. Putting your face down there. A woman doing that."

"What is wrong with that? You do it to men."

"It's more disgusting with women."

"Have you done it?"

"What do you think I am?"

"You have spent your life sucking men's cocks and letting them be stuck into you. You fucked men who tortured and killed your neighbors, and you say I am disgusting?"

Sibylle curled away from her. "I have my pride."

"Really? Where? You have been pitying yourself from the depth of your heart since I first met you."

"You're in no position to look down on me. At least I'm normal."

"What good has normal done for you?" Witold finished her coffee.

"I haven't sunk as low as I could go."

"Low compared to what? Do you take your measure from what people say? What do they say about you?"

Sibylle did not reply, resting her forehead against one raised knee. She felt like a glass cup that would shatter at Witold's next word. She looked at the torn grass where she had gathered stuffing for Witold's mattress and began to cry silent tears, blotting them on her shift.

Witold said her name softly.

"Oh no, no." Sibylle huddled into herself and wept. She was afraid that Witold would touch her, but as she emptied herself of emotion she longed for comfort. There was none. She wiped her face and looked around. Witold was watching bees forage in the blown flowers.

"You look so much like a man," said Sibylle.

"It is in how you hold your shoulders and head. My name is Bronia. Bron. I am not a man."

"No, you aren't. It's funny, when I look now I can see. I suppose people don't question the obvious."

"That is why it is easy."

"I wondered why you didn't have whiskers." Sibylle smiled wanly. "Do you enjoy being a pervert?"

"You should not use that word."

"Do you enjoy it, whatever you call it?"

"It is pleasant."

Sibylle gave a listless laugh. "Funny that we find each other degraded, isn't it."

"I do not think so of you."

"Should I get it over with? Do it and put it behind me?"

"Do what?"

"Fuck you, I suppose."

"Why would I want to do that?" asked Bron.

"I thought your kind were sex-mad."

"You believe everything told you?"

"So you don't want to."

"Not as part of your humiliation of yourself."

"I'm a useless whore. I can't even get a pervert to fuck me," said Sibylle. "I might as well get dressed."

Smiling faintly, Bron followed her inside.

Bron's clothes dripped from a drying line of copper wire. Sibylle found herself reluctant to take off her shift in front of her. She slid her day frock over it and sat on the bed to put on her shoes.

"Do you want me to get you a dress?" she asked her.

"What for?" asked Bron, startled.

"Well, because."

"I have to go to America. How far would I get in a dress? I would be incarcerated by well-meaning nuns or put in one of those United Nations camps. That is what happens to foreign women."

"Do you enjoy playing the man?"

"It has freedoms."

"Will you still take me with you when you leave Balmoigne?"

"Yes. To the coast if you want."

Sibylle watched Bron cut bread for breakfast. Bron looked the same as Witold. Sibylle was surprised to find the feelings inside herself the same as well. How could they be? Because Bron looked the way she always did? Was as she always was? Or because Sibylle herself had become strange? "Witold...Bron," she said tentatively, "I actually wouldn't mind if you kissed me."

"No?" The corner of Bron's mouth twitched.

"Not as self-humiliation. As a good thing."

"Oh, well, as a good thing." Bron put down the knife, walked over, and kissed her.

Sibylle was shocked. It was nice. Bron's mouth was softer than a man's but not disgusting at all. Bron started to move away. Sibylle put her arms around her neck. Bron kissed her again more intently, not crushing her mouth like men did, not forcing her tongue in like a slab of meat, but moving lightly, running the tip of her tongue across Sibylle's upper lip. Sibylle stiffened. Bron broke away.

"Don't stop," said Sibylle.

"I do not—"

"Please," said Sibylle.

Bron was unenthusiastic. "All those men. I would not—"

"I clean myself afterward, every time," said Sibylle, stabbed with hurt. "You think I'm soiled. Tainted. That's what you think."

Bron stood still, as if listening to something or someone inside her head. "No," she said slowly, "you are not."

"But you won't," said Sibylle.

"For you, yes. I will." Bron kissed her again.

Sibylle pulled Bron onto the bed. The weight of Bron's body made her feel as she had when a girl, when boys first touched her, when her body was still curious. They kissed for a long time. Bron's arms around her were nice. Sibylle did not know what to do next.

"Sibylle," said Bron, "what do you want?"

"I want..." Sibylle was unable to say it. Not to a woman.

Grinning, Bron stood up and took off her greatcoat.

"How can you fuck me when you're a girl?" Sibylle giggled, looking at her nakedness.

"Wait and see." Bron lay beside her and put a hand on her breast. Her fingers moved, and Sibylle caught her breath. Bron traced the seam of her frock from top to bottom. Sibylle pulled both frock and shift over her head. Bron put her hand on Sibylle once more, and now it was different. Bron kissed her mouth. Sibylle's head swam. Bron kissed her breasts, Bron kissed everywhere but one place. Was this all girl perverts did?

Then Bron did kiss her there, and Sibylle squeaked. This had never been done to her. Bron stayed there. The familiar sensations built inside her and Sibylle lay still, disappointed, until suddenly she was beyond what she had ever felt, was gripped by something sharp and shocking. Her breath panicked in her throat, she reached for something, anything, for assurance, found Bron's hands and grabbed them, holding hard as she fought against, longed for, what was coming, her eyes shut tight. It came at last, tearing through her, leaving her shuddering and drenched with sweat. Bron was beside her, holding her.

"Sibylle." Bron kissed her gently.

"I'm sorry," Sibylle breathed. "I'm sorry I said those things to you."

She could feel Bron's chuckle rumble in her chest.

"Why are you laughing at me?" she demanded.

"I am not laughing at you," said Bron.

"Do you love me?"

"I love Pascale."

"How can you fuck me when you love someone else?"

Bron's fingers slid along the curve of Sibylle's stomach. "It is because I do."

"You're crazy," said Sibylle.

"No, I am trying to be properly human."

"By fucking another woman?"

"What you need is important to me."

Sibylle blinked quickly. "More important than being faithful to Pascale?"

"Pascale would say that I am so. It is Pascale's rules that I obey. They are not like other people's. They are for people like us."

"Like us." Sibylle tasted the words. Had she become a pervert?

"Would you like to do it again?" asked Bron.

"Can we? So soon?"

"What stops us?" Bron's hand moved to her hip.

"I'd like to do it to you."

Bron hesitated. "There is no need."

"Don't you want me to?"

"I want...nothing that is pretended."

Sibylle's eyes stung with tears. "I know that. I won't treat you like a customer, I won't. I won't."

"I am sorry," said Bron. "I do not want to be—"

"Serviced?"

"I want it to be not work."

Sibylle pushed away. "It wouldn't be."

"I am sorry," said Bron.

"I haven't pretended with you. I won't ever."

"Okay," said Bron, but saw that she could not make it right.

Sibylle got up. "Do you want coffee?"

"I am sorry, Sibylle."

"Someone needs to buy bread. Where will you get money now?"

"I still have the money Gilles gave me two nights ago."

They ate breakfast in silence, Bron glancing at her, unsure and troubled. Sibylle went out to the shops.

Madame Perronet pursed her lips. "You're in hot water and no mistake this time, my girl."

"What have I done?"

"René, you know, René Nabeaux, one of Gilles' stevedores, tells me your man warned Gilles away from you."

"My—he did?"

"It's the talk of the river," said Madame Perronet. "I'd keep my head down if I were you. No one's given Gilles Roche ultimatums since the Boche left."

The baker, in his turn, gave her a curious look, as if to one not long on earth. Sibylle hurried home, her heart hammering her chest. Bron was not in the house, though her clothes were still on the line. Sibylle dropped her bundles on the table. Bron was not in either of the back rooms. Sibylle found her asleep under the pear tree, wrapped in a blanket.

"Bron." Sibylle knelt. "Bron."

Bron blinked awake. Sibylle shrugged off her clothes without thought and lay down, relishing the way her sweat-sticky skin met Bron's. She kissed her and made love to her.

At first Bron was quiet. Sibylle felt unsure, clumsy. Bron put a hand on her hair and Sibylle was encouraged. In a minute Bron hissed in reaction and, as Sibylle put her mouth on her, began to pant lightly and tremble in her arms. How strange this was, how easy. She could feel Bron tense, then gather and come with a quick lurch and groan. Sibylle looked up in the silence. "Are you all right?"

"Of course," Bron answered sleepily.

Sibylle lay close to her. This was what it was supposed to be. Bron kissed her and fell asleep again. Sibylle stayed, feeling Bron's breath warm against her skin.

Bron woke when the sun was low. "It is cold."

"I don't want to go inside," said Sibylle.

"If you stay here, the snails will make love to you."

"I wonder how that would feel?"

"Slimy," said Bron.

"I heard in town that you told Gilles not to come here. Is that why he threw you in the water?"

"I told him I would kill him."

"How could you do that? He's twice your height. He has a gun and knives and knows what to do with them."

"He is a brainless thug. I have killed smarter than him."

"This isn't a joke!"

"You think I would let someone like that touch you?"

"Oh, Bron!" Sibylle clenched her hands together. "He really will kill you, and me as well."

"So he said in front of his men. On his own he will be less bold."

"How can you be this stupid?"

"I had a little fight with one of his men on my first night," Bron confessed. "Gilles knows I am good with a knife."

"You had a fight. A 'little fight'. Bron, you're a woman."

"Should that stop me?" Bron got up and wrapped the blanket around herself like a toga. "Perhaps my clothes are dry."

The French radio announcer was summarizing the day's proceedings in the Pétain trial when Sibylle's first customer knocked. Sibylle jumped, slopping her coffee. She looked at Bron and shook her head. "Not tonight," Bron called through the door. The man grunted and went away.

"You have no lamp?" Bron asked her.

"They knock and speak," said Sibylle. "If I don't answer, they wait or leave."

"If you are going to keep whoring, a lamp would be better."

"I don't want to!" Sibylle burst out, surprising herself with her vehemence. "I don't like it!"

"Then stop," said Bron.

"How will we eat?"

"I will look after you."

"How can you look after me when you can't get work?"

"I will steal," said Bron. "We perverts have to take care of each other."

Other men came. Bron answered them. Leon argued that it was his usual night, shouting angrily over Bron's head to Sibylle, but backed off when he saw Bron's knife.

Sibylle smiled tremulously as Bron bolted the door. "I'm finished in Balmoigne."

They went to bed and made love. In the morning Sibylle woke to find Bron sitting cross-legged on the bed, looking at her.

"What's the matter?"

"You are nice to look at," said Bron.

"I'm no beauty."

"You have a good face." Bron's finger brushed her cheek, then her breasts. "This must not happen again."

Sibylle looked down at the bruises Yves had left. "With Chief Ponty's compliments."

"Let no one hurt you like this again, man or woman," said Bron. "Not even the chief of police."

Sibylle snuggled against her. Bron slid a slow hand down her back, making her press closer. They made love as the day became hot, growing slick with sweat. Afterward, Sibylle cooled herself with a wet rag.

"If Pascale won't have you, will you come back to me?" she asked.

"I will be in America."

"A long way to go for a gamble," said Sibylle.

"It is not a gamble to me."

"How can you be certain?"

"Because I am certain."

"I'll never be loved like that," said Sibylle. "I'm not a nice person."

"Yes you are," said Bron, surprised.

"Not as nice as you."

"If that is true, it is not my doing. Fear made me wild and horrible like a beast. Pascale brought me back."

"Not wild? Then why were you cut across the belly when I met you?" Sibylle traced the long red line.

"The Italian held a broken bottle to my neck. I had to attack him first."

"Just how a tamed beast acts." Sibylle kissed her. "Let's get out of Balmoigne before Gilles kills you."

"As soon as I find better clothes for you. And a coat. We will also need food."

"I'd rather be out of Balmoigne than have a new frock."

Bron shook her head, got dressed, and went out. Sibylle bathed and brushed her matted hair. It was not as short as she had thought. Perhaps she would be all right in a new town. She ran her hands down her own naked body. Those things Bron had said in the night about being lovely and beautiful might be true.

Bron returned at midday with two fish wrapped in leaves.

"Where did you steal those?" asked Sibylle.

"From the river, with a bent pin." She slapped them into the frying pan. "I have heard that the harbors of Normandy are full of Americans. Armies mean jobs. I will teach you to make change, as I did in my father's tavern. You could be a waitress. A shop assistant."

"Where will I get a wedding ring?"

Bron grinned. "Everything is for sale on the black market. I will buy you one."

The day grew hotter. They stripped and sat listening to the radio, playing at arousing each other until they were in earnest. The heat made Sibylle's desire almost suffocating. Bron rose afterward for water to trickle down her body.

"Last summer," said Sibylle, as Bron's cold wet hands stroked her legs, "I was hiding from the bombs. It was hot, but we didn't dare leave the cellar, not for days. The three of us nearly went crazy with waiting. It was a relief when the Germans retreated. Clothilde went with them. She came back later. Monette took up with Gilles. I met Aaron. I thought I'd be safe, but he left."

"You should rely on no one."

"Not men, anyway," said Sibylle.

In the cooler evening, Sibylle mended Bron's vest, then took the blanket from the bed and cut it into squares with the kitchen knife. She began sewing the pieces together into a satchel. Bron's mouth twitched as she watched her.

"I know I'm no needlewoman," said Sibylle defensively.

"It will take you weeks to finish. I thought you were anxious to leave."

"I am, but not without luggage. I won't get work if I'm carrying a bundle like a beggar."

Her customers came again that night.

"I've heard about you," Edouard said to Bron. "You can't keep her to yourself forever."

"Then stop me," Bron challenged.

"She isn't worth it." Edouard spat on the threshold and left.

Sibylle flinched.

"You care what he thinks?" Bron asked her.

"I suppose not."

"Suppose not! You should not care at all. He is filth."

Sibylle's laugh was ragged. "That's what they say about me."

Bron crossed the room and kissed her roughly. "This is what is true. You remember it."

The next day was as hot. They listened to the European Forces station announcing an air attack on Tokyo.

"Won't be long now," said Sibylle.

"Perhaps the Americans will then attack the Communists," said Bron.

"Why do you hate Communists?" said Sibylle.

"Because they are liars and cruel. They force their victims to agree that their punishments are just. Communists love to degrade."

"Capitalists don't?" asked Sibylle angrily. "We had American soldiers throwing cigarettes and chewing gum to us from their trucks as if we were zoo animals."

"At least you were not tortured," said Bron. "Or killed. The Americans will go away from France. The Russians will never leave Poland."

Sibylle sighed. "We ought to get a better world after all this."

"Not if men like Gilles are still living in it," said Bron.

The next morning, Bron interrupted Sibylle's sewing by taking her out to the cool grass. Sibylle let Bron make love to her, knowing that the smell of grass would remind her always of these days, of Bron. Then her mind was riveted onto what Bron was doing and thought ceased.

Afterward, nibbling Bron's neck, Sibylle said, "You don't seem in a rush to go to America."

Bron's arm tightened beneath her. "I am." Her voice was iron. "But I have responsibilities here."

That night, once the few customers had been sent away, Bron left. Sibylle woke in the morning to find her asleep on the bed, fully clothed. It was ridiculous and unsettling. Bron looked too much like a boy. She ought to undress before coming to bed. Sibylle rose and shook open the bundle on the table.

Bron's thieving had gained a linen frock, cotton stockings, a pair of women's shoes, a bottle of wine, a coil of sausages, two cabbages, and a dozen carrots, damp from the earth. A tin of paté clattered from their midst.

"Does it fit?" asked Bron, yawning.

Sibylle held the linen frock against herself. "It's beautiful. The woman who owned it will miss it."

"Whoever lived in that house can afford another. You would not suspect shortages exist."

"Those sort didn't suffer during the war either." Sibylle looked at the shoes. "The chief of police is known for beating his prisoners. Don't let him catch you."

"I will not be caught," said Bron.

Sibylle finished the first of the blanket-cloth satchels and started another. Bron made cabbage soup.

"What will you do when you find Pascale?" Sibylle asked. "Will you live with her?"

"If she wants me to."

"If she doesn't?"

"I will stay as close to her as she permits."

"How will you get money?"

"Women work in America, too. I will find something."

"Will you like wearing dresses again?"

Bron chopped carrots. "How can I say? The last time I wore one I was seventeen. I know I will not wear a corset."

Sibylle laughed. "You, in a girdle?"

Bron grinned. "I cannot wear trousers and tie all my life."

"Send me a photograph," said Sibylle.

"I will not know where you are."

Sibylle bent over her sewing. "It's strange to think that one day we'll never see each other again."

"I hope I will remember you somewhere that is not Balmoigne," said Bron.

Sibylle imagined herself in a shop, a clothes shop, say, or a milliner's. She could dress smartly then, rent a room, perhaps share with another woman. They would have parties, go to bars, stay at home to listen to the radio. She wondered how it would feel to live without men. Perhaps always as nice as this.

Bron did not go out thieving that night. They lay on the bed and let the night breeze cool their bodies. Bron's hand rested lightly on Sibylle's side. Sibylle could smell her own sweat, the scent of her body and Bron's, and smiled. The aftermath of sex was almost as delicious as sex itself. Right now, she could imagine never bathing again.

"This is the best thing I've ever had," she said.

"Hmm," said Bron.

"Don't you think so?"

"It is nice," said Bron. "Very nice. I am glad to do it."

"But you think it'll be better with her."

Bron muttered something in Polish and did not look at her. Sibylle realized that Bron was afraid. She could say nothing to reassure her; what did she know of this beyond Bron?

The announcer on the French station told them of Pétain's sentence the next afternoon.

"Death," Sibylle repeated. "Good. He said surrender was the best thing for France. He said collaboration was the wisest course. Look where it got me."

"You did not have to listen to him," said Bron. "Why did your family not stop you?"

"My father left us long before the war. After the Germans came, my mother took my brother and went to live with her own family south in Orléans. She disowned me."

"Will you try to find her?"

"No," Sibylle said rigidly. "I won't forgive her."

Bron said nothing.

"You think I should," Sibylle accused.

"Would good come of it?"

Sibylle sneered at herself. "I could tell her I've given up men. She'd like that even less."

Bron went to buy bread with the last of their money, waiting until the end of the day when loaves sold cheaply. Sibylle wandered into the last evening light of the garden to see if the Clicards' pears were ripe. She shook the branches to see if any would fall. One did, and as she bit into it church bells began to ring. She dropped it, startled. A few minutes later she heard a burst of radio and Bron's voice shouting, "What do they say? *Victoire? La fin de la guerre?"*

The announcer was detailing the terms of surrender.

"Japan?" asked Bron.

"Yes," said Sibylle. "All the war is over."

They decided to open the stolen bottle of wine to celebrate. Bron sipped cautiously, saying, "The last time I drank alcohol I had a surprise: a woman came to my bed."

"I'll drink to that sort of surprise." Sibylle raised her glass.

She had most of the bottle and decided to dance to the victory music. Bron straddled a chair and held out both hands as Sibylle swirled around her.

"I could teach you," Sibylle said breathlessly.

Bron shook her head.

"Then let's go to bed."

"That's what all the citizens of Balmoigne will be doing tonight," said Bron. "A good time for me to hunt."

Sibylle could not sleep after Bron had left. She sat on the bed with the rest of the wine, sipping and dozing, not thinking what the police, what Yves Ponty, would do to a Polish girl thief.

In the early morning, just as it was light, someone pounded on her door. Sibylle woke with a lurch, heart racing.

"Sibylle, let me in! Sibylle, you're in there! You're there with your Polish pimp. I know! Send him away, Sibylle, I have things I want to do. Sibylle!"

Gilles was jerking the door. He would break the latch. Sibylle slid off the bed, wine bottle in hand, and stumbled to the hallway. She could not push the corrugated iron away from the exit hole without Gilles hearing it. He was bellowing and kicking the door. She felt her way in the darkness to a rubble-filled enclosure that had been the scullery and crouched beneath its fallen roof timbers. Gilles was shouting what he would do to her, all those things no other prostitute would let him do. She shivered.

"Sibylle! I'm losing my patience, Sibylle!"

The corrugated iron scratched across brick. One of Gilles' men, sent around the back to stop her escape. She heard a clank, his boots in the hallway, the front door slam open.

"You little bastard," said Gilles, then grunted.

Sibylle shrank into the corner of the room. She tried to silence her terror against her sleeve, but the wine had slackened her self-possession and she whimpered as she heard scuffling footsteps.

Silence. Were they waiting for her? She strained to hear breathing. The front door creaked on its hinges. She got to her feet, wanting to get it over with, and edged into the hallway. She stumbled over a sack. The front door was open and the room was empty. She stepped outside. Wet darkness was spattered across the threshold and door and was pooling in the dust of the road. The wheelbarrow was gone. She could see the line of its wheel up the road and off into the trees. She closed the door and went to the latrine to be sick.

Bron came back three hours later, filthy, her face stiff as wood.

"Bron! Thank God! Thank God." Sibylle came to her but dared not touch her. "What did you do?"

"I need to sleep."

Bron stripped and, despite the heat, wrapped herself in the blanket from her room. She lay on the bed and closed her eyes. Sibylle sat without moving until she was asleep, then gathered her clothes. Bron's boots and trousers were sodden with water. They smelled of the river. Her jacket and vest were matted with dirt and oil and blood. Sibylle quietly ran water and heated it while she emptied Bron's pockets. Here was Bron's fishing line. A tin-opener with its handles sawn off to fit her pocket. Bron's knife, a German army one, well-rinsed. She washed Bron's clothes and hung them on the pear tree, then spent the day sewing the second satchel. It was restful to know that she would never see Gilles again.

She was simmering the duck from Bron's sack of loot when Bron woke.

"Are you all right?" Bron asked her.

Sibylle turned. "You ask *me* that?"

Bron sat and rubbed her head with the heels of her hands. "You found the duck."

"And the wallet and the hat and the candlesticks."

"Those last we can sell on the road."

"And the tins of goose. The police will be going from house to house to find you."

"If a crime is not known, who will look?"

"I'm not talking about these tins and things," said Sibylle.

"Who would miss them?"

"Bron—" Sibylle tried again.

"I want a bath. Where are my clothes?"

"Bron, I—"

"My boots?"

"Drying." Sibylle gave up. "I'll fill you a bath."

Sibylle went to the shops the next day with the coins from the stolen wallet, mostly to hear Madame Perronet's gossip. Madame was eager to discuss the commutation of Pétain's sentence. "It would have been shameful to execute that old man. He tried to do his best, poor fool. The Nazis duped him."

"How nice if every fool escaped punishment," said Sibylle.

Madame Perronet hesitated, then said, "There's to be a victory celebration tomorrow in the town square." Seeing Sibylle's surprise, she continued, "We're finished with the war. My cousin in the south tells me the grape harvest will be the best in decades. It's a new world. Time to forget the old. You should come tomorrow, bring your man. Let him enjoy himself before Gilles returns."

"Is Gilles away?" Sibylle asked cautiously.

"So I hear. When he gets back, your man should pack his bag. Gilles has sworn to kill him."

"That's not easy to do," said Sibylle.

Madame Perronet was unable to resist a smile. "Even Chief Ponty interviews Gilles with a pistol in his pocket. I'd say you should dance with your man while you can."

"I will," said Sibylle.

Bron was listening to the European Forces station with a scowl of frustration as Sibylle came in, saying to her, "How can I learn when they talk so fast? I hear only the words I know."

Sibylle told her about the town's victory party.

"Who will be there?" asked Bron.

"Everyone from the mayor to the river men," said Sibylle. "You're not going hunting, are you?"

Bron shook her head. "The police know that houses will be empty."

"Do you want to go to the party?" asked Sibylle.

"Do you?"

"I told Madame Perronet I would, but I can't. I'll be attacked."

"We could find a safe place to sit."

"Beside the priest?" said Sibylle scornfully. "In the middle of the Sisters of Ste. Clare? Why do you want to go?"

"The end of the war is not good reason enough?" asked Bron.

The next evening Sibylle dressed in her skirt and blouse, and hid her short hair under her new hat. Bron put on her tie. They walked along the darkening streets, hearing music and voices echo off the buildings. The main square in front of the church was filled with long sheet-draped tables, each decorated with tricolor rosettes. The memorial to the Great War was garlanded with flowers.

Sibylle balked at the crowds. "I can't."

"You can," said Bron, taking her hand.

Sibylle heard a man say, "It's the German-fucker," as she passed, and women hissed, but Bron persisted until they were in front of Father Pierre.

"Good evening," said Bron, taking off her cap.

Father Pierre looked from her to Sibylle in consternation until Bron's expectant smile forced him to mutter, "Good evening. Please sit down."

Bron moved along the table until she found two spaces beside a woman Sibylle recognized as Father Pierre's housekeeper.

"We can't," Sibylle whispered.

"The priest has given us permission. It is too late for anyone to object."

Sibylle took a chair. Bron perched on a piano stool beside her. Sibylle saw several men hurry to Father Pierre, glaring in her direction. The priest shrugged. No one approached her. She relaxed in spite of Madame Fourner's rigid presence.

The band played, the mayor and every other eminent citizen made a speech, Father Pierre prayed and blessed them, blessed the town of Balmoigne, glorious France, and the Allies. They stood to sing the Marseillaise. Sibylle found herself crying. She took Bron's hand. Perhaps she did not have to leave Balmoigne. Perhaps she was forgiven.

After the speeches, the supper, and after the supper, dancing. A police officer came up behind Sibylle and said softly, "Chief Ponty tells me not to spoil the festivities, but if you make one wrong move, I'll arrest you faster than lightning, you little piece of shit."

Sibylle said nothing.

"I don't want to see you enjoying yourself." He moved on.

Bron held Sibylle in her seat. "Do not run away. I want you to know you faced them."

"What's the point?" Sibylle's voice grated.

"It will be important to you later."

Wretched with humiliation and fear, Sibylle stayed in her chair, pretending to watch the dancing. No one spoke to her. Nothing happened, and after a while she eased and began listening to the band's songs. What a pity Bron did not dance. They could defy that pig of a policeman, dare him to arrest them for celebrating peace.

Sibylle looked at the couples bobbing across the cobbles, at the mayor and Yves Ponty chatting to each other at the head table, at the moths floating like confetti among the lights. She remembered the Nazi banners that had hung from the town hall and the police station, the armored machine-gun truck that permanently guarded the square. She wondered how she could have been so stupid, so unthinking. It had not occurred to her to help her neighbors or to spy on the Germans for the Resistance. No wonder Balmoigne did not want her.

The celebration ended at midnight. Father Pierre called on the revellers to join him at mass.

"Go to church," said Bron.

"To church? I'm not a believer, I'm a communist."

"Go anyway."

"Are you going?"

"No. I have other business. I want you in a safe place."

Sibylle grabbed her sleeve. "What are you going to do?"

"Get you into church," said Bron.

Sibylle joined the crowd. She sat alone in a pew, the townspeople passing as they saw her. She was silent through the responses, her mind's eye on Bron somewhere in the darkness of town, and remained on her knees as the mass ended, not praying, but concentrating as if she could keep Bron alive. An hour later she realized that only she and two others were left in the church. She stayed, not knowing what else to do. It was cold. She sat and looked around, remembering when she had come here as a girl with her mother, glad to escape her drunken father, enjoying the church's dark peace.

She was almost asleep when a shuffle made her look around. Bron was there, edgily alert, eyes darting around the nave.

"Home," Bron whispered.

Sibylle touched her hand. "I thought I might never see you again."

Bron's mouth tightened. "Now we go home."

Even so late, people were still celebrating in the street, laughing and talking over record music, their doors open, or giggling and panting in the shadows. Bron was as feral as a wild dog, watching everything. Sibylle was recognized and cursed by drunken men. At last they were down the hill. Sibylle locked the door and sagged against it. "Tell me what you've done."

Bron shook her head.

"Why won't you tell me? I know you haven't been stealing."

"I am tired." Bron shrugged off her jacket.

"Show me your knife."

"It is gone."

"It's in someone, isn't it?" said Sibylle.

They lay in bed without touching. Sibylle listened to Bron's ragged breathing slow to sleep and wondered if anyone could change forever. Bron had said Pascale had tamed her, but that was not true. Would Sibylle one day find herself looking at a man again, taking his money? Or would what Bron had done for her always stop her?

The next morning she worked on the second satchel. In the afternoon, three police officers hammered on the door and hustled them into a black van.

"Bron..." Sibylle whispered as the van lurched up the hill.

"Say nothing. Nothing."

They were unloaded at the police station and taken to a small, dirty room. Bron's face was expressionless. Sibylle sat on the single bench, her hands clenched around the half-finished satchel she had inadvertently brought. Two police officers came in.

"Sit down," said the older officer to Bron, ignoring Sibylle, who was quickly translating. "We want to know where you were last night around midnight."

"I was in town celebrating," said Bron. "Then at church."

"You weren't at mass."

"I do not go to church drunk. After I was sick, I went."

"When was that?"

"After I had finished a bottle of cherry brandy."

"We know you worked for Gilles Roche."

"A few days. When I found out he was a black marketeer, I quit."

"That's not what we're told," said the older officer.

Bron shrugged. "Who told you? That gossip box René Nabeaux?"

"We want to know what you saw last night."

"I saw the town, I saw wine, I saw someone's pocket being picked—which you did not see. I was sick all over my boots, and I went to church sorry for my sins."

"You're a smart one," said the younger police officer, looking up from his notebook. "You weren't at the river?"

"No," said Bron. "What was at the river?"

"The chief of police's been murdered. Gilles Roche has disappeared. We think Roche attacked him; Captain Ponty was killed with a German weapon."

"A sad end," said Bron.

"But Roche's men say that Gilles has been gone for days."

"Then he could not have killed your boss," said Bron.

"Maybe you did," said the older officer.

"From all of Roche's gang, why choose me? Because I am foreign?"

"We haven't eliminated anyone from our inquiries."

"Look at my size. Could I kill an ox like Chief Ponty?"

"Stand up," the older officer told her. "Reach as high as you can."

Bron did. The younger police officer whispered to his colleague, shaking his head. They both rose.

"We want you to stay in Balmoigne for a few days," the older officer told them, glancing at the satchel Sibylle was clutching. "We might have more questions."

"I want to go to the coast to find work," said Bron.

"Later. When you do, take her with you," said the older officer, jerking his head at Sibylle as they left.

Sibylle and Bron sat side by side. Hours passed. They said nothing to each other. Sibylle endured by wrapping herself in old, familiar sullenness. A young officer finally put his head around the door and said, "You, you're released."

Bron led her through the evening light, the empty town, past the fancy shops and big houses. Sibylle hated every brick, every cobblestone, every tree to her house.

She went to the standpipe to wash police stink from her hands and face. She was angry to see her hands shaking. "Why did you do it?" she demanded. "You could have been guillotined, and me as your accomplice. Gilles! Yves! They weren't the worst the world's ever seen. Why?"

"They were the worst for you."

The plop of water into the bucket was loud in the room. Sibylle said, "If you did that for me, what would you do for Pascale?"

"Anything," said Bron.

Forced to stay in town by police decree, they spent days in the garden and evenings by the radio. Bron insisted on listening to the European Forces station, with Sibylle patiently translating. Bron went on a raid Monday night and returned with a wristwatch and a fish pie.

"We still have the money in that wallet," said Sibylle. "You don't need to steal someone's lunch, especially with the police keeping an eye on you."

"The best time to steal is when the police think they have you," said Bron. "That money you must keep for your rent and clothes."

Sibylle spent the day hemming the linen dress. "I'll travel in this," she said. "I'll look more respectable."

Bron laughed. "How respectable can you be tramping the side of the road?"

The voice on the European Forces radio was pleased to announce the return of their usual evening program, broadcast live to New York and the whole of the United States: *The View from Paris.*

"Oh, I like her," said Sibylle as the deep voice of a woman began. Sibylle translated for Bron. "She's talking about refugees this week."

"Before I speak of the less lucky ones, the ones in camps, the ones sheltering in bombed ruins, the ones barely existing, let me ask Witold Rukowicz, if he is listening, to come to Paris, where..."

Sibylle looked at Bron, who was frozen in her chair.

The voice continued, *"...is waiting for him. Witold Rukowicz, please make contact. I hope you find her—"*

"What?" asked Bron hoarsely. "What does she say?"

"Pascale's here!" said Sibylle. "Pascale's in France!"

Bron was on her feet. "We go now."

"Tomorrow morning," said Sibylle. "Pascale won't disappear overnight. We have to tell the police, and we'll be faster in daytime."

Bron was putting on her jacket as if Sibylle had not spoken. She stopped. "You are right," she said slowly, pulling it off. "Tomorrow."

"So you're taking me to Paris!" Sibylle tried to rally her. "Plenty of work for me there."

"Yes," said Bron. "How did that woman get my name?"

"Pascale will have been trying to find you, too. Now she has. She must be smart. I hope I'll meet her."

"Pascale!" Bron hugged her ribs and howled. "*Pascale!*"

Sibylle looked at her compassionately, suspecting that Bron would be useless from now on. Sibylle would have to do all the planning, navigating, and stealing that had to be done on the way. It would be sensible to take the kitchen knife.

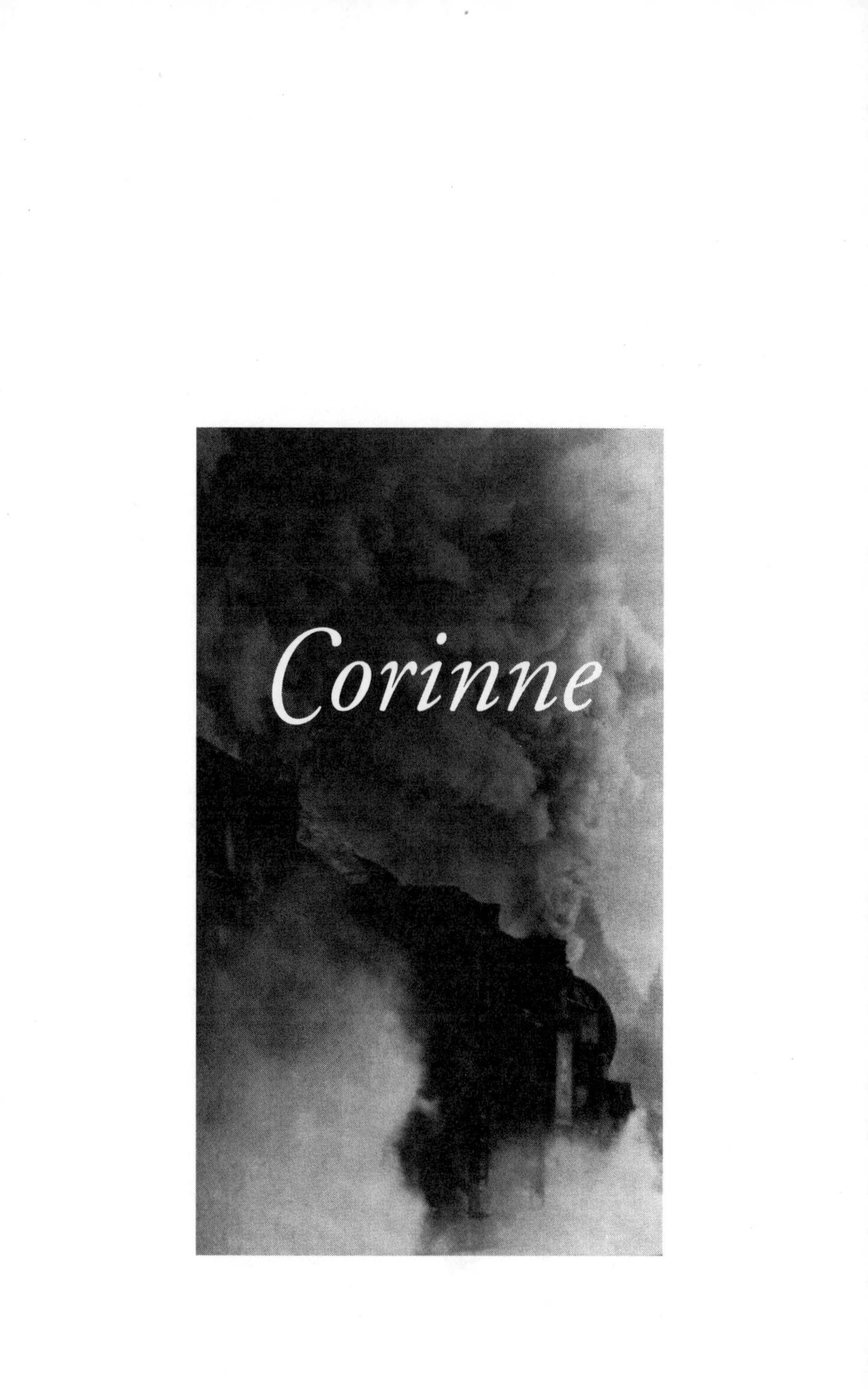
Corinne

"Ma'am," Sergeant Montellesi said over the internal telephone, "wonder if you can help with a problem we got downstairs."

"Certainly, Sergeant," said Corinne. "What is it?"

"Two young persons, Ma'am. They're asking for Pascale Tailland."

"Private Tailland? Who are they?"

"Little French girl, Ma'am, and a boy. Polish boy, I think."

"Oh God." Corinne put down her pen.

"You know 'em, Ma'am?"

"I think so. What appalling timing."

"Usually I call Captain Bassett, Ma'am, but he's not in, and as it's about one of the Wacs I thought maybe you could come down, especially since you speak the lingo."

"Fortune smiles on your choice, Sergeant," said Corinne. "I'll come at once."

Sergeant Montellesi was holding the door of the waiting room for her. "Right through there, Ma'am. You call if you need me."

Two dirty faces turned to her as she entered, a young woman in a badly fitting dress and a young man with an army greatcoat tied over one shoulder like a bedroll. They had shabby cloth bags at their feet. The boy stood up.

"How do you do," Corinne said to them both in French. "I'm afraid Private Tailland isn't here. Can I be of help?"

The boy looked at the girl, who said, "Madame, we have been told that. Where is she?"

"Who are you?" asked Corinne.

"My name is Sibylle Benard. I am a friend of...ah...his, Witold Rukowicz."

The boy took off his cap and bowed to her.

"So you're Witold," said Corinne. "How interesting to meet you."

He nodded at his name, but looked at Sibylle.

"He speaks no French?" Corinne asked her.

"A little, madame. But please—Mademoiselle Tailland?"

Corinne sat and looked at Witold. This little tow-headed tough was the one Pascale was hunting heaven and earth for? How could Nell Tulliver have wasted her time on that woman? Corinne had not wanted to believe it of Pascale, yet here he was, hot, dusty, unprepossessing, watching her with desperate patience.

"I'm sorry to have to tell you," she said slowly, "that Pascale left Paris two days ago."

Sibylle groaned and translated. Witold's face became stark.

"Madame," Sibylle nearly cried, "we came as fast as we could."

Witold wet his lips and said in French, "Madame, where?"

"Her regiment was ordered home to the States. They left Paris on Thursday. Her ship sailed this morning."

Witold sat down. After a minute he pulled himself erect and said to Sibylle in an amalgam of French and German, "I still have my first plan."

"I'm so sorry," Corinne said again. "Did you hear your name on the radio?"

They nodded.

"You should go to Miss Tulliver, the woman whose program it was. I suppose she'll be glad to see you."

"We've nowhere else to try," said Sibylle.

"Madame," said Witold, "Pascale, you know her?"

"Slightly."

"Her idea, the radio?"

"I don't think so. Miss Tulliver did it for her. When Pascale heard it she was full of hope. A week later she received her notification." Corinne waited while Sibylle conveyed this to Witold. He nodded and Corinne continued, "Miss Tulliver will know what to do. I'll see if I can take you to her."

Sibylle translated and Witold said, "Okay."

Corinne could not help smiling. "Okay? I see you're in training to be a Yankee."

He caught her meaning and grinned back. Corinne had to admit that, smiling, he had a certain limited appeal.

"I must get permission from my commanding officer," said Corinne. "Please wait here until I return." She ordered Sergeant Montellesi to give them water and to summon a staff car while she sought Major Schultz.

The major waved a hand at her. "Of course, Corinne. Don't forget to tell the public relations boys. After that broadcast, we don't want this story slipping through our fingers."

"Yes, Ma'am." Corinne saluted and telephoned TBC, who told her that Nell Tulliver was at the Reuss building. She loaded her two charges into the waiting staff car.

Sibylle looked around the interior with interest. "I've never been in a car as big as this. Are all American cars as big?"

"Yes," said Corinne, amused.

Witold asked, "Pascale, she knows Madame Tulliver?"

"Extremely well," Corinne answered dryly.

"To put my name in radio, this was good."

"For you, if not for her," said Corinne.

At the Reuss building, Corinne told the driver to wait, then ushered her charges into the vestibule, where she had Nell Tulliver summoned.

Nell rocketed down the stairs, her eyes on them.

"Lord in his heaven," she said, unhesitatingly going to Witold. "I don't have to guess. Witold Rukowicz."

He nodded at his name.

Nell looked at him for a full minute, her hooded eyes opaque. Witold held her gaze.

"I suppose so," said Nell at last. "Do you speak English?"

"A few words," said Corinne.

Nell focused on her. "Captain West? How are you involved in this?"

"They came to headquarters. Fortunately, I was the one asked to deal with them."

"Damn lucky. Who's the dolly?"

"That I can't say. She came with him."

"Him," Nell repeated. "I wonder what's going on here."

"I dread to surmise," said Corinne.

Nell grinned. "Ours is not to reason why. Does, uh, he know that Pascale's gone?"

"He was discomposed when I told him, but apparently has another plan to locate her."

"Like a goddamn homing pigeon. These waifs don't look like they've booked rooms at the Crillon. They'd better come to my place."

"How's your French?" asked Corinne.

"Lousy."

"Sibylle"—Corinne paused to introduce Sibylle to Nell—"Sibylle translates for Witold in an outlandish mix of French, German, and English, but she doesn't have enough English to talk to you. I'd better come along as interpreter. I've a car waiting."

Nell smiled at her appreciatively. "You're organized, aren't you, Captain West?"

"I pride myself on it, Miss Tulliver."

The driver shut her novel as they climbed in. Nell banged her shin on Witold's bag.

"What the hell's in that?" she demanded as Witold moved it, saying, "Excooz me."

"My radio," said Sibylle.

"Radio! Why are they hiking around a radio?" asked Nell.

Corinne consulted. "Apparently they have all Sibylle's worldly possessions in these bags. The radio was a gift from Aaron."

"That explains it." Nell lit a cigarette and offered one to Corinne. "Looks like I'm going to have to deal with her, too."

"What are you going to do with him?" asked Corinne.

"Pascale and I discussed this possibility as soon as she knew she was shipping out. I said I'd try and get him to the States as a staff member of the *Baltimore Morning Mail* or TBC."

Caught by Pascale's name, Witold's attention riveted on Nell.

"Kind of cute, ain't he?" asked Nell caustically. "Like a faithful terrier. I sure as hell wish I spoke Polish. I need to talk to him."

Polski, said Witold, pulling a stained, battered Polish-English dictionary from his pocket.

"Resourceful little bastard," said Nell, taking it. She looked up various words and wrote them in her notebook, then tore out the page and gave it to him. He puzzled for a few minutes, then asked Nell, "You are as Pascale? *Gleich?* Same? Her also?" He gestured to Corinne.

Nell said, "Yes."

He laughed delightedly. "Yez!"

They stopped under the flags of the Hôtel Scribe. Corinne ordered the car back to headquarters, to the driver's disappointment. Nell led them upstairs, pausing to bang on a door which was opened by a woman wearing a rubber pinafore stained with chemicals. "Drina, this is Witold Rukowicz."

"Holy smoke," said Drina. "It worked."

"And this is Captain West. Corinne, Adriana Scott."

The two women shook hands. Nell continued, "Witold's brought a friend with him. The girl is Sibylle Benard. They've got to be cleaned up before I feed them. Can you take her in hand?"

"For an exclusive, I'll scrub her back myself," said Drina. "Shall I deliver her in, oh, an hour?"

"Please," said Nell.

Corinne explained to Sibylle, who nodded and patted Witold's shoulder before going into Drina's room.

Nell showed Witold a bathroom, pointed him in, and gestured upstairs, saying, "*Ma chambre, aprés.*" Corinne snagged a passing chambermaid for towels. Witold locked the door behind him.

"Want a drink?" Nell asked.

"Love one."

Corinne looked around as Nell opened the room's single window. Here was the typewriter on which Nell wrote her stories. Those were her notebooks. Nell waved her to the stuffed easy chair, taking the wooden one herself. She poured two tumblers of whiskey, tapped out cigarettes, lit Corinne's, then sat back, crossing her outstretched legs—good legs, Corinne noted—and shook her head.

"I can't believe it. I can't believe he actually exists. I can't believe he missed her by forty-eight hours."

"What's your plan?" asked Corinne.

"Keep him out of sight."

"He can't stay here. This hotel's full of journalists."

"Don't I know it," Nell grunted. "I'll take him off the premises, feed him, stash him at, oh, the Club Sevastopol, then sneak him back after the parties here are over."

"I doubt Witold would be welcome at the Sevastopol," said Corinne severely.

Nell cawed a laugh. "Oh, hell, why am I keeping up appearances? I thought you might have guessed that Witold's a girl."

"Jesus Christ."

Nell's eyes glinted. "One of the Chicago, Denver, and Pacific Railroad West clan swearing?"

"Miss Tulliver, this is a blaspheming matter."

"I feel that way myself."

Corinne swallowed a slug of whiskey. "I owe Pascale an apology. I thought she was having it both ways."

"Not Pascale."

"I didn't like the idea of you being involved with that sort of woman."

"I didn't know you were paying attention."

"I was, rather," said Corinne, maintaining her sang-froid. "Now I understand why you were so steadfastly on Witold's trail. May I ask—or is it none of my business—why?"

"Why I was hunting Witold when I was dating Pascale?" The corner of Nell's mouth turned down in self-mockery. "Let's say I made a promise before I realized the cost."

"Now that Witold's found, must you do more?"

"What do you think?"

"How much self-immolation do you owe Pascale?" Corinne said into her drink.

"It's not like that. I'd be churlish not to finish what I started."

"I don't see how you can help him...her. Even if you get your newspaper or TBC to hire her, there'll be a medical somewhere along the way."

"Maybe not, if I can get my pal Rosie back in New York to pull strings."

"Thanks to your broadcast," said Corinne, "the Great American Unwashed are acutely interested in Witold and Pascale. The WAC office has been deluged with telegrams. If those two ever get together, surely reporters are bound to stalk them, and then their secret will be out."

"TBC'll sweat blood to prevent it," Nell grinned. "They and I are going to be locked in one hell of a Mexican stand-off."

"While you're putting your career at risk, those two will be living happily ever after?"

"That's up to them." Nell fetched her bathrobe. "Witold will be freezing to death: the system only manages an inch of hot water a day."

She came back with Witold's clothes, followed by Witold wrapped in the bathrobe. Witold paused when she saw Corinne.

"*Vraiment lesbischen?*" she asked cautiously.

"Yes," said Nell. "*Ja. Oui.*"

"*Beaucoup lesbischen Americaine,*" Witold grinned, sitting cross-legged on the bed.

"Each to her own," said Corinne.

Nell's mouth twitched. "Not your type?"

"I'm not drawn to Modern Primitive."

"Can you communicate with her?"

"My German is laughable," said Corinne, but a knock on the door took the task from her.

"Hello!" Drina came in. "One French girl, clean and presentable." She laughed as she saw Witold watching them interestedly, head tipped. "I can't wait to find out his story."

"You'll get it," said Nell. "But keep it under your hat for now."

"I'm going nowhere but that wee rubber looney bin called a portable darkroom," said Drina. "I'm incommunicado for the next few hours."

"Thanks for helping, Drina," said Nell.

"*Por nada.*"

Sibylle, wearing a clean dress of Drina's, sat beside Witold.

"Captain West," said Nell, "I'd appreciate it if you'd get her to explain my plan for Witold."

Corinne did. Witold said something that made Sibylle laugh disbelievingly. Sibylle turned to Corinne. "Are you really both women who fuck women?"

"I wouldn't have put it quite so delightfully directly," said Corinne, "but yes, we are."

"Are you two lovers of each other?"

"Regrettably, no."

"Bron and I were, but not now."

"Who's Bron?"

Sibylle put her hand on Witold's knee, saying, "Introduce yourself properly."

Witold stood and bowed. "Bronia Rukowicz, mesdames."

"Bronia," Nell repeated. "I liked Witold better. Does she understand how I hope to send her to the States?"

"You understand," Corinne said to Bron, "that this is for you, not your friend Sibylle?"

Sibylle explained herself at length. Corinne could feel Nell gather her patience like a cloak. When Sibylle had finished, Corinne turned to Nell. "Sibylle hopes you'll get Bron to America quickly, but she herself has no interest in emigrating. She likes the look of Paris. She was a prostitute in a town called Balmoigne, near Rennes I believe. Bron happened to meet her. The details are obscure. Sibylle took her in, they became lovers, and it was from the radio in this very bag that they heard your plea." Corinne lit a new cigarette. "Far be it from me to cast the slightest cloud over Pascale and Bron's romance, but Sibylle rather complicates the purity of the narrative."

"No more than I did," said Nell.

"I can't say I find it delectable," said Corinne, "but I'm the old-fashioned sort who demands reasonable fidelity."

"Nothing that either Pascale or Bron does with someone else is very real to them," said Nell. "Not compared to what they are for each other. We're moonlight to their sunlight, mere reflections of the greater glory."

"Ah, True Love! How appealingly it trivializes everything except itself," said Corinne.

Nell smiled. "Tell Sibylle that I'll make sure she's taken care of."

Corinne, having no intention of permitting Nell this further burden, said to Sibylle in French too rapid for Nell to follow, "I'm a rich woman, Sibylle. I'll give you money to help you live in Paris. Do you want a job? What can you do?"

"I haven't been a prostitute for weeks," said Sibylle. "I'd prefer other things. Why would you give me money?"

"Because that's what we sort of women do for each other."

"It's very nice," said Sibylle.

"Do you mind Bron leaving you?"

Sibylle shrugged. "She always was. I'm not in love with her, madame. I like her. This passion Bron and Pascale have for each other is strange, isn't it?"

"Passing strange," said Corinne. "I'm eager to reunite them."

"Does she understand?" asked Nell.

"Yes," said Corinne. "It occurs to me that I could telegraph Pascale aboard ship about Bron's arrival."

"First thing in the morning," Nell agreed. "All deliberate speed. You'll have to consult your officers, and these two look like they could use a night's rest."

"Where will they sleep?" asked Corinne.

"Right here, I guess," said Nell. "I can get cots or something sent up."

"Let me arrange it; that way your colleagues won't smell a rat. I'll also find them decent clothing. It will take me a few hours," said Corinne, and went downstairs to the hotel manager's office to leave a large deposit for silence and a room.

She took a taxi to the Ritz. The manager, Claude Ausiello, was somehow waiting for her. "Captain West." He bowed slightly. "I am happy to see you again. How may I help you?"

"I have a rather strange request, Claude," she replied, explaining what she needed.

"This presents no problem, Captain. It will take me but a little time."

"Thank you. I'll have a cocktail."

He had her escorted to the bar, where Georges mixed her usual martini. A few men raised their eyebrows, but no one approached her.

She stirred her cocktail as she thought. Drinking in uniform was against regulations, but so was the whole situation. This was the sort of vulgar romp she intensely disliked, yet here she was, having agreed to set up a whore in Paris, planning to assist an illegal alien to enter the United States. Buffoonery, and for what? The possibility that a certain woman might look at her once the damage had scarred over.

Less than an hour later, Claude delivered a large paper parcel. Corinne took a taxi back to the Hôtel Scribe, where she found Sibylle and Bron poring over a pocket atlas of the United States.

"I'm showing them where Boston is," said Nell.

"Are they enlightened?"

"Lord knows. Bron finds it fascinating."

Claude had surpassed Corinne's expectations. From her descriptions and estimates of size he had assembled lingerie, a puff-sleeved frock in dark green, a short-waisted jacket of the same color, hose, shoes, a hat, and a handbag. Sibylle exclaimed and stripped off without hesitation. While she dressed, Corinne gave Bron a young man's sports jacket, shirt, tie, underwear, trousers, socks, and a pair of black brogues. Claude had had the imagination to include combs, toothbrushes and handkerchiefs. The man was a master. Corinne looked forward to receiving her bill.

"These clothes are yours to keep," she told Sibylle and Bron.

"You're a genius," said Nell.

"Organized and rich," Corinne replied. She saw Bron standing anxiously, holding her clothes, and suggested to Nell, "Shall we step outside?"

Waiting on the landing for Bron to dress, they smoked while looking down the light-well to the floors below.

"This place was a zoo last summer," said Nell. "Reporters were perched on every window ledge around here, typewriters on their laps, pounding away like maniacs."

"I heard that Hemingway was here."

"He visited the bar. This hotel was a bit rugged for Ernie. He preferred the Ritz."

Sibylle and Bron joined them after a few minutes, both in their new clothes, with Bron looking, to Corinne, unpalatably masculine.

"I know a rather good and discreet restaurant," Corinne said to Nell. "I don't think we'll find any of your news fraternity there."

It was clear from Bron's and Sibylle's entranced bashfulness that they had never seen such opulence as that of the Place de la Madeleine. Corinne felt sure that Bron had never been in a restaurant before. The head waiter greeted Corinne by name and led them to a secluded table. Corinne ordered simple meals for the two young women, not wanting to overwhelm them. When Bron's and Sibylle's broth was set beside Corinne's sweetbreads in truffle sauce, Bron's look of unjudgmental amusement made Corinne both squirm and revise her opinion of her.

"If these two spend the whole night in my room being sick, I'll blame you," said Nell as wine was poured.

"They'll be two floors below you, number fourteen."

"What, Jerry's old room? He went back to Minneapolis weeks ago. Couldn't wait to get home."

"Are you looking forward to returning?" asked Corinne.

"I'm not going back. *Storace's* has asked me to stay on as their European correspondent."

"That's wonderful!" said Corinne. "You'll be based in Paris?"

"Yes. Don't get me wrong, I love the States, but I'd rather be here right now. There's still plenty going on. I want to write more about displaced persons and to see how much of a yes-man outfit this United Nations will turn out to be, not to mention finding out what the Russians will do with their half of Europe."

"I'll be staying in Paris myself once I'm discharged in December," said Corinne. "I have an apartment in the Montparnasse."

The waiter took their plates. New cutlery was laid.

"More?" asked Bron in wonder.

"Tell her that this is how Americans live all the time," said Nell.

"I'll do nothing of the sort," said Corinne, explaining courses to the younger women.

"It was places of this sort that Gilles supplied," Bron said to Sibylle.

"Who's Gilles?" Corinne asked.

"A man Bron killed for me," said Sibylle sunnily.

Corinne blinked. She hoped that Pascale could convince Bron that hostilities were over. Nell raised an eyebrow, wanting to know what had been said, but Corinne shook her head and resumed the earlier conversation by asking her, "You were in Paris before the war, weren't you?"

"Yes, I spent a lot of time here, though you wouldn't know it by my French. I was also in England, mostly catching ships."

"I was in Paris from '35."

"Yes, I remember. I didn't hang out with your crowd. I recall a tidbit about an Italian countess."

"A mistake," said Corinne. "She was limpetlike in her clinging power, but ultimately unpersuasive."

Nell tasted the Chateau Léoville-Poyferré and said, "I could get used to this."

"If you're staying in Paris, perhaps you will."

After their meal they went to the Pigalle, Sibylle and Bron silent in the taxi, glazed with excess.

"Do you think you should take Bron to the club?" asked Corinne. "What happens if someone gossips to reporters?"

"At the risk of exposing themselves?" Nell shook her head. "Pascale's the only woman I've known who truly didn't care who knew."

Ahmoud, the doorman, barred the way, despite Corinne's explanations, until Blanche emerged from behind the bar.

"Hold open your coat," said Corinne.

Bron did so, but leapt back, fists clenched, as Blanche placed expert hands on her.

"Yes," said Blanche. "Come in, mademoiselles."

Bron firmly buttoned her coat as they entered. Corinne had explained the nature of the Club Sevastopol in the car, and Sibylle looked around with frank interest. There were hostile comments until Blanche announced, "Mademoiselles, do not trouble yourselves. I have myself ascertained that this person is female."

Corinne smiled to herself as half the room looked at Bron speculatively, the other half measuringly. It would have been no different in the drawing rooms on the Rive Gauche.

They sat in a booth and ordered drinks. Sibylle and Bron, mur-

muring between themselves, darted glances at the women in the room, Bron earnest and Sibylle considering.

"They look like they're hatching a plot," said Nell.

"Bron's suggesting that Sibylle might meet someone here who could look after her," Corinne explained.

Nell laughed. "Not a doubt. She's young and pretty enough. I might have picked her up myself twenty years ago."

"Is she your type?"

"At that age, anything was my type."

"Now?"

"How about you?" asked Nell. "The Club Sevastopol isn't your usual stomping ground. Do you go to the salons?"

Corinne accepted the diversion. "I go where I can meet the women I want to meet."

"This isn't where they're found."

"Perhaps you think I check a woman's name on the social register before I condescend to have a drink with her."

"Or perhaps I could pick myself up by the collar and throw myself out for being a jackass."

"Or we could simply forget it," Corinne smiled.

Blanche cranked the record player and put on Duke Ellington.

"Now *that's* music," said Nell, holding out her hand. "Let's dance."

Corinne took it, and they swung onto the dance floor. She looked up into Nell's face—she seldom had to look up to any woman—and thought, *I could get used to this.*

Madame Grevaniski emerged from her private room. She pointed a finger at Bron and asked in her deepest voice, "Is this a man I see?"

"No, Madame," said Nell. "Her name is Bronia. She's Polish and has escaped to Paris in disguise."

"Aha? Ha!" Madame waddled to the table, arms outstretched. "Another victim of the Bolsheviks! My poppet, you are welcome here."

Sibylle translated in a terrified hiss. Madame snatched Bron into her arms and planted kisses on both cheeks.

"If we don't rescue Bron, she'll be in Madame's boudoir being force-fed Turkish Delight before you can say Rimsky-Korsakov," whispered Nell.

"Leave this to me," said Corinne, and advanced. "Madame Grevaniski, I see you have much in common with my special friend."

"Special?" Madame's small eyes swivelled to her. "Friend? Am I intruding? The friend is not this so-charming French one beside her?"

"No, I myself have that pleasure."

"Then you, too, are welcome here. Also this famous one," said Madame, with a stately nod to Nell. She ordered brandy for the party of this brave *émigré* before returning to her room.

"Is she lonely?" asked Corinne, watching the elderly woman close the door behind her.

"With Blanche?" Nell took Madame's vacated place. "I don't think so."

A tough-looking young woman at the bar, having listened without a qualm, crossed and said to Sibylle, "I'm Toni. If you're not with her, let's you and me dance."

Sibylle looked at Corinne, who stood to let her pass.

"That didn't take long," said Nell.

"It won't come to anything," Corinne prophesied. "That creature is more interested in out-doing Bron than having Sibylle."

"She's not the only one."

"You could have cut Bron out had you chosen."

Nell shook her head. "Not a chance."

"Pascale was simply using you," said Corinne hotly.

"Of course she was," said Nell, "but not in the way you mean. She didn't exchange favors for my help. If anything, I used her."

"Nonsense!"

"No, she said it and she was right: I wanted to live a romance."

"You've no need to be more romantic than you are," said Corinne.

"Don't kid yourself that a reporter is any kind of hero."

"I'm not talking about your work."

"Let's finish that dance," said Nell.

They danced for most of the evening. Sibylle had several partners, the hard-boiled Toni more than once, but also an older French woman with cropped hair and a Canadian WAAF.

"What about Bron?" Corinne asked Sibylle at one point.

"She doesn't dance," said Sibylle. "Can't."

"Too bad," said Nell. "Pascale's a great dancer." She paused, surprised. "Kind of like you, Captain."

"In the circumstances," Corinne suggested, "shall we proceed to first names?"

They returned to their table at last. Bron was asleep, her head cradled on her arms.

"I suppose they've been tramping since dawn," said Nell. "Let's fetch Party Girl and go home." In the taxi, she said to Corinne, "I'm grateful for everything you've done today."

"It's been interesting," said Corinne, smiling at her in the dark, but Nell's eyes were on Bron asleep against Sibylle's shoulder.

Corinne was at headquarters early the next morning to make telephone calls before her day's work began. She rang a friend in the WAVES who was coming off night duty. Julia gave her the number she needed. She reached a young man with a Texas twang who promised to ring back with the information.

Corinne looked through the papers in her tray while she waited. Her mother had wept when Corinne had joined the WAC, wondering why a daughter of Vernon West had chosen to become a clerical worker. Even the life—her mother had faltered—the life Corinne had been living in Paris was preferable to army service. Corinne could not now imagine returning to that life. She had acquired a taste for being useful. Her plans after the service would not please her mother at all.

The telephone rang. "Captain West, ma'am? About the telegram? The regiment you asked me to look up is scheduled to board the USS *Gordon Cray* tomorrow morning."

Corinne began to write. "Excuse me? Scheduled?"

"Yes, Ma'am. Engine fault's kept the *Gordon Cray* and the *John Wrigley* in Le Havre. They'll be loading personnel from 0700 hours tomorrow morning."

"Good God," said Corinne. "Thank you, Sergeant."

She drummed her fingers on the receiver, her mind racing like a tabulating machine, then went to Major Schultz and outlined her plans.

"Have you spoken to the public relations office yet?" asked the major.

"Not yet."

"Do it now, but stay on top of this. I don't want them dictating WAC press coverage."

Corinne saluted and went to Jack Smith in public relations, who said, "Holy cow!" and leapt to the telephone.

"Contact Captain Landis in Le Havre," he told her as he waited for a connection. "He'll roll out the red carpet. Press?"

Corinne said, "Nell Tulliver from TBC, of course. And a photographer from, I believe, the Griffin Photo Agency."

"Good. Have Greg Landis phone me when you've briefed him."

Corinne went back to her office and made more calls. Sergeant Montellesi had a staff car waiting. It dropped her at her usual garage, where she hired a Renault touring car. She stopped at several shops near the garage, then re-crossed the river to the Hôtel Scribe. In less than an hour after talking with the Texan she was knocking on Nell's door.

"Who the—" Nell appeared, slinging on her dressing gown, a cigarette in her mouth. "What's up?"

Corinne walked in. "Pascale's at Le Havre."

"The hell you say."

"Her ship was delayed. She sails tomorrow morning."

"Hell and lightning! There is a God. We'd better make plans."

"I've a car waiting. The army public relations office has been notified. We can be at the coast by midday."

Nell squinted at her through cigarette smoke. "You're frightening. Let me get dressed and we'll fetch the young'uns. What else?"

"It's your story," said Corinne. "The PRO will help you in any way they can."

"I bet." Nell scrambled for clothes and began pulling off her pajamas.

"I'll rouse Bron and Sibylle," said Corinne, leaving quickly, not wanting to try her own powers of endurance.

Sibylle answered the door, hung over. Bron was already up and dressed, standing at the window looking at Paris. Sibylle called out the news and Bron turned as if lashed. "Pascale here? Here?"

"We're going to her," said Corinne. "My car awaits."

Bron put her ammunition boots and greatcoat in her bag and

said, "I am ready."

"The simple life," Corinne murmured. "Sibylle, will you come with us?"

"Until we find Pascale, who else can talk to Bron?"

Corinne met Nell on the landing.

"I promised Drina," said Nell, knocking on her door.

Drina opened it crossly. "Keep it down! Andy's been awake half the night."

"Pascale's still in France," said Nell. "We're leaving for Le Havre as soon as you climb into your girdle."

"Don't move until I'm with you," Drina warned, shutting the door.

Nell took a handful of *jetons* from her pocket. "I've got phone calls to make."

Bron followed her to the foyer, expecting to get into a car, and looked murderous as Nell settled into one of the phone cubicles.

Drina emerged with two cameras and cases of film and flash-bulbs. She saw Bron pacing and said, "Get that boy out of sight! The mob will be down for breakfast any minute and I'll lose my scoop."

Corinne loaded everyone into the back of the car while Nell was telephoning. Bron drummed her fists on her knees.

"This is going to be a fun trip," said Drina, eyeing her.

Nell got in the front. "Let's start the parade."

Corinne opened the throttle almost before her door was shut.

When they were in the suburbs, Corinne said to the three in the back, "That basket holds pastries and flasks of coffee. I didn't have time for more."

Nell grinned at her.

"Maps are in the pocket beside you," Corinne replied. "One of them is Top Secret. I beseech you to look at nothing but the route, then forget you saw it."

"Forget that we must be running on black market gas, too," said Nell. "At least it won't be *my* stripes."

They were clear of Paris. Corinne put down the accelerator and they flew past villages and open fields, the first leaves of autumn tossing in their wake. Traffic thickened as they drove north, army trucks and half-tracks condensing into a single mass toward Le Havre.

"How is sh...he doing?" Corinne asked. "How's our lad?"

"He'd be a rocket if he could," said Drina. "He's burning more energy sitting still than I use in a month."

"Tell him," Corinne's eyes dropped to the map across Nell's knees, "tell him we've at least three hours to go." To Nell she said more quietly, "We have a problem to sort out."

"Shoot."

"The army will want a happy ending to this story, and they won't have it with...," she hesitated, conscious of Drina, "...with Witold left on the pier waving good-bye. The army will take charge of him, perhaps with a view to a final reunion in Boston. We can't let them get their hands on him."

"Damn right," Nell agreed. "Why do I suspect you've figured an angle?"

"It would be best if no one, especially no one in authority, is given time for second thoughts. Let's rush our fences, get Witold on board the *Gordon Cray* with Pascale, and tidy loose ends later."

"How will we do that?" asked Nell.

"They'll have to marry."

Nell choked on cigarette smoke.

"Yes!" cried Drina, overhearing. "It's perfect. A wedding on the quay, makeshift veil—great pictures! A Wac and her...what's the opposite of a war bride? War groom?"

"We can't!" Nell was scandalized. "It would be—" She boggled. "It can't be done."

"Don't be a spoilsport," said Drina. "It's a great idea! If a padre won't do it, one of the officers can, or maybe the captain of the ship. Don't you think the public relations office will love it?"

"Troop ships don't like taking civilians," said Nell desperately.

"They loathe taking women, too, but the *Gordon Cray* will already be up to its gunwales in Wacs," said Corinne. "One civilian man won't add to the horror."

Nell looked beseechingly at her. "Are you out of your skull, Captain goddamn West? What happens when, you know, cat and bag and the whole shebang? We won't be able to control it."

"Witold survived the war," said Corinne. "I think he'll cope.

Pascale will protect him on board ship, and you can have one of your cohorts waiting in New York to make sure he's rushed off without the usual formalities."

Bron demanded something angrily.

"What are you talking about?" Sibylle asked for her.

"We're discussing what we'll do when we arrive," said Corinne over her shoulder. "Witold can't go with Pascale on her ship unless he marries her."

Sibylle gasped, sputtered, and burst out laughing. "Oh, no! No, madame! You won't get away with it!"

"The army PRO is a powerful organization," said Corinne. "It can be done."

"Pascale will kill me for engineering this," said Nell, appalled.

"If Pascale has a better idea, I'll be delighted to listen," said Corinne.

"We'd better tell Witold," said Nell.

Sibylle, when Corinne suggested this, said, "Don't. Don't say anything unless you can make it happen. To get Witold's hopes up and then fail would be cruel."

"Good thinking," said Drina. "Him not knowing will make the reunion that much more natural."

"Very well," said Corinne.

Bron was waiting for an answer. Sibylle told her, "We're trying to think of the best thing to do when we reach Le Havre."

Bron nodded and went back to watching the fields blur and pass, her fists thrust into her pockets.

Late in the morning they reached Rouen. Corinne stopped at a hotel.

"No!" Bron ordered. "Go!"

"I need rest, and we need to eat," said Corinne.

Bron's face turned mutinous as she listened to Sibylle translate. "*Tak to jest jezeli muśis polegać na innych,*" she growled.

"What's that?" asked Nell.

"I don't know," said Sibylle, "but I think we should be quick."

Bron's silence strained them all. Corinne found herself gulping her coffee. In less than half an hour they were on their way again.

Pressure for space in Le Havre compacted the traffic at twenty kilometers distance. Corinne could no longer weave her way through the trucks. They had a glimpse of sea, but it was an hour before they reached the outskirts of town. Corinne rolled down her window and asked directions from the military police. They directed her off the main route to the harbor. She threaded through the town to the WAC's temporary station.

"Everyone stay here," Corinne said as she parked. "Let Army deal with Army."

She had the guard summon an officer from Pascale's unit. A stocky woman came to meet her.

"Lieutenant Francine Bergman," the officer saluted. "How can I help you, Captain?"

"I believe you know why I'm here," said Corinne, stripping off her driving gloves.

"I don't, Ma'am."

Corinne blinked. "You haven't been told? I think Army's trying to keep this from WAC."

"Wouldn't be the first time they've done that, Ma'am," said Lieutenant Bergman.

"We won't let them get away with it," Corinne smiled. "I'm trying to locate a Private Pascale Tailland."

The lieutenant's eyes flicked over her. "Private Tailland and the others are on liberty this afternoon. They've gone to the old harbor. May I ask what this is regarding?"

"Witold Rukowicz."

A muscle bulged along the lieutenant's jaw. "We'd better talk privately."

"I agree," said Corinne, following her into an office. "From your reaction, I surmise that you're the lieutenant who wrote to Fontaine's commandant."

"How did you know that?"

"I heard the whole story last night. Am I correct?"

"I'm sorry to say you are, Ma'am," said Lieutenant Bergman. "I don't suppose you got a cigarette on you."

Corinne proffered her pack. "Witold—Bronia—is outside in my car. You know about Nell Tulliver's broadcast?"

"Do I ever," said Lieutenant Bergman. "The girls in her unit went dippy at the thought of the great Nell Tulliver trying to find Witold for her. Made my blood run cold."

"Nell Tulliver is also in the car, and Drina Scott, a press photographer. I'm going to try to have Bron sail with Pascale tomorrow."

"That's not possible, Captain."

"It might be," said Corinne, and explained her plan.

After a silence, Lieutenant Bergman said, "You're all crazy." She worked on her cigarette. "Let me tell you, Captain. I was part of the first intake into what was then the WAAC. I was one of the first commissioned officers. If they keep the WAC going, I want to be in it. I love the army. I'm not going to do anything to jeopardize that, not even for one of us. There are too many complications and it's going to blow up in your faces. It's illegal. It's nuts."

"Would you intervene if it were arranged?" asked Corinne.

"I'd have to."

A commotion in the hall brought a harried corporal to the door. "Lieutenant, you'd better come."

Bron, followed by Nell, Drina, and Sibylle, was storming down the hall, issuing demands in Polish and trying to repeat herself in German and French. She recognized Lieutenant Bergman and stopped in front of her. "Pascale," she commanded.

"I wish this wasn't happening," said the lieutenant, retreating before Bron's ferocity. She turned to Corinne. "Captain, I'm going to my office and I'm staying there for the rest of the day. You don't need my permission for anything. Captain Thorsby's the one in charge. Her office is upstairs. If she asks, I never heard a word of this cockamamie plan."

"Thank you, Lieutenant," said Corinne to her disappearing back.

Drina was puzzled. "You'd think Pascale's lieutenant would want to get in on this."

"I don't think she approves of Witold." Corinne turned to Bron. "Pascale is somewhere in town."

"Come," said Bron, tugging her toward the car.

The town was crowded with soldiers who, undiscouraged by the overcast sky, were taking their last wander in Europe before heading home. There were far too many Wacs for Corinne's comfort. Each time a party of them was sighted, Drina's or Sibylle's squeak would have her braking. Each time they were disappointed.

The fishing fleet, crowded into one corner of the harbor, looked like miniatures beneath the towering tankers, freighters, and troop carriers of the Allied navies. Corinne kept the car at a crawl along the old quayside. Here, sightseers formed a solid stream.

Nell herself was beginning to be agitated. "There! Not her, there— is that? No."

They inched forward.

"We'll have to split into hunting parties," said Corinne.

Clusters of soldiers, nurses, and Wacs were strolling along the narrow piers. From one group, just setting forth, a woman turned as if called, turned and looked at the car.

Bron was out, running. Corinne slammed the brake.

"Too damn far." Drina struggled with her camera.

Nell got out of the car. Corinne went to her side.

The woman, Pascale, watched Bron run down the steps and along the pier. She held out her arms. Corinne heard Nell make a noise of pain beside her. Bron slowed, reached out, took Pascale's hands. Corinne wondered how much it would cost to have this scene obliterated from Nell's memory. Pascale kissed Bron. Sibylle sighed sentimentally. Nell shifted and looked down. Drina was making her way to the two women as Pascale's friends began to realize that something was happening.

"We don't need to be here," said Corinne. "And we have work to do. Nell, can you help me?"

"Sure, of course," said Nell.

Corinne put her hand on Nell's arm to turn her away and kept it there as they walked up the road.

Pascale

10

Pascale turned in the middle of one of Binty's jokes as if someone had called her name. She saw a large black car on the road. A door opened, a young man leapt out. It was Witold.

In the seconds it took Witold to run down the steps to the pier, Pascale's vision darkened and focused until Witold was the only thing she could see. She did not know she had raised her hands until Witold was bending to them. She gazed down at her with a strange illuminating pain. Witold straightened. The pain was joy. They looked at each other. Pascale asked, "What is your name?"

"Bronia Wladka Czelanczowski. Bron."

"Bron." The name fit, made for Pascale's mouth. "Bronia."

"Pascale Tailland." Bron's voice cracked; she lowered her forehead to Pascale's shoulder.

Pascale put a sheltering hand on her hair. Time wrapped around them. Finally Bron stirred. Pascale cupped her face and kissed her.

The shock of it stopped all sound, all light; all sensation disappeared but Bron's lips on hers. Now every action would have this as its context. Now the world had its center.

People, noise, slowly intruded upon them. Someone was taking photographs. Binty, Dot, and Marie were crowding round. Pascale glanced up to the road and saw Nell hurrying away with a WAC officer.

"What's happening?" she asked at large, then in Polish, "Bron, what's happening?"

"I found your friends in Paris. They brought me to you."

"You nearly missed me."

"I know."

Binty was saying, "I can't believe it! It's like a fairy tale come true. Wait till the others find out about this!"

"Can you two kids look over here?" the photographer called.

Pascale flinched as a bulb flashed, making Bron step between her and the camera.

"Now what's going to happen?" Marie complained. "Are we going to have to hide him again?"

"Don't be ridiculous," said Dot. "This is front page news."

"Gud afternoon," Bron said to them all. "We go, okay?"

"It talks," said Marie.

Taking Pascale's hand, Bron said, "Come," and led her to the black car.

Marie and the others followed, the throng of staring soldiers and sailors letting them through. A young woman by the car watched with friendly curiosity as Bron and Pascale approached.

"Pascale," said Bron, "this is my friend Sibylle Benard. She helped me. Sibylle, this is Pascale Tailland."

Pascale looked at the French girl and knew. She held out a hand to her and said, "Thank you for helping Bron. Thank you for making her happy."

"Not as you will," Sibylle smiled.

Nell came back with the WAC officer.

"Captain West." Pascale frowned, perplexed. "You're involved in this? Nell, what's—"

"Shall we save the briefing for a more private place?" said Corinne. "I've telephoned HQ and they're waiting for us."

"Why?"

"Trust your friends," said Bron, and Pascale allowed herself to be shepherded into the car.

"Hi, I'm Drina Scott." The photographer shook Pascale's hand as she got in beside them. "Are these girls part of your unit?" Binty, Dot, and Marie were squeezing inside.

"Drina Scott!" said Marie, awestruck. "How do you do? I'm Marie O'Dowd, one of Pascale's closest friends. May I introduce you to the others?"

"We've got tongues," said Dot.

The car moved off, Corinne at the wheel. Pascale sat within the flurry of introductions, looking down at her hand in Bron's, desperately wanting everyone to be gone. Bron turned her head to brush her lips against Pascale's hair. The car, the crowd, faded. Only Bron was real.

At army headquarters, Binty and Dot formed an honor guard around Pascale and Bron as they were taken down corridors to an empty room. Corinne came in, swept out everyone but Pascale, Bron, and Nell, then turned to Pascale. "You must realize that things have become complicated."

"With you, the army, and the press involved? I have," said Pascale. "How did you find Witold?"

"Bron," Corinne corrected. "Yes, I know her name. I know the entire story, but Nell's photographer friend doesn't, nor does anyone else. You can see Bron's still in disguise. As for finding her, she found us, thanks to Nell's radio appeal."

"When and how are we going to break the news to everyone about Bron being Bron?" asked Pascale. "Particularly in light of that broadcast? I'll get you into trouble, Nell."

Hearing Nell's name, Bron said, "I have not thanked this friend for saying my name on the radio. Please tell her."

"I will," said Pascale. "It's the most wonderful thing anyone has done for me."

"Her need is to do all that she is able."

Pascale controlled a flare of anguish. Bron touched her hand, but said, "You must accept what she does for you. It is her right." She sat back. "Now listen to your other friend," and Pascale realized that Corinne was waiting for her.

"I'm sorry," she said, and to Nell, "I'm sorry."

Corinne looked at her austerely. "Pascale, you should know that arrangements are being made on your behalf. You don't have to assent to them, but you have only this time here and now to decide."

Pascale's heart paused. "What arrangements?"

"We're hoping to have you married."

Pascale jerked as if touched by ice. "Married? To whom?"

"To Bron, of course."

"Bron! How can I marry Bron?"

"If Bron stays Witold."

Eyes on Pascale's face, Bron asked, "What does she say?"

"Marry legally?" Pascale stared at Corinne. "Or rather, illegally? Commit a—a complete fraud, a lie?" She looked at Nell. "You're part of this?"

Nell's mouth twisted. "It's the only way. You know I was hoping to get Bron to the States as an employee, but now that the army's got the bit between its teeth I don't have that choice."

"Does Bron know about this plan?"

"Not yet," said Corinne.

"Pascale," Bron said patiently.

Pascale put a quick hand to her cheek. "Let me learn more." She turned back to Corinne. "This is absurd. Why would we do this, even if we could?"

"It should be clear to you why," said Corinne astringently. "As to how, that requires nerve and wit, which I assume you and Bron can summon between you."

"We can't possibly carry off such an imposture."

"The public relations machine is already in gear," said Corinne. "Once rolling, it crushes everything in its path. Right now it wants a happy ending to this story—a story, I must remind you, that you started. If you disappoint them, prepare for a long separation from Bron. If you tell them the truth, prepare to shake hands forever."

"Marriage isn't possible," said Pascale. "Bron won't get through the medical examination."

"Do you think the PRO will allow anything to upset their exclusive? Bron could be phosphorescent with germs and they'd still proceed," said Corinne. "They're sorting a double cabin for you on the *Gordon Cray* even as we speak."

"It's not the—not just the tests," said Pascale, trying to gather her shrilling thoughts. "It's not just the problem of being caught—or even the marriage ceremony. It's the marriage. Marriage. Don't you see? If the army and U.S. immigration accept Bron as my husband, then my husband she'll be forced to stay. Always. To everyone, to my family and friends. To the world. If we're not found out, it will be because Bron and I will be lying all the time, for the rest of our lives."

"Pascale—" Nell began.

Pascale hardly heard her. "Where could we go? There'll be nowhere on earth to live honestly. The press will be watching us for months—years. If anyone finds out, it's over. We'll be taken away from each other. What will the fear of that do to us? How can we live with that? And we will be caught. How can we not be caught? Eventually?"

"What's your other choice?" asked Corinne. "It's beyond Nell's control now even if she could suppress the story. You should have anticipated what would happen when you first involved her."

"How could she?" Nell cut in quickly. "Even I never imagined for a second that it would turn out like this." She turned to Pascale, grey. "Not like this."

Pascale steadied herself. "Beloved Nell. You once told me I should wait until this moment to tell you that I owe my happiness to you. To thank you. I do thank you, Nell, no matter what happens."

"Keep a civil tongue in your head," said Nell with a ghastly attempt at a grin. "My dearest, I'm sorry it's become this tragicomedy. I'd do anything to rewrite the script."

"Never be sorry," Pascale said fiercely. "You've given me my heart's desire."

Nell turned away, a hand over her mouth. Corinne made a small throat-clearing noise to draw back Pascale's attention and said, "Pascale, I know this marriage is both repugnant and dangerous to you, but consider: Bron is merely another poor refugee among millions. She has nothing to recommend her. The only thing that makes her exceptional is you. Doors won't open for her except in connection with you and this news story. You could gamble that Nell will contrive to get Bron to the States some way, some time, but I think you should hang onto Bron while you have her. Anything might happen otherwise. If you keep her under these terms, yes, the cost is staggering. If you don't, remember that she's in army custody. You'll almost certainly never see her again."

Pascale stiffened. Bron said, "Now you must tell me what they are saying to you."

Pascale, unable to speak in front of Nell's pain, under Corinne's gaze, got up and crossed to the window. It faced the blank side of a building. How apt. She felt cold and sick. Out of the corner of her eye she saw Bron taking off her jacket, undoing her tie, coming to her.

Now Bron looked what she was: a slender woman, her throat white below the tan of her face, shoulders not so wide without her coat, her sleeves a little too long, her eyes on Pascale, anxious and determined. She said, "You are angry, Pascale. You are afraid."

"We're trapped."

Bron was unalarmed. "Tell me of this trap."

"Since Nell's broadcast, the army has wanted to find you and reunite us, but they've understood that you're a man."

"Of course," said Bron.

"Corinne thinks that if we tell the truth, everything will be stopped. We will be stopped. Separated from each other. But if we don't tell the truth, the army will take us to the States. We will also have to be married. Today."

"Married? How can this be?"

"The army wants a fairy-tale ending. It won't let anything get in the way. No examinations. No waiting for reports. Corinne says that arrangements are already being made."

"Married." Bron considered it. "I stay disguised." She shrugged. "This I can do. But you do not lie. It is not right that you lie."

"We'd both have to, all the time."

"It is not new to me. It is new to you. Because of me, you have started. I have lied to strangers, but you would be lying to your mother and father, to your friends and the women you love. Could you do it? Would they believe you?"

"My family would be delighted."

"Your friends would feel betrayed."

"Yes." Pascale thought of their distress and revulsion. "They would be."

"*You* would feel betrayed."

Pascale studied the wall across the way. "I've never hidden the truth about myself. Now that I have you, I want to shout it from every skyscraper in the world. Not you, Witold, but you, Bronia."

"You are responsible for all those who would be made brave by your truth, who should be told the truth?"

"Yes."

"Then to do this would be to fail them. This you would have to accept. Lies hurt them, but the truth will kill us. I have already sacrificed being honest with the world. I have nothing else to lose but you, and I will not."

"Oh, God." Pascale put her palms on the cool panes of the window. "It hurts."

"It will always hurt."

Pascale could see her life stretching out, a terrified scramble through the hostile years, throwing one thing after another to keep the hounds at bay: truth, integrity, comfort, moral courage.

Bron said, "You told me on our first day that life is the one imperative."

"Yes." Pascale stopped trying to see through the mist of her own breath on the glass. To cut off a hand, to gnaw off a leg. "Yes. I can endure the loss of anything except you. I would die without you. You are my life."

"For me," said Bron, "it is the same."

They looked at each other. Unsmiling, they turned to Corinne. Pascale said, "We'll do it. We're grateful."

"I'll get Captain Landis," said Corinne quietly. "Nell, will you come?"

Nell rose. "I...yes, sure."

They left, shutting the door.

Alone with Bron, Pascale paced the room. "If we're ever caught, you know we'll be arrested. Once our secret's known, I'll be put in a mental asylum or jail and you'll be deported. That means prison. Death. This will hang over us every minute we live."

"For me, it will be no different than it has been already," said Bron. "Truly, you also will become accustomed. We cannot be the first to have dared such a deception."

"Do you think so? I've never known anyone—to my knowledge." Pascale considered. "Though one has heard stories. I never thought they could be true. Now we'll find out if it's possible."

"You are an intellectual," said Bron, fastening her collar button. "I have cunning. It is possible."

Pascale smiled waveringly. "That's a nice tie."

"I am glad, since I am going to be photographed in it." Bron knotted it around her throat.

Pascale's smile collapsed. "Bron, I don't have your courage."

"Yes you do."

A knock on the door made Bron grab her jacket. Corinne came in with an officer from the public relations office. As Bron buttoned herself in, Corinne went to Pascale and said softly, "This is it. Good luck."

"Private Tailland? Mr. Rukowicz? Pleased to meet you," said a spectacled older man. "I'm Captain Landis. Private, I need to ask you a few questions."

Pascale was taken through the history of her WAC service, the captain checking the details in the file he held.

"You're too modest," he smiled as she finished. "I've spoken to your lieutenant and she's sung your praises."

"How kind," said Pascale faintly.

He asked about her family and background, then about Bron's, sucking his teeth sympathetically as she told him what she knew, but saying, "No relatives at all? No one who might want sponsoring to the States? I'll admit that helps."

Pascale looked down to hide her rage as he made a note and closed his file.

"That's it for now," he said. "You understand that the army requires you to cooperate with the press in all this?"

"Yes, Sir," said Pascale.

He smiled at her expression. "We won't be too tough on you, Private."

"Thank you, Sir."

He joined two MPs who had come in with a translator to question Bron separately. From across the room, Pascale watched Bron play the part of a Polish peasant too stolid to tell anything but the truth. Pascale's heart lurched every time one of the officers frowned, every time Bron hesitated. When Bron finally stood to shake hands with them, Pascale found her fists had clenched together in her lap, the joints white. She relaxed them as she glanced around, and saw that the room had filled.

WAC personnel had settled themselves behind desks, a PRO contingent had commandeered the corners and were jabbering into telephones as they dashed off copy, MPs had self-importantly set their own guard outside the door. Jeeter, Dot, and Binty rushed in, ignoring them.

"Here you go, professor." Jeeter handed Pascale a pair of earrings in a jeweller's case. "Something new."

"This I borrowed from Norma, and this is mine," said Dot, giving her a bracelet and a blue scarf. "I've always thought it would look better on you."

Pascale panicked. Not these—these terrible, kindly gifts. Bron came to her and asked, "Presents now?"

"It's traditional to give them to the bride-to-be."

Bron beamed at the women. "So much gud friends."

"We won't be if we're late for your wedding," said Binty. "Girls, look at the time! We've got to get changed."

With quick embraces, they dashed off.

"You perceive," said Bron.

Pascale did. All of her friends, this whole roomful of people, and none of them questioned what was in front of them, none of them saw. She looked at Bron, who raised a sardonic brow.

"Just a cotton-pickin' minute!" Drina's voice came from the corridor. "I'm in this show and I—Captain West! Will you tell these lugheads I'm on their side?"

Corinne said something to the guards and Drina came in, flipping a bulb from her case. She spotted Pascale and hoisted her camera. "Sorry, folks, but there's no getting away from me."

"This is a persistent woman," said Bron as the camera flashed. Drina caught Pascale's answering smile with her next shot. A roll of film later, she was shunted aside by the army's own photographers, who took Pascale and Bron to another room, where a sofa, a lamp, and a framed picture of Niagara Falls had been arranged in mock domesticity. Pascale and Bron sat, rigid as cards.

"You can do better than that." One of the photographers lowered his camera with a sigh.

"Come on, lovebirds," another cajoled, "give us a kiss."

"They're not performing seals," said Corinne frostily from the door.

"You'd think they didn't want to get hitched," grumbled the first photographer.

The cameras leveled like artillery. Pascale looked at Bron flaring to white in the popping flashes and thought, *Now we can never disappear.*

Corinne permitted the photographers ten minutes, then took Pascale and Bron back to the WAC office. A sergeant had prepared a pile of papers for them. On the top was a marriage licence. Avoiding it, Pascale riffled through the rest of the stack. Army, Federal, Immigration. *I swear to uphold the laws of these United States....* The words billowed like barrage smoke. *I declare the above to be a true statement....*

The sergeant was offering two pens.

"These papers will make us official?" asked Bron, taking one.

"Yes," said Pascale, "and makes what we're doing a crime."

"Breaking bad rules is not a crime," said Bron, writing *Witold Grzegorz Rukowicz* on the marriage license where the sergeant tapped a finger.

Pascale took her pen, looked at Bron's signature, and signed below. It was done. She turned to the next document. They worked down to the desk, reading and signing, the sergeant and Corinne countersigning where necessary. The sergeant tidied the stack and handed Pascale a message form, saying, "I figure you'd like to telegraph your folks."

"No—yes—" Pascale flailed.

"What does she want of you?" asked Bron. When told, she said, "It is expected. You must ask them for their blessing."

"I don't want them involved in this."

"You will disappoint them soon enough."

Pascale felt a flicker of amusement. "No grandchildren." She took the message form from the sergeant and wrote words as if translating from a surreal text: *...being married today...he...him...son-in-law....*

Velma came in with a young man, whom she introduced as Lieutenant Mitchell. The lieutenant said in rough Polish, "Mr. Rukowicz, will you come with me?"

Pascale instinctively reached out to save her, but Bron asked calmly, "Where am I being taken?"

"You'll want to get washed and tidy for the ceremony," said Lieutenant Mitchell.

"Thank you, yes." Bron gave Pascale a reassuring smile as she left.

"You've got to get ready yourself, professor," said Velma. "Your kit bag's been brought over."

Pascale followed her to one of the WAC washrooms. Her dress uniform had been hung up. She washed and changed in silence, refusing to catch her own gaze in the mirrors.

"You okay, honey?" asked Velma. "You're as white as dough."

"It's a big step," Pascale managed.

"You said it. Not to mention pretty sudden. After all, you haven't seen the guy in months."

"I know."

"And you'd only had a day to get acquainted. It wouldn't be wrong to be having second thoughts." Velma stubbed out her cigarette. "Don't let those PRO johnnies hustle you into anything you don't want."

"No second thoughts," said Pascale.

"Let's go, then. Captain Thorsby's waiting to give you away."

It was dark when they crossed the courtyard. Velma stopped her at the door of a briefing room. Pascale could see pale shapes where maps had been taken down. Opposite her, a mass of flowers was banked against the wall. Her whole unit, seated in the first rows, were turning in twos and threes to see her, their faces pleased, disbelieving, envious. Francine faced stiffly forward, no doubt wishing she had thrown Bron off the train that first day. Nell and Corinne sat together. What Nell was wishing Pascale could not bear to contemplate. Sitting behind the Wacs were the men from the PRO, and behind them the rest of the chairs were filled with reporters, who must have flown from Paris to be here. As they spotted Pascale their pens hit their notebooks. Pascale knew that tomorrow's newspapers from Cape Cod to San Diego would be describing her as radiant.

Captain Thorsby came out, nodding to Velma, who slipped away and returned with a cascade of roses bound in white ribbons.

"Thank you." Pascale accepted them dutifully and arranged them on her arm. "How beautiful."

Captain Thorsby turned her directly into the doorway, scrutinizing her like a stern grandmother, then smiled and said, "Come, come, my dear. This is the happiest day of your life!"

Pascale, unable to answer, looked over Captain Thorsby's shoulder and saw Bron, rosebud in her lapel, hair slicked back, standing next to Lieutenant Mitchell. Bron's expression did not change, but as her eyes met Pascale's her face suddenly suffused with light.

"That's better," Captain Thorsby was saying. "And here's the music."

A piano paced them up the aisle. Bron held Pascale's gaze until they were side by side, then turned to face the presiding officer as he began to speak, her head tipped for Lieutenant Mitchell's running translation. The men's voices rolled over Pascale like a chant in another language. Her life, all that she had lived for, had come to this, to these voices and a woman beside her whom she barely knew.

Then Bron began to repeat the vows Lieutenant Mitchell was translating: "I take you, Pascale Katarzyna...," and Pascale felt the air around Bron's words crackle with power.

Lieutenant Mitchell passed Bron a ring. Bron put it on Pascale's finger. It seemed heavier, colder, than gold could be.

The presiding officer turned to Pascale, who repeated his phrases directly to Bron in Polish: "I take you, Witold Grzegorz, to be my lawfully wedded husband...," she looked up to meet Bron's steady eyes, "...from this day forward...."

When she finished, the presiding officer spoke the final solemnities and said to Bron, "Son, you may now kiss the bride."

Bron did, a chaste peck. Pascale could see the muscles tight in her jaw. The presiding officer shook hands with them both, then the piano's recessional marched them down the aisle.

In an adjoining office, the WAC sergeant waited with another stack of papers: the register, marriage certificate, a dozen visa and entry documents. Pascale signed her new name below Bron's on each one: *Pascale Rukowicz. Mrs. W. G. Rukowicz.* Drina was there to reap the moment, her flashes creating sudden shadows under Pascale's pen. The photographers came in with flowers from the briefing room. Pascale and Bron were arranged in front of them, Pascale's hand adjusted to show her ring to advantage.

"Thanks, that's great!" the photographers chorused. "Now turn to each other. Hey, smile, won't you? You just got married!"

Drina, again elbowed to the fringes, took pictures of the photographers kneeling before them.

When they returned to the briefing room, Pascale found it transformed. Trestle tables had been brought in and draped with cloths and flowers, the lights had been wrapped with colored paper, and someone had hung two huge cardboard horseshoes from a map hook. Captain Thorsby escorted Pascale and Bron through the applauding guests, her smile triumphant. *Yes,* Pascale thought, *it is a triumph, of fear over truth.* She was seated at the head table. Every eye was upon her, every eye was approving. Pascale tightened her hold on her feelings. To become accustomed.

A platoon of catering staff from the nearby army camp emerged through the double doors, bearing trays.

"They must be what Aaron was," said Bron, looking interestedly at them.

Pascale's smile came from far away. "Aaron?"

"A man Sibylle knew before I met her. He gave her a radio."

Pascale's smile warmed. "My thanks to Aaron."

The catering staff served them tinned turkey and potatoes. Pascale knew that Bron was watching her toy with her food. Bron said nothing, but Captain Thorsby was not as perceptive. "Try to eat a little, my dear. You mustn't let the cooks down."

"This is pleasant, but army food only," said Bron. "Pascale waits for my *pierogis.*"

Lieutenant Mitchell leaned forward. "Did you hear that, ma'am? Most fellows can barely rustle up bacon and eggs."

"I am a treasure," said Bron, her eyes bright with laughter. Meeting them, Pascale felt the tightness within her ease.

The wedding supper finished at last. Captain Thorsby stood to make the first speech. Bron listened to Lieutenant Mitchell's translation as she followed Pascale's reactions, smiling when she smiled. Captain Landis took the floor with a necessarily general speech on the worthiness of this fine, fine young couple. Velma gave a laundered version of her first encounter with Witold, making the guests laugh and the reporters write while Captain Thorsby, hearing the details for the first time, kept her face rigidly genial. Velma grinned and winked at Pascale as she sat down. Pascale grinned back, but her smile faded as Nell stood up.

Nell thrust her hands in her pockets and said, "When I embarked on this crazy hunt for one misplaced Polish boy, I thought that the proverbial needle would be easier to find. I'd never played matchmaker before, and Lord knows I don't look like Cupid, so I didn't realize I was dealing with destiny. But the more I got to know Pascale, that is, Mrs. Rukowicz, the more I discovered that I'd better get used to the wings and bow, because I was looking at True Love. We all hunt for it, but not all of us find it. I'm honored that I could be part of bringing these two together and helping to create a bit of happiness in this uncertain world. Ladies, gentlemen, officers, will you join me in a toast?"

After the guests had toasted them, Bron quietly raised her wine glass to Pascale, drained it, and said, "Now this must serve no lesser honor," as she snapped the stem between her fingers.

Pascale felt as if she were seeing a promised land. "Br—" she began, "Witold—" but at that moment the catering staff wheeled in a wedding cake. As they proudly paraded it through the room, Pascale hurriedly explained to Bron what she had to do. It was placed in front of them. One of the servers gave Pascale a silver knife.

"This is as much ceremony as a church," said Bron, putting her hand over Pascale's as she drove in the blade.

"I have to feed you a bit."

Bron obediently opened her mouth. A camera flashed. They exchanged a glance Pascale knew they would be sharing too often. Bron swallowed. "It is good cake. Now they can photograph me smiling."

When the last slice had been dispensed, the tables were pushed back. A record player was carried in and a sergeant from the PRO arrived with a case of records.

Pascale told Bron, "We have to dance the first dance by ourselves, then you'll dance with Captain Thorsby and I with Lieutenant Mitchell."

The sergeant put on a waltz.

"I cannot dance," said Bron.

"Yes, you can." Pascale led Bron to the dance floor. "Hold me."

Bron did that willingly. Pascale began to dance, whispering through unmoving lips, "Listen to the music. It tells you what to do. Listen with all of you."

Bron followed Pascale's steps, studying her feet, then lifted her eyes to Pascale's. The music rushed between and around them. Bron began to move with Pascale as if Pascale were still speaking, as if she understood, and they were dancing. They were dancing together. Bron confidently circled the room. Pascale was closed off again, aware of nothing but the music, her hand in Bron's, Bron's arm around her waist, Bron's smile mocking anything that could harm them.

The music ended. The guests clapped. Another record, and Pascale was with Lieutenant Mitchell, who said, "Witold seems like a real nice fellow. He sure is crazy about you, and I can see why."

"Thank you. I'm pretty crazy about him."

"You know, I'm engaged to a girl back home. Her name's Anita. As soon as I get back I'm going to marry her."

"An excellent idea," said Pascale. "I recommend it."

Pascale could see Bron dancing less well with Captain Thorsby. Pascale claimed her again for the third dance to show her the steps, then Bron was loosed on Velma, who towered over her. Pascale danced with Captain Landis. Nell, she saw, was on Lieutenant Mitchell's arm. Pascale wanted to cut in, to dance with her one last time, to talk with her. Nell whirled past, chatting brightly to the lieutenant, eyes anywhere but on Pascale.

Record followed record through the evening. Pascale was with a warrant officer now, and Bron was dancing with Sibylle, who seemed to be teasing her. Pascale moved on to a PRO lieutenant, then was claimed by the officer who had married them. At the end of the record, thanking him, she looked around for Bron, heart hesitating as she could not find her. Then she did, and smiled, for Bron's hair oil had surrendered: her hair was bristling again as she passed her fingers through it, nervously waiting to be summoned for the next dance. She caught Pascale's eye and returned her smile wearily from across the room.

Pascale made herself focus on the blur of faces, on all these people who had worked to make her happy. There was Corinne, glancing up from her watch to look unguardedly at Nell. Pascale's gaze flinched away, only to find Nell herself, brave and desperate beyond Pascale's power to help, clutching a cigarette like a life raft as she listened to Captain Landis. Over by the record player stood Sibylle, glad for Bron, but already distant, fidgeting to go back to Paris.

Captain Thorsby drew Pascale to one side. "My dear, I think it's time you took your leave and let this party wind down." She looked at her fondly. "Have we given you a wedding to remember?"

Pascale propped up her enthusiasm. "It's been an amazing day."

"Quite wonderful," Captain Thorsby nodded. "Let's rescue that husband of yours so he can take care of you."

Bron came at her gesture, Lieutenant Mitchell on her heels. The photographers, sensing that this was the last moment of the drama, gathered round. One called to Pascale, "Hey, sister, you gonna throw that bouquet?"

The Wacs bunched together, squealing. Pascale launched her tired flowers through an explosion of flashing bulbs. It was Marie who intercepted them, their long ribbons cracking like whips as she snatched them from the air.

"Wouldn't you know it," Jeeter whispered to Pascale as the women said their good-byes. "She'll be like the prize pig at a state fair all the way home."

Drina took her last photographs and wished them happiness. Bron shook hands with her, with Nell and Corinne, then hugged Sibylle hard. Pascale took Nell's hand between her own.

"Nell, come visit us in Boston."

"In a few years," said Nell.

Corinne swept her firmly out to the car. They were gone.

Pascale saluted all the officers she could see, Bron thanked Lieutenant Mitchell for his service, and it was over. Someone put on an Artie Shaw record. Bron caught Pascale in her arms for a last dance and they spun round the room to the exit.

A young WAC public relations officer, waiting for them there, blushingly shepherded them to the big hotel on the city square and up to a double room. More flowers from Captain Thorsby had been placed on the washstand. Bouquets with messages stood in vases along the dressing table. Pascale's kit bag had been carried across and someone—Pascale suspected the awesomely efficient Corinne—had delivered a small suitcase of men's clothes and toiletries for Bron. Beside it stood Bron's artillery boots. Her greatcoat and Polish army cap had been hung behind the door.

"Bron," Pascale said, sitting on the bed, "this is a terrible fairy tale."

"Not terrible." Bron came to her.

They lay on the bed fully clothed, listening to the sounds from the square and the harbor. A church bell rang eleven times.

"We've been together less than half a day," said Pascale.

Bron rose to her elbow and looked down. "Also the day and night we met."

"And now we're here." Pascale stroked Bron's sleeve. "This has really happened to us."

"This did not happen to us. We made this."

"I tried to write to you. I could never reach you. I couldn't find you." Pascale gripped Bron's lapel. "I searched for you. Then I received my orders home. I planned to come back to Europe as soon as I could, get work somewhere, hunt until I found you."

"How fortunate that all this does not need to be," Bron smiled. "Now we go to America together."

"We'll have reporters on our doorstep for months. Thanksgiving with the Rukowiczes. Their first Christmas. America's most famous couple see in the New Year."

"Do you think the woman who lived with you will revenge herself through these reporters?"

"No, she'd be terrified that she'd be traced as the informant."

"Then there is nothing to fear. The reporters will tire of us eventually. We will look back and see this day as strange as the war is growing strange to us now."

"Yes." Pascale's torment fell away. There was no nightmare. They lay looking contentedly at each other. Pascale did not notice the transition from peace to their kiss. They were kissing. To have Bron at last. To have her at last.

Bron eased away, stood, and undressed herself. She was as beautiful as a young racehorse, strong and lean. Pascale stripped off her uniform, took Bron's hand, and lay down with her. She turned her face into Bron's shoulder, shaking with an ardor so intense that it seemed like fire from the center of the sun. Bron touched her. Pascale captured her hand and kissed it, kissed each finger while Bron watched in awe, as if not believing that Pascale could feel the same.

"I do," said Pascale.

Bron said, "You are so beautiful." She kissed Pascale's mouth softly, then roughly, then they were kissing as if starving for each other.

Bron's fingers traced lines of heat down Pascale's body, Bron's kisses branded her skin. Pascale's heart grew wild. She had to have her mouth and hands on Bron. She seized her, fought her for ascendancy, until she had her fingers in her hair, was holding her still, insisting that she accept her kisses. Bron was taut in her hands, breathless for her, and Pascale felt fierce triumph over everything that had tried to keep them from this.

Pascale moved from Bron's mouth to kiss the line of her jaw, of her throat, put hands and then lips to Bron's breasts. Bron groaned, rising to her mouth. As Pascale moved lower Bron went still in anticipation, almost rigid to receive her touch. Pascale gently lowered her head. Bron gasped in shock, with joy, and kept her hand on Pascale's hair until, writhing and shaking under Pascale's mouth, she flung wide her arms as she choked Pascale's name, arched, and came with a guttural cry. Pascale lifted herself across Bron's panting body, knowing a love deeper than harmony, a completion beyond understanding.

Bron stroked her with trembling hands. Pascale slowly slid up her body to kiss her.

Bron said, "Pascale, I must tell you. I was afraid. Twice, I was afraid to trust you. On our first day, and tonight. Twice, without reason. I am sorry."

"Not afraid enough to stop," said Pascale.

Bron smiled. "No."

They lay kissing, gloating over each other, touching each other's hair, hands, faces. Finally Bron said, "But you interrupted me."

"Because you're irresistible."

"So are you." Bron kissed her. "You are everything I want."

"Everything I have is yours."

Bron took it all, dropping kisses along her body: palms, breasts, hips, down to her toes, up her back to the nape of her neck, each kiss a statement, until Pascale could not doubt what Bron was saying, until Pascale felt entirely claimed, loved, desired.

Bron, behind her, glided both hands like thistledown across her breasts, fingers drifting along the curves of her body, circling her. Fire crackled across Pascale's skin under her touch; she felt herself become molten in Bron's arms. Bron moved slowly, her mouth on Pascale's breasts, on her belly and thighs, her mouth finally centered on her.

Pascale's heart was like red gold inside her body's furnace. She felt incandescent, wanted Bron everywhere, every way, demanded to be filled. Bron hesitated, then Pascale felt her, was soon no longer aware of fingers or mouth or sensation, but was rising within a fiery darkness of rapture that grew and grew until she came with an expanding wordless release that blazed through every nerve, every muscle and sinew, every drop of blood.

She found herself across the bed, lungs tearing in cold air. Bron lifted and turned her limp body until Pascale was lying full length on top of her, supported by her, Bron's fingers lightly holding her there. Pascale rested her head on Bron's shoulder and heard Bron's heart hammering like an engine. She kissed the softness of Bron's breast, tasted her sweat-damp skin, savored everything that was Bron.

Finally she put her hands on Bron's, which were instantly there for her use, raised herself, and looked down at her. Bron smiled her small smile. Pascale thought of the hundred and thousand times she would look at Bron, would kiss her, would have Bron's body against hers, and each time as amazing, more amazing than this time, but never like this.

"I love you," she told her at last. "I love you."

Later she said, "We can't let our pretense seep in and damage this. I couldn't bear it."

"We do not lie to each other," said Bron. "It is the only responsibility that matters."

"I would do anything, say anything, commit any crime, abandon everything, for you, Bronia."

"Ah," said Bron, "I worship you."

They slept tangled in each other's arms and legs, woke to make love again, slept and woke, talked through the dark hours. Bron told her of Lucia, of the night watchman who had given her shelter, of the nuns, of Madame Robichoux.

"I paid them with work," said Bron. "After the end of the war, people acted differently. They were kind. It was easier to get what I needed. The rules had returned for them."

"And yours?" Pascale feathered Bron's hair.

"My only rule was you."

Pascale said, "I never thought anyone could be what you are. Steadfast. Here," she kissed Bron's heart, "here, where it matters. Where it can only be."

Bron laced her fingers through Pascale's. "We are the same."

They made love, slept until dawn was insistent against the window, then rose and dressed, knowing they were to be fetched through an honor guard of press and photographers to the ship.

Pascale pulled back the curtain and looked at the harbor. Water and sky were the color of steel. The *Gordon Cray* was there, ready to take them home. Bron came to stand behind her, barely touching her. Pascale thought of Velma, Jeeter, Dot, and the others who had smuggled Bron from the war, of Lucia and Sibylle and Corinne. She thought of Nell with piercing tenderness. She said, "We have a responsibility to all those women who've helped and loved us. We have to make this succeed. We have to get away with it." She sighed and leaned back against Bron. "Can we live by any principles they'd understand?"

"They will know that our rules are necessary for us," said Bron, "and we will justify them by surviving."

"Will we survive?" asked Pascale. "How?"

Bron put her arms around her and growled in her ear.

Pascale laughed.